The Coven's Apprentice

Witches of Evanoir
The Coven's Apprentice
The Coven's Council

The Coven's Apprentice

WITCHES OF EVANOIR 1

JEN DAVENPORT

This book is a work of fiction. Names, characters, businesses, organizations, places, events, and incidents either are the product of the author's imagination or are used fictitiously. Any resemblance to actual persons, living or dead, events, or locales is entirely coincidental.

The Coven's Apprentice
Copyright © 2021 by Jennifer Huey

Published by Jen Davenport and Portal World Publishing
Visit the author's website at www.authorjendavenport.com
Visit the publisher's website at www.portalworldpublishing.com

ISBN : 978-1-955532-11-2

Cover design by Megan VanDyke
Copy edits by Jade Loren

This one's for you, kiddo.

CHAPTER 1

BEFORE I GRADUATED HIGH SCHOOL, everyone told me to go to college. It would be the best years of my life. They warned me the transition from teen to adult wasn't easy, but it was worth it. What my Coven and Mom failed to say was that I'd have no freedom to do what I wanted. Date the hot girl in my Bio class? Nope. It was against the rules. Use magic to finish a Chem assignment because I stayed out way too late the night before and almost missed lab? Hell no. That wasn't just against the rules, it was a punishable offense. I didn't know what the punishment was, since I did the work on my own—not with magic—and failed.

The worst "adulting" activity of all... Shopping day. Every Monday after witch training classes, we spent the afternoon trudging through the forest behind my mom's backyard picking wild herbs off of the Coven's list of supplies. We needed them for the next session, and one rule of the apprenticeship was that we could only do spells with items we gathered ourselves. Boring spells like making healing salves and potions for tea. Full members of the Evanoir Coven went to the store to get what they needed.

No freedom.

As I entered the woods through the thick trees, my best friend Tierney's voice rang out in front of me.

"Azami," she called out. "Come on, or we'll be late for the party."

"Tierney," Katie, another apprentice, scowled at her.

"What party?" I asked as I bent over and pulled a chunk of horsehound out of the ground.

Even though we were together pretty much 24/7, no one had mentioned a party. Just like they hadn't invited me to last week's party. Lately, I hadn't been invited to anything, not even into New Orleans for a shopping trip. Or maybe it had always been that way, but I didn't realize it until the last month or so.

I added another bullet to my list of reasons why college wasn't as great as everyone said. Friendships were hard, as in harder than I ever imagined. With the distance growing between me and my Coven sisters, I needed new friends. Ones I made on my own.

"Oh, it's no big deal. Just a stupid thing for Fraternity Row now that classes have started for the year." Katie waved her perfectly manicured hand in the air.

Last week's get-together was no big deal either. Katie said it was just a stupid thing for her sorority sisters to celebrate the last days of summer.

I caught up with the two of them, while Tierney trained her gaze on the path in front of us. Recently, she'd been canceling our study sessions, and I couldn't help but wonder if they were doing other things without me.

"Tierney, I thought we were hanging out tonight. You know, getting ready for the apprenticeship exams." I tapped a rhythm on my leg waiting for her answer.

She took off to the right without saying anything. A crow cawed above me. I tilted my chin skyward, hoping to catch a glimpse of the midnight black wings streaked blue by the sunlight.

"I can show you something your friends know nothing about."

A voice intruded into my thoughts. I jerked my head to the left and right. Both Tierney and Katie had disappeared.

"Tierney," I called out. "Where are you?" My voice shook.

There was no one around. The idea the crow spoke to me wasn't completely crazy: they were my family's familiar. But it wasn't like I made it a habit of talking to birds. The air around me dropped a few degrees and I rubbed my arms.

"You don't need her," the voice spoke again.

Whoever it was, they were wrong. I needed my friends. We were supposed to stay together. Family for life. It was the way of our Coven. For all my adult bravado, one thing hadn't changed. I still hated being alone. Especially when there were weird voices in my head.

The crow cawed again.

Crows—the symbol of bad luck or death.

The belief I'd read online, but I liked to think of them more as a symbol of mystery and life magic. Our family wasn't afraid of crows. My skin prickled as the one overhead dipped and rose through the sky. I fought my gut instinct to run as fast as I could, which wasn't that fast. Freshman year of high school I tried track. Turned out I was incapable of making it around the loop once without falling and skinning my knees.

This was just a bird. It couldn't hurt me. Besides, I hadn't found everything on my list. That still didn't mean I wanted to stick around. I picked up speed, glancing all around me as I headed in the same direction Tierney and Katie should've gone.

"Please be playing a prank. Please let this be Tierney or Katie," I whispered through clenched teeth as I gripped a bundle of herbs so tight my knuckles turned white.

I found the girls at the end of the trail with their heads together, whispering not so quietly. The herbs fell from my hands and I let out a long breath.

"Come on, Katie. We could invite her just this time. I'll

keep her with me all night."

Katie shook her head. "No. I'm not bringing along little miss goody-two-shoes. If any of us break one of the beloved coven rules, she'll run off to her mom and anyone else who will listen. Then we'll get in trouble. I'm not willing to risk it."

Tierney sighed. "She's our Coven sister, Katie. This isn't right. Besides, she's never snitched."

I sucked in a breath. A pile of rocks rolled around my gut. I was the good girl, even if I had no clue how I'd earned that reputation. Neither did Tierney, apparently. It could've been the hours of studying, but Tierney was usually there with me. At one time, I'd wanted to be the best witch of the Coven. I wanted Mom to be proud of me. Then I went to college. A year away from my mom changed my perspective on life.

Making her proud was still important, but I wanted to find my own happiness. So best witch no longer mattered. If Katie still thought of me as the goody-two-shoes, then I'd failed to relay the message. Our lack of communication went both ways.

"Yes, she has. How do you think Gwen found out about our trip to the old Coven house a few weeks ago?" Katie glanced over her shoulder in my direction. She paused but didn't seem to notice me. "Just because your crush blinds you to the truth, doesn't mean the rest of us don't see she's the favorite."

I had no idea what she was talking about. I couldn't tell our leader anything since I didn't even know they'd gone to the house. It'd been over a month since I'd even talked to the Coven leader. I scratched my head, trying to figure out what Katie had against me. We were never as close as Tierney and I were, but I didn't realize just how much she disliked me. For the moment, I ignored the crush part.

"Seriously?" Tierney's voice rose at the end of the word.

"Well, who else could it have been? She was the only one not there."

"Of course she wasn't there. You didn't invite her. We went without her. What's your real problem with Azami?"

I slowed, wanting to learn more. A branch snapped under my foot. Tierney jerked her head away from Katie.

"Azami, umm, sorry. We didn't realize how far we'd gone or that you stayed back there."

"Lies. So many lies," the strange voice entered my thoughts once more.

When I tilted my head to the sky there were no birds, crows, or otherwise. The crisp blue sky should have calmed my nerves—something wasn't right. A battle waged between my head and heart. What did the voice mean about lies?

Just my luck, I wasn't going to find out any time soon. It wasn't as though I could just ask whatever, or whoever was in my head to explain.

"Hey. I couldn't find you." I decided to keep my eavesdropping a secret.

"We, um, thought you were behind us. Sorry about that." Tierney lowered her lids and kicked the ground with the toe of her tennis shoe.

"Whatever," Katie muttered.

Katie, with her perfect blonde hair and curvy body that all the guys loved, and myself with my frizzy brown curls and not-so-perfect overly large curves. She was the popular girl. I was the nerd. Yet, we'd grown up together in the Coven. Our moms had too. The only thing we had in common was both of our dads had died. Mine before I was born and hers when she was only a year or two old.

"Listen, Azami, about the party. It's kind of invitation-only," Tierney started.

"And you're not invited. Simple really," Katie finished with more than a little snark to her words.

"I see." I nodded. For a few seconds, I contemplated how to react to the rejection. In the end, I took the opportunity for what it was. A chance to step out on my own. They didn't want me around, there was no reason to dwell.

Besides, it wasn't like I enjoyed the party scene. Tierney and Katie pledged to a sorority last year. They wanted me to join them, but the idea of being in a house full of females who ran around sharing makeup and planning parties wasn't my idea of fun at all. Sure, there were more academically focused houses, but not the ones Tierney and Katie found interesting.

Tierney brushed her hand down my arm then laced her fingers in mine. We'd held hands a million times, but after learning about her crush I had to wonder. Did it mean the same for me as it did for her?

"You're not the type that would have fun at this kind of thing. You know?"

At least one of them knew me well enough.

"Azami, I'm here. Let me show you something that will have your friends begging to spend time with you instead of pushing you away."

The hair on my forearms rose and a tingle began at the top of my spine. That stupid voice. A crow cawed above us once more. The white tuft of feathers on the top of its head was hard to miss, it was the same one from before.

"Are you talking to me?" I sent the telepathic question toward the crow, unsure if I was crazy or not for trying.

"Come see what I've found."

"What's up with that crow?" Tierney asked. She shielded her eyes with her hands to scan the sky above us.

Katie and I shrugged. I still wasn't sure it was even the crow speaking to me. But I wanted to find out, and even though I'd just decided not to care about what they thought of me, if I was honest with myself it would take more than a few seconds to change. So yeah, the crow was right. If there was a way to get their attention, I was interested.

The voice spooked me, but I was going to face it head-on. It was time to cut the Coven strings and do things I wanted to do.

"Show me what you've found," I replied.

"You two go on. I'm going to go that way to finish off my list. I'll catch up with you later." I pointed over my shoulder at the way we'd come.

Tierney stepped closer and wrapped her arms around my waist.

"I'm sorry, Azami. Really, I am," she whispered into my ear.

Her hold was a little longer than comfortable and I could've sworn she sniffed my hair. I pushed all of that aside, hugged her, and then pulled away. I didn't want any part of it. She'd rejected me once, and I wasn't about to make the same mistake twice.

"Right, see ya." Katie headed in the opposite direction without even a glance over her shoulder.

The air turned cooler and filled with the scent of a burning campfire as I continued down the path. The crow cawed out again, two quick calls then a long one. Behind me, a branch snapped and I tugged the strap of my leather bag higher on my shoulder. I still didn't know who the voice belonged to or why the crow was following me. The urge to find out grew, making me walk away from the other two even faster.

A gust of warm air brushed across my neck. A glance over my shoulder revealed nothing. I stood silent, hoping whoever, or whatever, it was would leave. I took a slow step forward, then another as I tried to convince myself I'd worried over nothing.

"Head toward the farm house in the field."

I changed direction, one step at a time nearing the edge of the woods. *Never go beyond the edge of the forest to the field with the old house,* our Coven had reminded us the day before.

As if they didn't tell us as often as possible. The Coven leaders told us the house held spirits of long ago. Ones intent on revenge for wrongdoings. They told us we could be harmed by entering. Except, Tierney and Katie were fine.

It was my turn to see if the stories the Coven gave us were true, or just a tale to keep the kids from going into some rundown, unsafe place. My money was on the latter.

The sun slowly disappeared behind the trees.

"Here." The voice was clearer like he was nearby.

As I tiptoed across the field, the house grew closer, no longer a gray blob in the middle of an open area. Pieces of siding dangled from the walls. Gray shutters swayed on a single nail. Weeds cluttered the front of the house and a hole engulfed the middle of the second step. The front door was the only piece of the house that didn't remind me of a five-hundred-year-old home.

Creaking wood followed a gust of wind. I shuddered at the idea the thing wouldn't even withstand a thunderstorm. If I went inside I'd have to watch where I stepped, or make sure I didn't push a beam to make it come crashing down.

The crow that had followed me perched in the right corner window of the top floor.

"Come inside, Azami. Explore the place I've brought you to."

I followed while my head screamed to go home. The place was dangerous. A disaster waiting to happen.

"Are you the one who brought me here?" I asked out loud.

The crow cawed in response. Not words. I stepped back, ready to go home. This wasn't a good idea. From the way my skin tightened across my arms and the warnings in my head about going closer, maybe I should've listened to the Coven and not gone to the field. They were older, wiser, more experienced. If they told us not to go inside, they did it out of experience. Not some crazy attempt at controlling us with lies.

When I lifted my foot to turn around, my leg jerked forward like I had a puppet string tied around my ankle. Losing my balance, I threw my arms out to the side to keep from falling.

"What's—"

"It's just inside." The crow swooped down and landed

on the railing of the front porch. He tipped his beak toward the door.

I wasn't crazy. The crow had guided me here. It spoke to me.

"What's inside?" I asked.

"You must enter to see." This time the words weren't in my head. Its scratchy voice reminded me of those people who hold the wand thing up to their neck when they have a hole in their neck.

Did I go inside, knowing I was breaking the rules? Yes. No. If I didn't go inside, I'd never know why it led me to that point. He was our family's familiar, surely whatever it was couldn't be bad. I wanted to do things for me, explore on my own. Choosing to listen to the Coven was the exact opposite of that.

Using the swaying rail as support—a bad idea, but I didn't have much to choose from—I made my way up the stairs, one step at a time, careful not to fall into the hole in the middle of the second one.

The door slowly swung open with a whine. A gust of wind blew strands of hair around my face. I stopped short of crossing the threshold. I wanted to take the step, but going against everything I knew wasn't easy. At least, not like I thought it would be. If I turned back, then I hadn't technically done anything wrong. The Coven couldn't suspend my training, something they threatened us with often. They wouldn't accuse me of breaking any rules.

Worrying over breaking rules was worse than pouring salt in an open wound. If I wanted to break away from their tight hold, I had to do things on my terms.

"What's so important in there?" I whispered, afraid to disturb the spirits—if there were any.

The crow promised I could entice my friends, but didn't tell me why. Even if I did want to break the rules it would be careless to go inside the house without knowing a little more. I had to be smart.

My crow guide cawed, tilted his beak toward the door, then flew toward me and back to the porch.

"Do you want a chance to show your friends how wrong they are for excluding you? You want to prove you're the one who knows how to have fun? Show the Coven you're more powerful than any of them could hope to be."

I narrowed my eyes in the bird's direction. Show the Coven my power? As far as I knew, there was nothing special about me. Tierney was the best at potions and brews. Katie excelled at transformations. Me...I did fine, but there wasn't anything I'd say I was a specialist in—or the best at. Adrenaline raced through my veins. Did the crow know something about my power that I didn't?

The unknown inside drove me to move closer. What if I found an ancient relic? What was the point of being a witch if all I ever did was make potions to sell in town? What if there were spirits? All we ever did in training was simple, harmless magic. Maybe I had the power to control spirits. I could make them do my bidding.

As soon as I stepped into the massive entry, the scent of mothballs transported my thoughts to Grandma's house. A staircase started on my left and my right, meeting high in the middle of the entry. Shadows fell over the room, except for one spot just to the right of the center. A table stood in the spotlight of sun shining through an upper floor window. One of the rickety, wooden back legs of the table bowed with age.

In the center of the circular tabletop was a book, black and leather—maybe—I had to get closer to see. Cracked and peeled gold lettering adorned the front cover.

Mort d' Evanoir

"Why is this named after the town? What does mort mean?" I attempted to recall what little French I knew. Grandma spoke some, but I'd never learned.

"Death," the crow answered.

"Death of Evanoir?"

My fingers slid over the print and across the soft leather.

Curiosity piqued, I pried open the cover. Faded black cursive lettering lined the first page in two columns. In the left column were names. I scrolled down the list with my finger, searching for someone I might recognize. Some of the last names were familiar, but that was it.

A breath stuck in my throat as I read the right column.

Fire. Drowning. Cut off their leg and bled to death.

"What is this?" I asked aloud.

A buzz of magic brushed over my skin, making my muscles tense. Like the stinging of bees. Our trainers described this as dark magic. The metallic taste in the air signaled death magic. Everything about the moment felt wrong and right. Cold seeped through my tennis shoes, as though my feet were frozen to the wooden panels of the floor. An out of body moment began, where I watched myself study a book I shouldn't touch with magic I wasn't supposed to know beyond a few errant details.

I flipped to the halfway point to see more names, more death beside the names. Some of the people I recognized from stories Grandma had told me.

Someone, or likely multiple people, had kept a record of every death in Evanoir. I couldn't imagine tracking so many names. The book had to be more than a thousand pages with fifty or more names per page.

Close to the end, the people became more familiar. Some classmates who graduated a few years ago, grisly descriptions by their names, but none of them were dead as far as I knew. It couldn't be a record. Maybe a prediction. Except, that didn't make sense. The deaths were so precise.

The room darkened with the setting sun. I slammed the book shut, not wanting to see the end. My skin tightened once more and my whole body shivered at the idea of reading my name, or my fellow Coven members.

Knowing how they died was way more power than I needed to have. All I wanted was the chance to do more with my magic, not control death. If that's what the book's purpose was.

"Take it," the crow urged. *"You're the first person to open this book in nearly fifty years."*

The lower corner of the book shifted to the edge of the table without me touching it. I jumped back with a squeak.

Beads of sweat formed on my upper lip. My mouth went dry. The Coven leaders failed to tell the whole truth about this house. It was full of magic I had no idea how to use or defend myself against. Dark magic. Death magic. Now things were moving without my guidance. Maybe it was the spirits. I didn't want to stay any longer to find out.

Leaving the book on the table, I turned toward the door, ready to run all the way back home. This house was haunted and full of things I had no reason to be around. My muscles ached with the need to move.

"Don't leave, Azami. If you do, you won't be able to find the book again. Take it," the crow taunted me.

I paused. The book would disappear. A book of death. It would have been wrong to leave it for someone else to find. If the next person tried to work the dark magic within it, it'd be my fault for leaving it. The crow said it'd been here for fifty years.

"My Coven sisters were here not too long ago. How did they not find this book?"

Slowly, I twisted toward the table and wrapped my hands around the leather. The book warmed beneath my touch.

"Take it," the crow whispered. *"They aren't as powerful as you. I told you, this book is yours. Not those girls. They are weak."*

"I shouldn't." I could leave it and tell the Council to recover it. They could make sure no one ever used the magic within. I'd keep everyone from being harmed.

Except...

I could take it, and then find a safe place to keep it. We weren't supposed to use black magic, but if I never performed any spells then no one would know I had the book. Besides, if I was more powerful than my fellow witches, they didn't need the book. It was my responsibility as an adult to protect others. At least, that's what I told myself.

The book called to me. Its warmth wrapped around me like a blanket.

"Maybe I should take it to the Council."

"No. Keep it for you. They won't know what to do with such a book."

The crow's voice turned hard. Dark. The temperature in the room plummeted and the air around me grew thin. My hands shook.

"Why not? Even I've heard of this book. It's in our history of Evanoir classes. I mean, no one talks about it, but the Coven knows what it is."

"That woman you call leader is no leader at all. She wants the book to destroy life."

Our Coven leader wanted *Mort d'Evanoir*. I wondered if she knew it was in the house. It would make sense that they told us to stay out. Maybe our leader was waiting on the person who could open it, which was me.

"What if I don't take it?"

"Do you see your name in the book?" the crow asked.

I shook my head. A creepy-crawly sensation started at the tip of my fingers and made its way up my arms. I tried to rub it away, but no matter how hard I scrubbed my arms, the tickle of a thousand spiders crawling across my skin wouldn't stop.

"Why would I try to find my own name? What does it matter if it's in here or not?" I asked.

"You never know, if you don't take the book your name could end up on the list." The crow flew across the room and landed on a three-legged stool next to the front door. *"Maybe it will, maybe it won't."*

The magic was even darker than I thought. Slowly, I tucked it in my bag and jogged out of the house. It was my responsibility to protect everyone from whatever chaos the book was sure to cause. I had no idea what it did or how it worked, but it wasn't good. That much I was certain of. If our leader wanted it, but couldn't open it, then I needed to know more before I took it to them.

"Just for a day or two."

"Keep it. Do not give it to anyone else. Mort d'Evanoir *belongs to you, Azami."*

The crow cawed and nodded with his beak.

CHAPTER 2

FIVE HOURS OF SLEEP WAS NOT enough for me to function. Thanks to my recent magic acquisition, I'd stayed up too late the night before reading the names of residents of Evanoir and how they died.

"Azami, get up. You're going to be late." A warm touch caressed my cheek.

The face in my dreams didn't match the voice. My dream girl had long, black hair with a stripe of purple and sapphire eyes. Her touch warmed me like a plush, minky fabric. The voice, on the other hand, wasn't a deeper soothing tone like my dream girl's. More like the high-pitch scratch of fingernails being dragged down a chalkboard. I squeezed my eyes tight and prayed Tierney would go away.

"Oh, please. You're pathetic sometimes, Tierney. She's old enough to get up on her own. If you keep babying her, we'll be late for class, too." Katie's soft lilt pulled me out of my dream.

My preferred alarm clock was the trill of my phone. I'd have to talk to my roommate about visitors.

"Ugh. It's too early," I moaned into my pillow. The first day of classes was always the hardest.

Coffee was a must.

"You never oversleep. Especially not on the first day. Are you okay?" Tierney slid her hand under my hair and cupped the back of my neck.

I shook off her hand and sat up in bed, pulling the covers to my shoulders. After learning about Tierney's crush, being around her with nothing but a sleepshirt on was more than a little uncomfortable.

"I'm fine, just stayed up late."

Katie huffed. "See. I told you. She's fine. Can we go now?"

Yes, please. With the most restraint I could manage, I didn't say the words out loud. There was no point in hurting my friend's feelings.

Tierney glanced from me to Katie and back to me. "Do you want us to wait? We can walk to class together."

"No. Go ahead. I've got to go the opposite direction anyway." I needed them to leave soon to avoid them finding the book.

"All right. Well, there's coffee and a pastry on the table." Tierney lowered her chin to the table and shrugged. "Guess I'll see you later."

After they left I rolled out of bed, changed from my nightshirt to a pair of lace shorts and a lavender v-neck short sleeve shirt, and slid my feet into my favorite pair of sandals. Late spring was my favorite time of year—shorts, sandals, and sunshine. The only hard part was keeping my hair off my neck. Humidity plus thick curls did not equal easy hair dos. I pulled it into a messy ponytail before checking my appearance one more time. The freckles on my nose weren't as noticeable as they were in the winter when my skin paled due to lack of sun.

As I began to pull open the door to my room, a dark spot on my dresser caught my eye. The night before, I'd spent hours staring at the book. Debating whether or not I should open it, read the names. When I almost caved, I'd remember reading the way people had died and I'd find something else to distract me. Then the debate started all over again. I continued the cycle until three a.m. when my eyes refused to stay open any longer.

Mort d'Evanoir.

It wasn't a dark spot, it was a big, black mark of wrongness that called to me.

Outside my window, a crow squawked. The little hairs on the back of my neck stood straight out and chill bumps dotted my arms. Oh, goddess. I had hoped the crow was a one-time thing.

"Azami, are you ready to have fun?" it whispered in my thoughts.

I shook my head.

"No. No. No. Not today and probably not ever."

Leaving it at the house would have been a much better idea. The crow messed with my head. I wasn't thinking straight. It was just a crow. A bird. He couldn't do a lot to me. No one else had opened the book. It would've been safe.

Except, I didn't know for how long. Taking the book had been the smarter choice.

"The things in the book...those were done by my direction."

He killed the people in the book.

"Does that mean I will kill people and their names will show up too?" I choked out the question while saying a silent prayer to the goddess it wasn't true.

"Doubtful. There's no chance you're half as strong as me." So the crow had a much larger ego than a bird should have had.

A lump the size of a tennis ball formed in my throat. I might have been wrong about bringing home such a dark item of magic. Coffee threatened to spill over the edge of the cup as I tried to take a drink thanks to my shaking hands. Entering the house the day before had been a mistake. I'd wanted excitement, to sever the control the Coven had. Maybe find something forbidden. Not death and murder. Definitely not with dark magic.

The Coven council could vote to strip me of all abilities

if they found out what I'd done. Breaking rules like entering the house was forbidden. They said if we broke one without thought we'd break another and another, eventually turning to dark magic. It seemed far-fetched, but they were older, our elders. They would know the consequences.

From the rumors, being stripped of magic was worse than death. It was emptiness and loneliness for the rest of our life. We used magic to heal people, to bring them happiness. To protect our town. If those abilities were taken from me, I'd be nothing.

Along with first-day jitters, I was going to spend the whole day second-guessing my decisions. Wonderful. What a way to start my junior year of college.

"Morning." Either my voice didn't crack too much or my roommate didn't notice anything wrong.

A pop rang through the tiny kitchen area of our suite. My hand flew to my chest and my gaze darted around the room as two pieces of toast popped out of the toaster.

"I'm going crazy," I mumbled.

"What was that?" they asked.

"Nothing." I yanked my bag off the hook on the wall and slung it over my shoulder then grabbed the pastry and my coffee and headed for the door.

I gave a quick wave on my way out the door.

***

The puke-green hybrid clunker of a car my grandparents

got me for my birthday two months ago squealed to a stop in the parking lot out front of Haberdash Hall. I'd usually walk, but Tierney was right about being late to class. I wasn't—ever. My heap of metal made more noise than it was supposed to and my six-month-old cousin's regurgitated lunch was prettier, but it ran and the gas was cheap. I couldn't complain since I didn't pay for it and didn't have a job to buy a new one.

A horrifying squawk came from above the building in front of me. Goosebumps rose on my arms. I pulled the strap of my messenger bag against my chest when I crossed my arms. I didn't need to see what was above to know what made that sound. That didn't stop me from raising my eyes just enough to spot at least twenty crows lined the edge of the building. Black ones. Blueish ones. Black and white ones. The one in the middle, my stalker, stood taller than all the others. It had to be mine with the way its beady eyes stared down at me and the white tuft of feathers on top of his head.

"Well, that's weird." Josh, the third apprentice of our group, preferred the term witch over warlock, stepped to my side and wrapped his arm around my shoulder before tucking me into his chest.

The lump in my throat refused to go away, no matter how hard I swallowed.

"Umm. Actually, I could use your help with that."

He gave me a side-eye. "Go on..."

"That crow in the middle, well, I followed him to the forbidden house in the fields."

Josh raised his palm. "Wait. You, Ms. I-don't-like-to-break-the-rules went to the field last night because a crow told you to."

I needed help with *Mort d'Evanoir*. I had no idea how it worked, or what it was. His jab at my willingness to do whatever I was told stung, but not enough for me to care at the moment.

"When I got to the house, I found a book inside. There's something dark about the book. The magic residue is a metallic taste like blood. It's disgusting. But I tried to leave it and couldn't. The magic, or something about it, drew me back. The problem is I don't know what to do now. The book is a mystery. I've read about it in the Coven library, but they don't have a lot written."

"And?" Josh asked.

He didn't get it. People's names, ways to die, images of some of the gruesome things listed flashed through my mind. Goosebumps rose on my arms and the air around me chilled. Just thinking about the book felt out of place. The damn crow's words about it being mine and making me powerful kept me from saying much more. All the back and forth in my head about what to say and what not to say made me nauseous. Car sickness was better than the indecisiveness I was putting myself through.

"And, what would you think if you found a book titled

Mort d'Evanoir?"

"Cool." Josh grinned.

"I'd read it, and figure out how to use the magic you mentioned." The voice of the last person melted my senses away.

The soothing, deep tone matched the face in the dream Tierney interrupted. The one that made my nights hotter than the summer sun. The tingles down my spine weren't from fear. Josh glared at her, but I stood frozen with my mouth wide open like the fool I was.

Mila Hutchings. My crush. A witch who wasn't part of our Coven, since her family had been banished when they performed black magic without permission. The Council forbade us from socializing with her. Of course she'd be the one to figure out how to use the magic in the book.

Soft fingers brushed across my lower back. Her warm breath caressed my neck right beneath my ear. I'd spent more time than I'd willingly admit imagining what dating Mila would be like. The only reason I hadn't made a move? Stupid rules that I didn't want to follow anymore. Okay, that and my insane fear of taking a leap like asking a girl out on a date. I wasn't going to go there. Using the Coven as my excuse was much better.

"Mmm. I could show you how to use the magic. But that would mean you'd have to associate with me. Wouldn't want to disappoint Mommy or your precious Coven."

Her words lit a fire under my skin that made me want to kiss her and punch her at the same time.

Mila tossed her head back and laughed as she walked away from us toward the front door. I stared at her back, loving the way her jeans showed off her curves and wishing I didn't care what people thought of me and my extra curves. She flaunted her blue and purple hair and grinned the sexiest evil grin I'd seen. Personally, she could have worn a brown bag and I'd have found her more attractive than most of the women I'd met. Josh hated her zero-creativity use of neutral-colored makeup. I envied her ability to make gold eyeshadow highlight her blue eyes.

"She could really use some color in her wardrobe. All black is so retro. No one should dress like that anymore." Josh shook his head and tugged the strap of his bag.

It seemed he wasn't going to help. Mila's offer was tempting. Very tempting.

CHAPTER 3

TUESDAYS WERE MY SHORT DAYS with only two classes back to back in the morning. By noon I figured the annoying crow sidekick I'd picked up wasn't going anywhere soon since it flew alongside my car as I drove home after Bio.

"Are you going to follow me everywhere?" I asked my empty car.

"Mort d'Evanoir belongs to me. You stole it."

My jaw fell open. "How could I steal a book you forced me to take?"

"It was not me who chose you, but the book. While I claim it as mine, Mort d'Evanoir does what it wants. Now, it has picked you to release its bindings. For a reason I will never understand."

I shook my head. My world flipped upside down again. For the last twenty-four hours, I'd debated with myself about the rightness of taking the book from the house. The crow, who urged me the night before to take it, changed his tune.

Wait. What did he mean by "release its bindings"? That couldn't be right. My coven wasn't even allowed to learn, much less practice, any sort of dark magic. *Mort d'Evanoir* had no reason to choose me. I was a nobody. Everything would've been easier if I took the book back to the house—dumped it and forgot about it.

Except...the idea of not having it left an empty spot in my soul. The desire to learn more was greater than the right thing to do, which was to get rid of it. I slammed my hands against the steering wheel, yanked the car to the side of the road, and got out.

"What do you mean, release its bindings?" My words didn't come out as shaky as expected. The curiosity outweighed the fear of what the bird's answer could have been.

"I told you, Mort d'Evanoir has been closed for fifty years. Even though I was the protector, I really had nothing to protect since it went missing. It found you in the house and you opened it. You released its bindings." The crow hovered at eye level.

"But why me?" I asked. "And what is a protector?"

"Don't know. Don't care. The protector should still be me, but the book has other ideas. I was the one designated to keep the book from being destroyed." An egotistical and pouty bird. Even better.

"So if you're not the protector, then why are you still here?" Thank the goddess no one drove past to see me flailing my arms and talking to a crow.

Rather than answer my question, the bird took off.

Our Coven had no reason to use dark magic. We were taught dark, or black, magic to be unworthy of our families. I slumped against my car door. My friends had been taught the same thing as me. The only person I knew who might have some knowledge of dark magic was the one whose family had actually used it.

My phone buzzed with a text.

Meet me at the park.

M.

I didn't recognize the number. The letter M was the only clue I had to who was texting me. Mila was the first person who came to mind, but she didn't have my number. At least, I'd never given it to her.

Another text came through seconds later.

Tierney: Josh mentioned some book you found. We're hanging at the bowling alley. Spill the tea.

I ignored both of them until I made it back to my dorm, happy to find my roommate gone.

In the quiet of my bedroom, I considered the two messages.

Tierney wouldn't stop until I answered her questions, but instinct told me not to tell her about the book. Then again, Tierney wouldn't have any idea what to do with an item like *Mort d'Evanoir*. Mila might.

Me: Can't make the alley. Have something I need to do.

T: Are you not coming to class tonight?

Me: Yeah. I'll be there.

T: Okay, we can talk then. Don't think you'll get out of it.

Mila and I didn't have many classes together. We'd gone to the same school since kindergarten and I'd never once attempted to talk to her. I chewed on my lip as I sent a quick text agreeing to meet her. It was time for me to shift our relationship from one in my dreams to real life. Who knew what the future held for us.

When I arrived, Mila sat at a picnic table tucked under an oak tree. Spanish moss hung from the limbs of the tree in a curtain of pale gray. A bold contrast to her darker skin tone. Even with her back to me, her blue and purple hair was hard to miss.

The woman I'd crushed on for the last couple of years sat waiting for me. She was the forbidden fruit, and for the first time, I had no hesitation to take a bite.

A few minutes had passed when Mila glanced over her shoulder and quirked an eyebrow. Our gazes met and she checked the watch on her wrist then her eyes were on me again. I rubbed my hands up and down my thighs.

Message received. I'd delayed getting out of the car

long enough.

I straightened my T-shirt, tightened my ponytail, and smacked my lips to make sure I had enough lip gloss. Not that I had any plans to need said lip gloss, but it never hurt to be prepared. I got out of the car and took my time appreciating the calm surrounding Mila.

The way the blue streaks in her black hair fell down her back reminded me of trips I'd taken camping and watched the waves crest on the lake. That inch of skin showing between the bottom of her shirt and the top of her pants begged for attention. Since the first time I noticed her love of crop tops and jeans, I imagined how smooth and soft her skin would be when I brushed my fingers across her lower back as I wrapped my arm around her waist.

A crow squawked from the tree to the left of where Mila sat. I cursed at the bird, hoping it heard. That was a bad influence. Mila was not.

"*Not likely,*" the crow said. His caw laugh was creepier than a clown's laugh. My whole body cringed.

"Did you bring it?" Mila asked as soon as I was in range.

"No. Wanted to talk to you first." I deepened my breathing and tried to slow my racing pulse.

Mila cackled like the witches from the movies. She wiggled her fingers in the air.

"Scared of me, little girl?" she trilled.

"How could I be scared of someone so cheesy?" I awkwardly settled onto the bench seat, nearly falling off backward.

"Oh no, you're scared of getting caught. Being seen with the *evil Hutchings girl*."

I rolled my eyes. "Grow up. The Coven might be pissed if they knew, which is why I don't intend to tell them."

The sudden bravado made me want to smile, but I bit my cheek to hold it back. There was no reason to let on that my insides trembled while my words sounded confident.

"I'm an open book. What do you want to talk about?" Mila propped her chin on her hands.

"You know about *Mort d'Evanoir*." I couldn't take my eyes off her.

More questions centered around kissing her and running my hands through her hair sat on the tip of my tongue. It was going to take a massive amount of restraint to stay on topic.

"I know a little, not a lot." Mila smirked.

Whether she read my thoughts or just liked playing hardball, I wasn't sure.

"What do you know?" I asked. My feet swung beneath the bench. The answers needed to start flowing or I'd have to leave with nothing new.

"How about you tell me what the whole metallic taste was that you told your friends about?"

I swallowed. My swinging paused. She'd overheard

more of our conversation than I thought.

"It's nothing. When I found the book I got this taste of blood in my mouth. I'm sure it's related to the dark magic, since the energy from the book raced through my body at the same time that nasty taste hit."

"Hmm. I'd say you're right about that."

The crow with a white tuft of feathers above us gave a low, hoarse caw. Despite it being almost ninety degrees outside the air around me felt like the middle of winter. I hated that crow. Mila's gaze went to the tree then back to me.

"A friend of yours?" she asked.

There wasn't any humor or sarcasm in her voice.

"Kind of." I traced a heart someone had carved into the wooden table. The earlier bravado dissipated.

"That doesn't make sense. Either the crow is yours or it isn't." Mila leaned forward, closing the distance between us.

"That crow—" I pointed over my shoulder "—led me to the book."

Mila clapped her hands together. Just as I was ready to ask how she knew about the book, the distinct sound of tires squealing through the parking lot interrupted us. Next to my rusted-out piece of crap was a sparkling silver Camaro. Katie.

No one knew I'd gone to the park.

When Mila began to turn around I had to act quick to

have a chance at keeping our meeting a secret.

"Who—" she asked.

I reached across the table, grasped her head with both of my hands, and prayed to the goddess she really was into girls like I suspected. Then I kissed her on the lips.

She moaned into my mouth, and what I thought would be awkward turned into an experience forever etched in my memories.

Mila's lips were soft, smooth. They pressed against mine with the perfect amount of pressure. Not that I'd kissed a lot of girls. She was my first. But the moment felt...flawless.

As she took my face in her hands and held us close, my mind began to wander. Did I slobber? Would she kiss me again? Did I want to kiss her again? Should I use more lip gloss next time?

Our mouths parted and I sighed at the loss.

"She'll know it's not real if you can't relax."

"It's not fa—"

Mila smashed her lips to mine once more as she slid her hands from my cheeks to my neck. If she thought I was faking it, then I had to try harder. I closed my eyes and forced my brain to shut off, to enjoy the moment, then lifted off the wooden seat and planted my hands on the table. Our kiss grew more intense with each passing second. A growl rose from one of us, but I wasn't sure who. Her tongue slid into my mouth, a soft caress, hesitant but confident. Mila had far more experience than I did.

"What the actual fuck? Wait until everyone hears about this. The Coven is going to flip out." Katie clicked her tongue.

I jumped back at her voice. No. No. No. My attempt to keep her from seeing us failed. The hair lifted on the back of my arms and my hands turned clammy. I struggled to get air into my lungs. If she told the Coven, I could be removed from training. Mom could be banished, too. I was her daughter—a representative of her and the witches of Evanoir. All my fears I'd decided to overcome flooded back. Like a rubber band, their control and influence over me snapped into place.

"What are you—" I started but Mila held a finger over my lips to silence me.

"Tell anyone, even your old, putrid cat and I swear on my life, I will spill your shit all over this town. What happens between us is our fucking business. Got it?" Mila stood tall, right in Katie's pale face.

Katie nodded and her wide, brown eyes turned in my direction. There was nothing more to say. Not that I could have followed Mila's threat anyway. She'd stunned me into silence. I thought she hardly knew me, and yet, she stood up for me as though we'd been lifelong friends, or dating for a while.

"Wait until I fill in our mentor on what you're doing outside of the apprenticeship. It should make training very interesting." Katie winked.

Without thinking, I bolted from the picnic table toward my car. Not because I kissed Mila. The thrill and desire strumming through my veins battled with the other emotions from Katie's threat. Embarrassed. Scared. Ashamed. Pissed the eff off. These were the reigns I wanted to break from.

"Azami, don't—" Mila called.

I didn't turn around. Didn't want to risk seeing shock or disappointment in Katie's face, but as I sped past her car I gave a flick of my wrist. The back passenger side tire let out a loud hiss. A flat tire would give me more time to run.

In less than twenty-four hours, I'd broken more Coven rules than I had in twenty-one years. Never before had I used magic against one of my Coven members. Nor had I used it so destructively. Get rid of a pimple, sure. Blow a tire on a car, nope.

For a split second, I considered taking the book to the Coven, telling Mila it was a mistake, and returning to my life of studying and cooking potions. That seemed less risky. Less drama. Less damage. Regulated.

In other words, boring. At most—a way to save face with the Coven. The burning in my veins, the sudden need for adrenaline coursing through, held me back from giving it all away.

Instead of go home, I hid out at my favorite seafood restaurant. The place was small, only eight tables in the dining area. Unlike most restaurants, the counter to order was at the front of the restaurant with seating in the back near the kitchen. They served meals in the plastic red baskets with a paper liner covered in little sketched shrimp. Mom and I had been eating there for as long as I could remember.

The delicious scent of fried crawfish etouffee balls permeated the air. My mouth watered. They were the perfect distraction from seeing Katie at the park. In a couple of hours, I'd have to face her at training, but for the moment, my favorite comfort food could sweep me off to a place without stress and drama.

A red basket slid across the table to me. Nothing out of the ordinary, except for the slender hand with bright pink nails passing the food over. Slowly, I raised my head. I knew that hand. Had just felt those fingers brush my skin as our lips touched.

"Mila," I whispered.

Metal scraped against tile floors when she slid out the chair across from me.

"Azami," she replied.

Her smile melted my insides and decision to return everything, forget about my crush, and get back to normal.

"Why did you follow me?" I asked before stuffing my mouth full of fried crawfish.

Her calculating, irresistible eyes screamed she wanted something.

"I wanted to make sure you were okay. Katie wasn't too happy at the park. Apparently, she must have run over a nail or something because one of her tires had gone flat."

I sucked in a breath and almost choked on a piece of crawfish. Then took a quick drink of water.

"Umm. Thank you. I'm fine. Bad luck for Katie."

Mila shook her head.

"You ran like there was some kind of invisible emergency."

Embarrassment warmed my cheeks. No doubt my forehead lit up like one of those flashing red signs. My skin hated me. When I was nervous or embarrassed the center of my forehead turned red and splotchy.

"Our Coven...ummm...we're actually forbidden from associating with your family." I shrugged. It was the weakest, but honest, answer.

"I see. So, when Katie showed up you what...got scared?"

I nodded and shoved a fry into my mouth.

"How do you feel about that rule?" she asked.

An easy question.

"I hate it. There's no reason for it. The only thing the Coven has ever said was your family had a history of performing dark magic. Makes no sense to me."

"And Katie?" Mila rested her chin on her fist. "Is she really a friend? I mean, it seems to me a friend would keep a secret, not devise ways to get you in trouble."

"I'm not saying you're wrong, but I'd rather not think about that right now. Tonight is going to be hell."

"Good. Then that should make things between us easier."

With that, Mila snatched an etouffee ball out of my basket, took a bite, winked, and left. I sat in awe, watching her walk away. With absolute certainty, I had no idea what she meant about making anything easier. But I wanted to find out.

<h1 style="text-align:center">CHAPTER 4</h1>

I STAYED AT THE SHACK until the last possible second, hoping to avoid a chance for Katie to ask about the park.

Our Coven owned an old plantation-style home on the south end of town. It sat on twenty-five acres of land and most everyone stayed away, afraid we'd cast spells on them if they got too close—not true at all. As far as I knew, we'd never done anything to the people of Evanoir, but our Coven wasn't a secret. Our closest neighboring coven was at least an hour west past the university. I went to school with a few of their witches. My recent feelings of distrust and contempt against the Coven weren't new. When I was twelve, I learned they practiced more advanced spells than we did by age ten, I considered switching covens then. My mom and grandmother were the only reason I didn't.

Katie and Josh cuddled next to each other on the loveseat to the right of the study door. Their conversation stopped mid-sentence as I walked up. My skin tightened with anticipation. Wondering whether or not Katie would mention my afternoon meet and greet with Mila made my heart race.

"Cutting it a little close," Josh said.

"Nope. I've got—" With a forced smile I checked my phone. "Five minutes before lessons start."

I searched the room beyond the loveseat, but it was empty. Where was Amanda, our trainer for the night? If she'd been there, we could've skipped the awkwardness of the moment. Instead, we had to wait outside the study until we'd been invited in. Coven teachings said it was so we learned respect and patience.

"Hey, Azami. Who were you at the park with today?" Katie asked with a snicker.

I balled my hands into fists and the urge to tell her it was none of her fucking business sat on the tip of my tongue.

"Good evening, trainees." Amanda stood in the doorway of the study.

Saved by the trainer. I swallowed my anger and turned my attention to Amanda. Even if I didn't want to do everything our mentors said we had to, losing my connection with the Coven wasn't appealing. We'd been taught the connection helped strengthen our magic. To be cut out was to lose that boost. These were the people I'd grown up with. My mom and her friends shared memories of my dad. My friends and I had our own stories. Giving all of that up just to have some freedom seemed overkill.

"Good evening," we responded in unison.

During training sessions, all Coven trainees had to act as one in speech, movement, and decisions. Teamwork and respect and all that nonsense. They treated us like robots instead of human beings. Mom said it wasn't that way when she was an apprentice. These new rules had been enacted by Gwen, our Coven leader.

I hated it but hadn't questioned anyone before. If Mom didn't see a problem with the rules, then it reasoned to believe I shouldn't either.

"Before we review, does anyone have questions or something they want to talk about?" Our trainer's bright green eyes lasered in on me.

I flinched under her stare. Did she know about *Mort d'Evanoir*? Or Mila? Since she was Josh's mom, the only way she'd have learned about either would've been through Katie and her big-ass mouth.

The four of us stood in the doorway, silent. I crossed my arms over my chest and glanced to my right, where Tierney stood, and to my left to see Katie and Josh winking at each other. Whether they were trying to get me to out myself, or if they'd told his mom, it didn't matter. They wouldn't win. I dropped my arms and squared my shoulders.

"Can I say something?" I asked.

Amanda nodded.

"Do you think we could talk about dark magic tonight?" Katie blurted.

Our trainer shook her head and turned back to me.

"You had something to say, Azami?"

"Yeah, I thought you should know I think I found my familiar. Last night, while I was out shopping in the forest, I found a crow that seems to have the ability to speak telepathically."

It wasn't a lie. Not the full truth, but enough to keep Katie from trying to get me in trouble. She had no proof of the book. As far as Mila, I'd figure something out if necessary.

Amanda ran her hands through her hair. I bit the inside of my cheek.

"You'll need to talk to your mom about the crow. Familiars are her expertise, not mine."

"So, about dark magic?" Katie said.

"No, we won't be discussing that tonight. Dark magic is forbidden within the Coven. Only one family has used it in our history and they were banished as a result."

One family, Mila's family, used black magic, for a reason we didn't know, and they were banished. If the magic was so horrible, then I couldn't help but wonder what would cause someone to turn dark.

"But why aren't we allowed to at least learn about it?" The words fell from my lips before I had a chance to stop them.

Three pairs of eyes focused on me. Amanda froze; her gasp the only indication she'd heard my question. For the first time, I'd pushed one of our trainers' buttons.

"Because Coven law says you're not to be taught or allowed to use it. We will *not* discuss this further." Sparks flared from Amanda's fingertips.

The four of us took a step back. None of the mentors lost control. In fact, their extreme restraint of the use of magic was the reason they'd been selected.

"That makes no sense." I threw my hands in the air and paused. If she lit me on fire it would've been deserved. When Amanda didn't move, I continued. "How are we supposed to recognize it or protect ourselves?"

"Enough!" Amanda snapped. Her face turned sunburn red and her eyes grew wide. She pointed a well-manicured fingernail in my direction—sans sparks.

"You're released from this evening's class. I expect when you return this weekend you'll remember your manners and the expectations of a Coven trainee."

"But..." Katie started and stopped when Amanda's glare aimed in her direction.

"Why are you kicking me out? Katie asked the question." I stood with my feet together and shoulders back, silently preparing a spell in case Amanda did something stupid.

None of us had done anything wrong. Yet, I was being

punished.

"Katie didn't push the matter when I said it was done. You were disrespectful when you pressed beyond my direction. As punishment, you won't attend class tonight."

"That's ridiculous. This is ridiculous. We ask a simple question and this is the result."

I shook my head. Amanda started to say something else then stopped.

"Don't worry. I'm leaving."

She turned her attention to the other three.

"Now, if we are past these questions, the three of you can follow me to the greenhouse. If anyone else would like to continue with a matter you've been instructed to leave alone, you may go home with Azami."

I watched as Katie, Tierney, and Josh shook their heads no. When the room cleared, I remained in my spot, waiting for guilt, remorse, or even sadness to kick in. This was the first time I'd argued with a mentor. The first time I'd been kicked out of training. There should've been something. But my emotions ran between curiosity and a little confusion. Maybe some fear of punishment.

After another minute or so, I grabbed my bag from the table at the front door. My phone vibrated at the same time I put the car in reverse. I pulled my phone out of the front pocket of my bag.

Meet me at the park. Same table. We're not done talking.

Once again, I wondered how Mila got my number? And how did she know I could even meet her at the park? Like usual, I weighed the pros and cons of going home versus meeting Mila. It was a thirty-minute drive back to my dorm, but the park was on the way. Since my first class wasn't until ten, I did not need to rush back home. This time, I'd have to remember to ask who gave her my number.

"Why do you insist on talking to anyone about Mort d'Evanoir? *I can tell you everything you need to know."*

The sun had set, making it impossible to see where the damn crow was.

"As if I would trust you. First, you said you'd tell me what I need to know. This time, I'm going to decide what I need and don't need. Not someone else. Second, you're a bird and apparently no longer protector of the book. Given that, I don't see how you could actually offer much," I replied.

"I haven't always been a bird, you ungrateful witch. I have more knowledge than you could fathom." The sharp snap of his voice straightened my spine and tensed my muscles.

"What, the Coven scares you? Why are you so insistent that I don't get help?" I asked.

"Your Coven is the reason I'm a crow." Even in my thoughts, the animosity rang loud.

"But I'm a member of the Coven."

"Ahh. You're a child. Not yet a true member. Maybe that is why the book chose you. Impressionable."

Good to know. The crow underestimated me.

"It's not your book anymore and I'm not a child." I flipped on my blinker and turned into the park. Suddenly talking to a bird I couldn't see didn't feel so strange.

"Compared to my eighty-five years of age, you're most definitely a child."

I parked under a streetlamp and considered everything that had happened in the last two days. Once I'd decided to not let the Coven dictate my every decision, life shifted. Adulting wasn't that hard after all.

"Right, so no response about the book?"

Poking the crow boosted my confidence. He was a bird—an old one—and he seemed more obsessed with *Mort d' Evanoir* than hurting me.

A knock on my window made me jump. I may have squeaked a little too.

"You wanna sit in the car instead?" Mila asked.

I nodded and unlocked the doors.

"Hey," I greeted.

When her warm hand covered mine, I jumped. Being with Mila didn't scare me. She turned me inside out. My mouth watered. Her crisp, soft scent of fresh-cut flowers intoxicated me. Words failed to form. My thoughts on one thing...kissing her again.

"Azami, relax."

Her hair draped down her arms and my fingers ached to run through the locks. Warmth washed over me and I licked my lips. How did other people deal with these kinds of desires?

"How do you know about the book?" I asked.

"My aunt told me about it. She said the Coven used to have it in their possession, but someone managed to lose one of the most dangerous books in existence." Mila picked at her nail polish as she spoke.

"And I found it. Leave it to me to find a book of such dark magic. I don't even know what to do with it. How did I get so lucky?"

"Does this book have anything to do with the Coven's ridiculous rules about performing magic beyond their carefully scripted guidelines?" she asked.

"How do you know about those?" I'd wondered what rules, if any, Mila knew.

She scoffed.

"Azami, my family was banished because of using dark magic. Do I need another reason to know about them?"

Oh. Right. I hadn't considered the connection, but it made sense.

"Well, no. I guess I figured your family wouldn't want anything to do with us, so you wouldn't bother to learn our rules."

Mila shrugged.

"Mom and Dad don't want us to learn them. They

wrote off the Coven before we were even born. Mom's family isn't even from the Evanoir Coven. She won't say what coven she's from. Anyway, I wanted to know more. Going along with the status quo isn't my vibe. I did my research. Talked to a few people."

I nodded. If I were in her shoes, I'd probably have done the same thing.

"Did your aunt tell you anything more?" I asked.

When Mila didn't answer right away I moved my seat back and turned to her. The possibilities for her silence filled my thoughts. She knew something and didn't think I could handle it. Her aunt was an open wound I poured salt into. When she continued to stare out the window at the empty park I considered apologizing.

"Why are you so interested in this book? Why take it from that house?" Mila broke the silence with more questions I wasn't prepared to answer.

I popped the joints of my fingers one by one and tapped my foot against the floorboard. But maybe I could tell a partial truth. This needed to be a game of give and take. To expect Mila to share everything she had and me give nothing in return wasn't right.

"It's a part of my Coven—I think. Honestly, I'm kind of hoping it can help me become better at magic."

Okay, so it wasn't really the truth at all. While I was happy with what I'd done so far, the last thing I wanted was Mila to see a weakness and use that against me.

"My aunt didn't tell me a lot." Mila shifted her gaze from left to right then focused over my shoulder. A partial lie, maybe? "I don't think the book will help the way you think it will."

"Tell me what you know," I said.

The book had already helped exactly the way I wanted, and all I did was take it from the house and put it in my room. One act of defiance and I'd begun to find the courage to start making my own decisions without whispers from others to manipulate me into doing what they wanted.

"What she told me might not be true. I mean, Aunt Dot was a little more than crazy. Especially at the end, always talking about the winds speaking to her and how I needed to eat more vegetables to improve my spell work."

My heart softened as I listened to her talk about Aunt Dot. The story, her words, held so much love. Her gaze drifted as she spoke, but this time it wasn't because I believed her story to be a lie. It was more like recalling memories that brought Mila joy.

The Coven spoke of being a family, except family was the gleam in Mila's eyes right then, not the distance I felt growing between me and my friends. I reached out and placed my hand over Mila's, wanting to comfort her and selfishly hoping to experience some of the love she radiated. Our fingers laced together and she looked at me through lowered eye lids.

"I want to kiss you again," I whispered.

"The book is bound by a spell. No one knows what it is. Aunt Dot said it's a book of death. She used to tell me how it made people die when she wanted to scare me, which worked by the way. Her stories caused nightmares so bad I couldn't sleep for days afterward."

Wow. That was awful. Both what Aunt Dot had done and the fact Mila ignored my confession. Acid crept up my throat, leaving a burning sensation in its wake. Rejection was a bitch.

"And you liked her?" I gasped at my own question.

Mila laughed.

"Yeah. After the first couple of times, Mom found out what was happening and she made Aunt Dot promise not to tell me the stories anymore. Later on, when she talked about the book she left out a bunch of details. It wasn't nearly as exciting to listen to her as it had been."

I didn't know what to say about her aunt or my confession about our kiss. My first kiss and my first rejection on the same day. Mila must have had lots of experience kissing other people, because the memory of her hands on my face, the soft brush of her skin against mine, would forever be etched in my mind. Later that night I'd pity myself. Right then, there was one more thing I wanted to ask before I left.

"Did anyone ever tell you where to search for the binding spell? It has to be written down somewhere, right?"

"No." Mila opened the car door and got out, she walked around to my side of the car. I rolled the window down.

"What—"

I didn't get to finish my question before her mouth pressed against mine. Without thinking, I reached out to grab her waist, then tried to pull her back into the car with me. The clank of her head hitting the top of my car broke the moment.

"Ouch." Mila rubbed her forehead.

"I'm so sorry. This...I'm...wow. That was awful."

My cheeks heated and I was never more thankful for the dark night sky.

She smiled.

"It happens. Good to know I excite you that much." Mila winked before walking away.

I sat with my mouth hanging open and I still didn't know how she got my phone number.

CHAPTER 5

JOSH MET ME AT THE door of my building Wednesday morning.

"Can I tell you a secret?" he asked as he slung his arm over my shoulder.

I considered pushing him away, since we weren't really the kind of friends who told each other secrets. Not anymore, anyway. Since he and Katie became besties our junior year of high school, most days Josh and I were friends bordering on acquaintances.

We walked a few feet down the sidewalk before I answered.

"Umm...sure."

"You have to promise not to tell anyone what I'm about to tell you." He checked over my shoulder before looking over his own.

His hand shook against my back. Whatever he needed to tell me was important. We'd grown up together and I'd never seen him so jittery. Energetic. High strung. Yes, to both, but never paranoid and jittery.

"I'm not going to make any promises, Josh. We both know it's dumb to make a promise about something without all the details."

He blew out a puff of air. "Fine. It's about Katie and the Hutchings."

My heart actually stopped beating for a count of five. There was only one connection I was aware of between Katie and the Hutchings. Mila. My gut instinct was to deny anything he knew, but I stopped short as my brain finally worked out the fact he wouldn't ask me to keep a secret about myself.

"All right. I promise." The words left a sour taste in my mouth. The last thing I wanted to do was promise to keep a secret about one of the people who had something to use against me.

Of the four of us, she was more likely to use secrets to her advantage. Of course, knowing one about her would give me leverage in return, but I wasn't that kind of person.

"I think she's dating Dustin Hutchings."

Josh nearly tripped over his feet when I came to a stop in the middle of the path.

"Say what?" I screeched.

He rolled his eyes then paused between each word as he said them again. "I. Think. Katie. Is. Dating. Dustin. Hutchings."

Less than twenty-four hours before Katie threatened to tell everyone, but no one said a word at training. An idea began to form. Had Katie kept her mouth shut because she had her own secret?

"Josh, did she...did Katie...umm..." I wanted to ask if she'd told him about me and Mila but hesitated. If she hadn't, then I'd out myself.

"You want to know if Katie told me about the park yesterday."

"Guess I know the answer."

"Why do you think I came to you with this news? You have a reason to keep it to yourself. If you tell Gwen, then Katie can tell her about you and Mila."

My theory for Katie's silence the night before didn't make sense, though. Since I didn't know about Dustin, she'd have had no reason to worry about me telling anyone. There had to be another reason she'd spared me the trouble.

Josh and I made our way to my first class in silence. If I'd been less focused on myself, I would've asked more about Katie and what he knew.

"Have you seen Tierney this morning?" I asked as we entered the building.

"Nope. She was supposed to meet me for coffee, but texted at the last minute and said she had some project due for her chemistry lab."

"Weird. I thought her Chem lab was on Tuesdays and

Thursdays."

"It is."

Josh's blank stare indicated he missed my point.

"Today's Wednesday. I didn't think the lab was available this morning."

"Hmm. Good point." He shrugged. "Maybe she got some kind of exception from the professor."

That didn't make sense, but who was I to try and argue. It wasn't like Tierney's classes were my responsibility. She'd promised to talk in her text, but after my rejection I figured I'd see her first thing that morning.

"Did I miss anything important last night?" I asked.

"Not really. Some basic recipes for protection spells."

"All right. Guess I won't have much to catch up on on Saturday. I gotta get to class."

Josh grabbed my wrist as I started to leave.

"Hey, Azami, there's something else."

I'd been checking my phone to make sure the ringer was off, but the icy tone to his voice drew my eyes to his lips.

"What's going on?" I held my books to my chest like they'd somehow protect me.

"You need to give that book to the Coven."

Whoa. A pocket of cold air blanketed us.

"Umm. Why do you say that?"

He leaned in closer, the whites of his eyes expanding until the brown irises almost disappeared. "They know and they aren't happy. You need to give it to them before they take it."

"What if I don't?" My voice quivered, no matter how hard I tried to let on I wasn't spooked by the sudden shift in his demeanor.

"Then people will die." His voice changed, unrecognizable to me, lower with more vibration.

Josh walked away without another word.

A short burst of laughter sounded from behind me, but I stood frozen in place.

"That didn't take as long as I thought it would. Are you going to give it up?" Mila asked over my shoulder.

My hand flew to my chest and I dropped my phone in the process. Without thinking, I bent down to pick it up and pressed my ass right into Mila. The bump threw me off balance, but Mila wrapped her fingers around my hips, steadying me. I didn't know if I should be turned on or embarrassed.

"Shit. Sorry." I slowly turned to face her. "Do you have a class in this building?" I asked.

"Nah, but I caught you and Josh walk in out of the corner of my eye, so I thought I'd come say hi."

She didn't smirk or laugh at me. The smile on her lips looked genuine. I checked her eyes for more truth, but they were clear. No hint of humor. I finally let out a sigh of relief. For once, I didn't become the butt of a joke thanks to an accident, something my friends were keen on doing.

"So, you going to give the almighty coven *Mort*?" she asked again.

"No." I moved past her to the doors of the lecture hall for my Government class.

"Good. I want to see what it can do."

I jerked to a stop. "What do you mean, *you* want to see what it can do?"

Mila waved her hand through the air. "Come on, don't act like you aren't curious. We both know it's full of sinister magic. It's got to have some kind of power. I think I can help you figure it out."

"Fine. You're right, but I have to get to class." She called my bluff. I did want to know more.

Mila blew me a kiss and sauntered off. The woman had a way of leaving me speechless.

***

My history instructor, Professor Trombull, turned off the lights like always. The bright glow of the white board illuminated the room.

"All right. Who wants to recap where we left off yesterday with the Romans?"

The class groaned. We did the same thing every day. Trombull went on for thirty minutes before blinding us with the fluorescent lights. Then we took a quiz over his lecture. It was my least favorite class.

Mr. Trombull's deep voice vibrated through the room, lulling half the class to sleep. A picture of a Roman colosseum appeared on the board at the same time the metallic taste of blood filled the back of my throat.

I bit the inside of my cheek. A warm, salty drop of blood splashed onto my tongue. In a way, the real thing was somewhat comforting. I searched the room; no one stood out as different. As far as I knew, I was the only witch in class. Except, that had to be wrong.

There had to be a reason I tasted the dark magic. Someone was using it.

I clenched my hands into fists. Every muscle in my body seized, paralyzed me. I couldn't move. The lecture hall disappeared, replaced by an empty field. I blinked a few times, but nothing changed. Somehow I'd been transported to another place. When I tried to raise my arm, nothing happened.

The field I'd been taken to was familiar. A blurry house-like structure sat to my left. The pointed roof reminded me of the house where I'd found *Mort d'Evanoir*. If only I could have gone closer to check.

A woman with long, curly, chestnut brown hair came into view. She wasn't blurry like the rest of my surroundings. The closer she came, the more I recognized her features. The hair, her honey eyes, and round face; she and Gwen could have been twins. I didn't know her name, but there was no doubt she and our Coven leader were related.

The woman wore an ankle-length dress layered with

bright fabrics and ruffled hems. The colorful mix of red, yellow, pink, orange, and blue plaid of the form-fitting, spaghetti strap top reminded me of a dress I'd worn for Easter when I was six. The vivid colors contrasted with the lackluster smoky gray sky and damp air. She was light in a dark moment.

She moved close enough for me to notice red streaks through her eyes and puffy skin beneath them.

"Who are you?" I asked.

She didn't respond or even acknowledge me.

Could she even see me?

The metallic taste on my tongue grew so strong I gagged. Part of me wanted whatever was happening to stop, but the other part needed to know the woman's story.

She clutched a black box against her chest as she walked toward a fire pit. Her lips moved, but no sound came from them. A few feet later, I recognized the box, only it wasn't a box. Between her arms, along the spine in gold lettering, were the words *Mort d'Evanoir*.

I had so many questions on the tip of my tongue. What was she planning to do?

Was she the protector?

No. I shook my head. The crow protected *Mort*. I needed to learn more to figure out who the mystery woman was and how she got the book.

Flames surged into the sky, turning blue at the bottom when she stopped in front of the pit. Her arms lifted overhead, her fingers white against the black leather of the book. She plunged the book into the center of the flames.

I gasped. Smoke filled my lungs making it impossible to breathe. Heat singed my body, burning me from the inside out. When I tried to reach for my throat my arms wouldn't budge. Still paralyzed, panic took over.

The field began to spin and the earth dropped out from under my feet. My chest tightened and my insides quivered as I plummeted down a black hole. Flames burst up around me. I was dying. Or she was dying. I couldn't say for sure.

"Don't betray me."

The words whispered through my thoughts before the field disappeared and my lungs cleared. Not a higher-pitched voice. It was lower, like a man's. So much like Josh's warning. The black hole shifted to the white walls of the lecture hall. One by one my classmates came into view. Before my sight fully returned Professor Trombull flipped on the lights.

"Any questions about the Romans? Today is our last day discussing them. Your midterm is next week."

The Romans didn't matter. I had to figure out who that woman was and what the voice meant.

The shock faded, replaced by goosebumps popping up on my arms. Thankfully, the panic attack didn't last long.

A paper football hit my shoulder. I picked it up to toss it in the trash on my way out the door only to pause when my hands warmed with a familiar sense of lighter magic.

The residual panic had faded but left my fingers chilled to the bone. It hurt to unfold the triangle-shaped paper. Slowly, words appeared.

Look outside.

I glanced to my left. Mila stood in the middle of the grass waving to me. Apparently, she knew cloaking spells since no one seemed to have noticed her yet. She wore high-waisted black shorts and a cropped sweater with a block of black at the top and black and gray stripes at the bottom. A perfect mix of warm and cool with the spring temperatures. Her hair was covered by a gray knit beanie, and she had on a pair of solid black low-top Converse.

The girl was so cute. I sighed. We needed to talk: the urge to tell her about the dream, or vision was too strong to ignore. Everyone else would laugh at me or tell me how dangerous it was to have the book and that it should be taken to the coven. Mila had yet to laugh. Her encouragement to dig deeper was more than any of my friends had done now or in the past.

One of the first spells we learned came to mind. I murmured the words, "Pen to paper. Words to thoughts. Deliver the message to Mila."

Then I wrote. *Something just happened. I need to talk to you.*

If the spell worked, my response would be delivered through the wind and she'd receive the telepathic message.

Of course, I had to hope she recognized it came from me and didn't ignore the voice in her thoughts. With my head in my hand, I stared out the window and waited for her answer.

Same. I talked to my dad about Mort. She replied telepathically.

That was something I hadn't experienced except with my crow. The Coven refused to use telepathic communication, stating it was too easy to intercept. More of the leader's logic that made no sense, but we didn't argue. I'd come to that realization a lot lately. After the reaction from our mentor at training, I wanted to keep asking questions from now on. Accepting things as they were without question no longer satisfied me.

I returned with *This class is almost done. Give me ten minutes.*

Mila nodded and crossed her arms over her chest. Her left foot pointed outward and her smile quirked.

Dad told me how the magic works. The book needs two people to activate the death magic. A wielder and a protector. Meet me at my car and I'll tell you more.

Two people. If that was true, then the woman in my dream could have been the previous wielder since the crow was the protector.

Fine.

It took almost twenty minutes for me to get out of class. Mila leaned against a sleek blue sports car, studying her fingernails. A tiny green dragon of jealousy reared its head. It seemed so strange for her to like me. I had a junker of a car, didn't have her good looks, and was part of a coven of witches that hated her family.

I shook my head. The swooning had to wait. There were more important things to discuss.

"We need to go somewhere we won't be seen. Any ideas?" I asked in greeting.

Mila shrugged. "My house?"

A gasp caught in my throat. No. That was a bad idea. Alone with Mila where no one would see us. There were too many bad, or maybe good in a bad way, things that could happen. Not that I was going to throw myself at her, but the idea made me smile inside.

"Maybe not. Anywhere else?"

"This is a small town, it's not like we have a lot of options and I don't have much time."

Right. Okay.

"Let's go to the Arts building. They've got that garden we can hang out in without a bunch of people around to overhear."

Mila walked toward the shed while I waited a minute or two just in case someone was watching us. Katie had seen us together and told Josh. I didn't need anyone else in the Coven learning about our friendship...relationship. I wasn't sure what to call us.

"So, what happened in class?" she asked as we sat on

a concrete bench surrounded by purple and blue Louisiana Irises.

"I had a vision. I think. This woman was holding *Mort d'Evanoir* and she tried to throw it in a fire. Then someone gave a warning not to betray them. It wasn't her though."

"Hmm. That fits what I learned." Mila pulled on a tall blade of grass and rolled it between her fingers. "Did she do anything else? Were you part of the vision or watching it from the outside?"

"I don't even think she knew I was there. It was like watching an old movie."

"Have you ever had this happen before?" Mila played in the dirt with the toe of her black and white tennis shoes.

I wanted to know where she was going with all of it but was afraid she'd stop if I asked.

"No. It's weird. Also, there was the taste of blood in my mouth again. But there couldn't have been anyone practicing magic. I was the only witch that I know of."

Except Mila was there almost immediately after the vision. She could've used magic.

"It was related to the book, maybe that's why you sensed the magic," she said.

I shrugged.

"Maybe. You said my vision fit with what you learned."

"Right. So besides Dad telling me there are two people needed for the book's power to manifest, he also said it's almost impossible to destroy. Apparently, when the book is at full strength it can do things. Like, keep that woman from burning it."

A book with that much power would be awful in the wrong hands. For the first time, I wondered if being its protector was a good thing. If I could keep it from having full power, then I could save lives. I'd have to learn more about it before I gave it to the Coven. There was too much at risk.

"Is there a way to find the wielder?" I asked.

Mila shook her head. "I'm not sure. Dad didn't say."

That made sense. If we knew who the wielder was we could stop them from using the book's magic. Of course, nothing was ever that simple, but I still understood. Regardless, I knew my next goal was to find the wielder.

"Well, umm, thanks. I gotta get home."

I stood and dusted off my shorts then awkwardly held out my hand to shake hers. Mila stood, shaking her head.

"You're different, Azami. Weird. But I like it." She didn't shake my hand, which only made it more awkward. "Want to go to lunch on Saturday?"

The vision scrambled the thoughts in my head. I had no idea how to process what happened or what it meant. My stomach fluttered in response to Mila's lunch request. For a second, I considered jumping up and down screaming yes. Then I reeled my excitement back in.

"A date?" I sat back down next to her and studied the bench with an intensity that made no sense.

There were so many ways a date with Mila could go wrong. We could have nothing to talk about outside of the book and magic. Someone from my Coven could see us and cause a scene, which would make her think I was too much work. I could say something stupid and she'd realize I wasn't worthy of her time. My feet became restless, kicking back and forth under the table, as I considered one scenario after another where I did or said something stupid and ruined my chance with Mila.

She slid a finger under my chin and raised my head until our eyes met.

"Yes. A date. You and me at a restaurant. People might see us."

I cared about people finding us, but not for the reasons she thought. That fear was easy to push away since I wanted to go out with her more than worry about other people.

"Want me to meet you there?" I kicked the ground with my toes. "Or I could pick you up."

"I'll text you where to meet." Mila held up her hand when I started to argue. "Right now you want to pick me up, but when Saturday gets here, I don't want you to back out in fear of your Coven."

Damn. She already knew me so well.

"Deal," I said.

CHAPTER 6

I TOOK THE STEPS TO my dorm two at a time. Once behind my bedroom door, I pulled *Mort d'Evanoir* out from under my socks in the top dresser drawer. Carefully, I unwrapped the bandana I'd used to protect it. The leather spine creaked as I opened it.

When I read the names I understood what the second column meant. They were descriptions of how people died. One person, Julie Ann, died in a fight when her neck snapped.

There was something gruesome yet curious about it all. Another person, Christopher, drowned when his car fell into the river.

Some of the deaths were as simple as a heart attack and others right out of the stories of nightmares. I slammed the book shut after reading that Thomas was killed when he fell onto an axe and cut off his own head.

"Impossible," I whispered.

A rustle sounded below my window. I peeked out between the curtains through the open window but didn't see anything. The crow was nowhere to be found either.

"Who's there?" I called out into the shadowy night.

For a split second, I could have sworn a guy ran from behind the tree. I squinted to see if I recognized him, but he wasn't there when I looked again.

More rustling. I tugged the curtain back further and waited to see if the mystery guy would make himself known. After what felt like forever, a dark head swept from left to right, teeth clacked together. Its four short legs slid across the ground.

"Stupid alligators. No more tonight. This is daytime-only research."

Twenty minutes later, I kicked my foot out from beneath the blanket then flipped to my stomach and back to my back. Sleep refused to take me. My mind played a video of images from the last few days. Mila at the park. Tierney in the woods. Katie. The book popped up between each new scene.

The woman from my vision at school took her rotation through the video. All of my questions about who she was and why I was having visions of strangers sat front and center.

Eventually, the images blurred until they faded completely to darkness and I fell into a sleep full of more dreams—or, better yet, another nightmare.

Tanned ivory skin with peach tones, short golden brown hair and hot pink nails burned into my memories.

Someone had spread a woman out on the beach, her arms in a V-shape and wrists tied to tent stakes. Her legs spread eagle with ankles bound just like her wrists. Blood dripped off her stomach onto the ground. Her black two-piece swimming suit shredded as if she'd been attacked by an animal.

She moved her lips, but no sound followed. I inched closer. The woman continued to talk, but the space around us stayed silent. Finally, I knelt and crawled to her head. There I could see chunks of hair missing, ripped from her skull. My gut rolled and I threw up all over the ground next to her. I hovered over her mouth in an attempt to hear what she whispered.

"Keep Mila safe," she repeated it over and over.

"Who are you?" I asked, but her only response was a whine of a breath.

"Keep Mila safe."

"From whom?"

She didn't answer as her head fell to the side. I watched her take her final breath. The last words on her lips. "Safe."

I shot out of bed, each breath coming so fast it made me dizzy. I buried my fists in my eyes, trying to force the image from my dream away. No luck. Even with my comforter tugged up to my neck I couldn't get my body to stop shaking.

Another mystery woman, but this one tied to Mila. She wanted me to keep her safe, but I had no idea who from or how.

One question had me stumbling to the drawer where I'd put the book before crawling into bed. Without knowing anything about the woman in my dream, besides her wish about Mila, I had to guess where to start. I started at the end of the book and went backward until I found the names of people my mom had talked about. Before I found anyone with Mila's last name, another entry froze me in place.

Marshall Durand.

The actual words next to his name didn't matter, I didn't have to read them. Dad's death wasn't a mystery. Trampled to death. The date, April tenth two thousand and four. Three days before I was born. I never had the chance to meet my dad. He died trying to leave a rock concert when the roof began to cave in halfway through the set. The crowd scrambled to get out, knocking him to the ground then trampling him as they fought to save their own lives.

Mom told the story many times. Showed me pictures of them growing up, getting married, all the good ones. The print of his name had faded, but that didn't minimize the pang of sadness that hit me under my ribs.

His death didn't hurt so much as the fact I'd never had a dad. The Coven fathers tried to be dads to me, except it wasn't the same. Or at least I imagined it wasn't.

I shook off the heaviness in my arms and legs to continue my search for the woman of my nightmares. Replace one bad time with another.

"It's not here. Why isn't there a Hutchings in the book? It has to be here."

"You must ask the source to receive the answer."

That stupid crow was back again. He'd been gone all night and returned when I needed him the least.

"Who the hell is the source? I thought that was you."

He tapped his beak against the window. *"No, it's not me. The source changes as the book desires."*

I pointed to my chest. "So I'm the source now."

"That is undecided."

"You're not making sense. Supposedly I unbound the book, but now it's undecided if I'm the source or not."

I threw my hands up, clueless what to do about the stupid bird who liked to give worthless advice. Mila was the only person who might have answers—again. The coincidence of the one person I wasn't supposed to associate with was the only one who helped me wasn't missed.

Except there were still a few more hours before the sun rose. I considered texting her anyway, but the conversation we needed to have wasn't one for text messages.

By the time I felt comfortable texting Mila about meeting up, I'd written and deleted my message at least a hundred times. She responded within seconds of my request.

All of my good intentions flew out the window the moment I found her waiting for me. Someone needed me to keep her safe, and I would do what they asked. One way or another.

"Do you have an aunt who would have hot pink nails?" I stood beside Mila in line at the cafeteria.

Electricity flowed through her skin to the tips of my fingers when the back of our hands touched. Warm. Comforting. Light. Her head dropped to her chest. I wanted to hug her. Tell her never mind.

"My aunt. Why?" Mila faced me.

"I had a dream about her last night."

Mila shook her head. "Why would you dream about her?"

"I don't know. The woman in my nightmare told me to keep you safe. Are you close to her?"

Mila chose her breakfast then moved toward the cashier. We didn't speak until we sat at a booth away from everyone else.

"We were. Aunt Monica was attacked on her camping trip this past weekend."

"Attacked? But how does that happen on the beach?"

"A bear, I guess. That's what Dad said." Mila took a bite of sausage.

The way she refused to meet my eyes and the somber tone of her voice should've been enough to keep me from asking more questions, but I couldn't stop.

"Do you know why she'd tell me to keep you safe? I've never even met her. We barely know each other. This is so...weird."

"You opened the book." Mila changed the subject. It wasn't a question, more of an accusation. I nodded. "How? The book isn't supposed to be opened. The stories I've been told say it's been sealed shut."

"I don't know. It opened like any other book. This wasn't the first time. What else do you know?"

"Some." She tapped the tip of her chin with her finger. "Have you had visions like this before?"

I shook my head. Were my visions tied to the book? The first one made sense, but not Mila's aunt. Unless the Hutchings family was somehow associated with the book, which would have given my Coven reason to banish them.

"What about your aunt? Aren't you upset?" I asked.

Mila swallowed. Her gaze focused over my shoulder. A layer of water coated her eyes.

"You know what, don't answer that. I'm rude and an idiot," I said.

"You're not an idiot. I mean, maybe a little awkward and have bad timing, but that's all." The small quirk of her lips didn't help ease my guilt. Tact was not one of my stronger skills.

I stretched my arm across the table and took her hand in mine. "Tell me more about you. What's your major?"

"I want you to help me clear my family's name."

If I agreed, I'd go against everything the Coven taught us. Except I couldn't promise something I knew I couldn't do. As an apprentice, I had absolutely zero say in the Coven's actions.

"How am I supposed to do that?" I asked.

"We could figure it out together, and I'll help you with *Mort.*"

Throwing *Mort* into the mix made it a much harder decision. Turning down her request put me back at square one with the book. Accepting it meant we'd spend more time together and both get what we wanted. Her name cleared and I'd...well, I wasn't sure what my fascination with *Mort d'Evanoir* was yet. Something about the book and the coven's strong opinion of dark magic intrigued me. I wanted to know more.

"Are you sure she'll give you what you seek?" The crow interrupted my thoughts.

The stupid bird came and went without warning. I couldn't see him and yet...he always had an answer. It didn't matter if I hadn't asked a question.

My heart fought with my brain. Guilt for not being upset for breaking another Coven rule weighed on my shoulders. While Mila drank her coffee, my gaze locked on the white wall behind her. The dirty paint blurred with my attention.

Mila squeezed my hand, startling me. "My major is

Toxicology. I want to know why chemicals go bad."

"What? I'm sorry, I zoned out for a second."

She smiled. "Toxicology. That's my major."

"I read about that degree but had no idea what kind of job I could get with it. Not that jobs matter for me. I'm destined to be the up-and-coming life of the Coven. All of us are. Once we become full members we can take over for our parents." My words dripped with enough contempt even I recognized the change in tone.

"So, that means what for you?" Mila asked.

"Mom manages the training schedule for apprentices. I won't take over for a while, which is why I chose to go to college."

Mila choked on her drink. After wiping coffee off the corner of her lips she said, "You're here to pass time while you wait for the Coven to give you a job? Did I understand you correctly?"

As I listened to her interpretation I realized how ridiculous the notion must sound. For the first time in three years, I began to realize how much of a mistake I'd made.

"Yeah, that sounds about right. They've got tight leashes on all of us." I added another bullet to my growing list of reasons convincing me the Coven wasn't all it was meant to be.

One part I wasn't sure of was when the Coven changed. Did our leader put us on this path of no choice or was it is before Gwen? When Mom told me stories of her years going through the apprenticeship it sounded like fun. That's when she truly felt alive and at one with being a witch. I had none of that. Mila had what my mom had, or it seemed like that to me.

"So what is your major?" she asked.

"General studies." I let the answer drift without further explanation.

Later that afternoon I planned to go to the student center and change my major. It was late, I only had one year left before I graduated, but General Studies would get me nowhere. One day if I decided to leave the Coven I'd have nothing. No skills. No education worth mentioning. That had to change.

The Commons buzzed with people coming in for coffee, a quick breakfast, or early morning study time. A couple of guys sat at the table next to us, yelling at their friends as they came in. Soon, their group grew to six smashed around a table for two. One of the men, extra sweaty and loud, pressed into my side. He didn't seem to care about personal space, not offering even an apology or asking if I minded his disgusting overgrown muscles smashed against me.

Mila wiggled her fingers and winked. In a split second, I went from uncomfortable to relaxed. The sounds of the Commons muffled. The clatter of trays and silverware disappeared. When I observed the area around us everyone appeared…blurry.

"Did you do something?" I asked Mila.

She nodded.

"Simple magic. I'm surprised you don't know the spell. It's great for making a personal bubble in a crowded space."

The ability to do magic when and wherever she pleased was something I knew nothing about. As thankful as I was for her spell, I wouldn't lie to the jealousy taking up space within the emotional blanket I'd crafted in my mind.

We sat with our hands locked together enjoying the stillness around us—or I did. Mila kept her gaze on the blurred group of guys beside me.

"What if you changed your major?" she asked. "Maybe tell the Coven to fly a kite and do what you want. Let someone else learn from your mom. Break tradition."

Mila's question mimicked the questions I'd spent the last few minutes asking myself. It hadn't seemed like a possibility until that moment. Everyone knew what their role in the Coven would be from the day they were born. I could be a teacher. Or maybe start my own business that used the skills I had learned from the Coven.

"You're not allowed to socialize with *her*." The venom in Katie's *her* dripped like acid through our private bubble.

"Who died and made you boss?" I asked in a lame attempt at a comeback.

Katie hissed at me, an actual cat-like hiss. "She's dangerous, Azami. We all know the Hutchings family is not a good family. I don't want to see you get hurt. Second, what's gotten into you lately? You tell us you found this book of dark magic, then get kicked out of training, and now you're hanging out with Mila."

More than once the last few days I'd asked myself what was going on in my head. The problem was, I didn't have an answer. Not a good one. The only change had been the book. Except logically that wasn't a good explanation.

"It's not just *a book,"* the crow whispered.

"That's interesting coming from you. Last I heard you and Dustin were a thing." Mila shot me a raised eyebrow. I figured she'd have known about her brother, but maybe I'd been wrong. I continued, "What's wrong with questioning what we've been told? I mean, haven't you ever wondered why the Coven has so many rules about dark magic?"

Katie tossed her hair over her shoulder and huffed.

"That's none of your business. I suggest you leave Mila alone, or you'll find yourself in her shoes."

What the hell did that mean? My jaw clenched shut and I pressed my lips together. Under the table, I balled my hand into a fist as Mila squeezed my other one.

"It's time to go," Mila said. "You should probably watch your back. The last time someone crossed my family it didn't end well for them. I mean, we're the banished ones after all."

We gathered our trash and left a gaping-mouthed Katie standing beside our table alone.

CHAPTER 7

BY SATURDAY THE CROW QUIT talking to me. I was too busy anticipating and worrying about my lunch date with Mila to miss the bird. It took forty-five minutes of standing in front of my closet debating what to wear before I found the best outfit. My roommate left twenty minutes into the process. Mila hadn't said where we were going. A dress would've been cute unless we spent the whole time outside walking around. Then I would've needed shorts and a cute shirt.

I settled on a pair of teal linen shorts and a flowy, cotton off-white tank top—cool and comfortable, but a little dressy too. Shoes were a little easier to choose since I didn't have that many options. I slipped on my favorite pair of brown flats. Once I finished getting ready, I decided to try a revealing spell I'd found in one of the Coven's spellbooks. I wasn't sure what I'd hoped to reveal, maybe that's why it didn't work.

The only sound in my room was the ticking of the clock as one turned to one-thirty and then two. I sent a few texts to Mila with no response.

I sighed and my stomach clenched. It seemed I'd been ghosted on my first date. Another hour passed without a word before I began to worry. If something happened to her and I'd been busy throwing a pity party, it would have been awful. I grabbed my purse and phone off my desk, to go check on her. Except, I didn't know where she lived or if she'd gone out for the day. The only way to contact her was her phone, and she wasn't answering.

"Azami, you here?" Tierney called from the front door.

I left my room for the living room. Tierney was leaning against the kitchen counter, studying her nails.

"What are you doing here?" I asked.

"Came by to see if you wanted a ride to training." She stopped checking her nail polish and took her time inspecting me.

Time slowed with the intensity of her gaze. I crossed my arms over my chest then uncrossed them and put my hands in my pockets. Tierney winked and licked her lips. I wanted to curl up in a blanket or throw a potato sack on to cover myself from her view. Her attention put me more on edge than the magic of *Mort*.

"A text wouldn't do? You had to come over unannounced?"

Tierney jerked, our eyes meeting.

"That's suddenly a problem? It's not like I haven't dropped by before. We're friends and Coven sisters."

Right. Before her visits didn't seem so...intrusive.

My phone buzzed with a text.

Tierney lurched forward. My phone hit the floor with a bounce, swiped up by Tierney before I leaned down.

I'm sorry, but I have to cancel our date. Please know I wanted to go, but something's come up with my family. Promise I'll make it up to you.

"You had a date?" The words rang with hurt and accusation. Like I'd done something wrong.

Cheated on her.

I shook off the ridiculousness of the implication that I somehow mistreated her. Tierney and I weren't dating. I hadn't crushed on her for years.

"Not that it's any of your business, but yes, I had a date this afternoon. She had to cancel, as you can see."

She shrugged. "Good. Then you can come with me to training."

"We don't have to be there for another three hours. What's the point in going now?" I didn't want to go with her.

Being stuck in a car with Tierney and forced to come and go since she was my ride, seemed like a bad idea right then.

"It's Gathering Day, so most—if not all—of the Coven members will be there. Today's the day to start making good impressions. If we show our leadership, we could be voted onto the Council after we're full members."

"You go ahead, kiss their asses. I don't want to be on the Council. Mom says it's not all we think it is."

Tierney tossed her head back and laughed. The temperature of the room dropped as she filled the small space with sound. I rubbed away the chill on my arms.

She locked gazes with me.

"Doesn't matter, you're coming to training with me. If you don't, then the Coven's going to learn about your new little girlfriend. I suggest you don't argue, just get your stuff so we can go."

If I'd thought her laugh was sinister, I'd been wrong. The hint of danger in her words straightened my spine. Arguing would've made things worse. So, I did as she instructed and we left for the Coven house.

***

Josh and Katie met us at the door of the Coven house. One on each side, they looped their arms through mine and tugged me toward the kitchen. Tierney said hello then wandered off down the opposite hall. As long as she left me alone, I didn't care where she went.

The house had one of those massive kitchens that had been built to cook for twenty people. There were two stoves, one on either side, two sinks, three refrigerators, and enough cabinets to hold a grocery store worth of herbs, spices, and whatever other food we kept on hand.

In the middle of everything was a gray marble-topped island, with a loveseat set into the back of it. We could sit and talk, or stand around the counter. I preferred to sit since the couch was the perfect amount of squish and firmness. But it was only big enough for two.

Sunlight glinted off the silver handles resting in the butcher block. An image of using one of the knives to cut out Katie's tongue flashed through my mind. I gasped and rubbed my eyes.

"Everything okay?" Josh asked when I gripped the edge of the island so hard my knuckles turned white.

"No. It's not." Even if I'd wanted to lie, I couldn't. Tears filled my eyes.

What had I just seen? I didn't like her, sure, but I didn't want to hurt her. Not that like. More importantly, I had no idea where the idea came from.

"Are you sure about that? She knows your secret. Wouldn't it be better if she couldn't talk?"

No. I mentally screamed at the crow. *I'm not that kind of person. I will own up to dating Mila if asked. There's no reason for me to hide.*

"Are you going to share what's wrong?" Katie asked. She cocked her hip out to the side with her hand fisted on top.

"You aren't afraid of what the Coven will do to you?"

I shook my head at Katie and the crow.

"That's good. You're growing. Soon you'll be ready to

take over protection without me."

Shudders seized my muscles. First I thought of maiming Katie then the crow told me I'm growing. Whatever was happening to me wasn't good, except I couldn't say I was unhappy about the shift.

"Josh told me about your find at the house. When are you going to share it with us?" Katie asked.

Josh shrugged. Katie's smirk said more than her words. She planned to use the information to her advantage.

"That knife is even more appealing now, isn't it?"

The crow could fly off for good as far as I was concerned.

"It's so quiet in here," I said, trying to steer the conversation away from me. "Too quiet."

"So?" Katie and Josh asked at the same time.

"You don't think it's weird the birds aren't singing or anything else for that matter, even though the windows are open?"

I walked to the sink. Through the open window, a gust of wind brushed across my cheeks. Cold. As chilling as the room I stood in. There was only silence. A body pressed against my back. Josh or Katie, I wasn't sure.

An arm with a tattoo of a black and gray snake surrounded by crystals and roses reached over my shoulder. Josh.

"Is that—" he started.

"Your girlfriend," Katie finished his sentence.

A putrid smell followed her words. Death.

The air in the kitchen drew in around us, suffocating me. A faint metallic flavor coated the back of my throat. I clutched my arms around my waist then doubled over from pain.

A second person joined the person who could've been Mila, but they were too far away to know for sure. I didn't want to believe it was her. The person had long, dark hair. They were curvy and wore a pair of ripped-up black jeans with a flowy black tank top. An outfit similar to what Mila wore the day before.

I didn't want it to be her. She canceled our date and said she had something to take care of, which didn't make sense if she was at the Coven house. There was no reason for her to be here. She was with her family.

"Right." Mom clapped her hands from behind us. "Let's go. We're working in the greenhouse."

The warmth of Josh and Katie at my back disappeared before I turned around. Josh stood in front of me, but he was alone.

"Where's Katie?" My voice cracked "She was just here."

Mom shook her head. "Only you two in here when I walked in. I haven't seen Katie and Tierney's already in the greenhouse."

"Josh?" I raised my brows, begging him to help me.

Surely I hadn't imagined Katie being there the whole time.

"I..." He cleared his throat. "I don't know where she is. One minute she stood right next to me, and the next she was gone."

I walked as fast as I could to get out of the kitchen.

"We need to find her." I swallowed and the metallic taste lessened. Whatever dark magic I'd sensed had faded.

"No. It's time for class. I'm sure she just went to the restroom or something. One of the other trainers will tell her where we're at. You two need to come with me so we can get started." Mom pulled me toward the back door.

Katie vanished out of thin air. I didn't know how, or why I was so certain, but there was no other explanation. Neither of us saw her leave, but she wasn't there when Mom walked into the kitchen.

A picture on the wall caught my attention. I'd never seen it before, or at least hadn't noticed it, and stopped to inspect it while everyone else continued on.

"*Stop.*" I didn't know where the command came from. The word was spoken to me, through my mind.

With one finger, I traced the frame of the painting then glanced around to see if anyone watched. No one. There was a spark of light smack dab in the middle of the picture. Like the flame of a candle, but not. It was a flare. Touching it sent electricity down my arm. I gasped but still traced the light to the hand holding it, and down the arm of a woman with long black hair and silver eyes like Mom's.

The woman held onto a pole at the edge of a white cliff.

"Who are you?" I asked.

"That's Rivka. She was one of the four founders of our Coven. That's why each group of apprentices has no more than four. Our Council used to be made of only four witches, but Gwen changed it to five. She said we needed an odd number to break any tie votes." Tierney's mom stood beside me.

Her quiet footsteps didn't alert me to her presence.

"Oh. Mrs. Clarke. I didn't think anyone was around."

An awkward silence settled between us. In the past, I'd have hugged her and we'd have no problems talking. Right then, being next to her felt...awkward.

"Hmm. Interesting. How long has this picture been here? I don't remember seeing it before."

She shook her head. "No. You wouldn't. Amanda found it in the attic a few days ago. She wanted to hang it up and this wall was empty."

"Cool."

Mrs. Clarke nodded toward the back door. "Get moving."

"Yes, ma'am." I checked the kitchen once more for Katie, but Mrs. Clarke blocked the entrance.

Katie never showed for training. I watched for her, sneaking a peek every time the click of the greenhouse door opening broke through our conversations, but she didn't return.

Tierney wanted to kiss more ass after our training, so we went back to the main house where more witches and their families had gathered. Mila hadn't texted anymore, and sitting in my room staring at Mort didn't sound like much fun at the moment.

While the other members mingled and gathered in various rooms, I searched each one for Katie. By the time I reached the library, I'd run out of places. In the library, I found Amanda with a pile of history books at her side and one in her lap.

We kept a written history of the Coven members, important events, and anything else the leader thought should be recorded. Even now, we handwrote everything. Gwen refused to enter the twenty-first century and break tradition to make our records digital. Josh, Katie, Tierney, and I volunteered to help with the transition.

"How can we preserve our traditions if we change the way we do them?" she'd said.

Her belief made no sense at all, but none of us argued. If she wanted it written, then that's the way it'd be done.

"Have you seen Katie?" I asked.

"Passed her in the hall earlier. She said she needed to take care of personal business and told me your mom approved of her leaving early."

Good. I didn't have to deal with her anymore. The thought left a sour taste in my mouth. Insensitive. Criminal. Like the image of the knife in the kitchen. A sick sense in my gut said I needed to search for her more, figure out what she needed to handle. My brain didn't agree, though.

Torn and unable to do anything more for Katie, I went in search of information on *Mort d'Evanoir*.

"I see," I said.

A while later, my phone vibrated in my pocket. I pulled it out to see who'd text. Mom.

Where are you? We need to talk.

In the library with Amanda.

Her reply came almost immediately.

Stay there. I'm coming to you.

The heavy double doors swung open. It wasn't just Mom who walked through. She'd come with Gwen, Pam, and Heather. Amanda joined them in a straight line. The full Council had come to find me.

I bit my lower lip to stop it from trembling. Whatever they came to do, I would not show weakness. A few days ago, I decided to break the rules, I'd accept whatever consequences came my way.

The five ladies formed a barrier between me and the door. Each of them had their feet shoulder-width apart. Their arms hung at their sides, while they had their hands shaped into the symbol for protection.

Their right hand made the sign for the letter "*O*" while their left hand made a shape like a "*C*" or a crescent moon. The sun and the moon were believed to protect our Coven from harm.

I lowered my eyes to the floor, hoping whatever came next wasn't as bad as the tightness in my shoulders.

"Azami, the Council has learned you're in possession of *Mort d'Evanoir*." Gwen's nasally voice didn't lack authority, but it did ease the tension in the room.

"Is this true?" The crack in Mom's tone made me twitch.

"Yes." Even though I refused to look Mom in the eye, I didn't hesitate with my answer.

"Speak up," Pam ordered.

I faced the firing squad. As I searched each of their gazes I understood. Wrinkles covered Pam's forehead. Gwen released the protection symbol and wrung her hands in front of her. Amanda studied her black patent leather pumps as if they were the most important item in the room.

This wasn't about me.

The book sat in my desk, wrapped up where no one could find it. These ladies, or their predecessors, had lost *Mort d'Evanoir*. I hadn't performed any spells. Sure, I'd tried, but none of them worked. Mila said the book wasn't supposed to open and I had no idea why it had, but that didn't make a difference. The rules I'd broken hadn't harmed anyone, but losing *Mort d'Evanoir* could have killed people.

They'd come into the library to intimidate me. Rather

than cower, I pulled my shoulders back, locked eyes with Pam, and spoke up.

"Yes. I have *Mort d'Evanoir*. I found it and I'm keeping it safe."

Which was more than they could claim.

"Well done," Mom murmured.

She smiled, a small one, but I caught it out of the corner of my eye.

"You support her?" Gwen snapped.

"No. I don't agree with my daughter having the book, but I'm proud of her. She stood up to us and owned her actions." Mom broke the Council wall by facing Gwen. "How does it feel to have an apprentice you can't intimidate?"

"Mind your place, Isabelle. You may be a part of this Council, but that can change. If it weren't for your mother, you wouldn't be here."

Mom's eyes narrowed. Her lips moved, but the sound didn't reach me.

"Isabelle, don't." Amanda placed a hand on her arm. "She doesn't have sole power to remove anyone, but if you complete that spell, we'll have no other choice."

Whoa.

"You will return the book to the Coven." Gwen focused on me.

"No. You lost it. I've got it in a safe place. I believe I'll keep it."

Pam and Heather gasped. I stepped forward to leave.

"Where did you find it?" Amanda asked. She wasn't angry. More curious.

"The old place in the field behind our house."

"Gwen, it chose her," Heather murmured. Pam nodded.

I didn't disagree, but that didn't explain why the book chose me. Not that any of them would give me any answers, either. They'd told us not to go in the house without a reason. It wouldn't have surprised me if the book and the ban on the house were tied together.

"I expect it returned or you'll face punishment." Gwen tried to step forward, only her feet didn't move. Her upper body fell forward until she bent at the waist.

To hide my laugh, I covered my mouth with my hand. Mom stood still, calm. Amanda's hands moved in a series of gestures I'd never seen. I attempted to study each movement, but the shapes changed so fast I wasn't able to keep up.

"Amanda, stop the spell," Gwen hissed. "Things will not end well for you either."

"This is not the way, Gwen." Amanda started. "The Evanoir Coven doesn't work by way of fear and threats."

"She must return *Mort d'Evanoir*." Gwen ground her teeth, the movement noticeable from where I stood a few feet away.

"Why must I return it? What does the book mean to

you?" I asked.

Gwen pursed her lips together. I found the courage to stand toe to toe with our leader. Amanda and Mom stepped back, while Pam and Heather held their ground. The change in positions gave me a pretty good idea who hung with who.

"The book called to me. It's mine." I pointed to my chest. "Are you familiar with the crow?"

Gwen nodded.

"The crow protects *Mort d'Evanoir*. If something happens to me or the book, the crow will destroy the one who causes harm."

Not true. At least as far as I knew. It sounded good and the quick inhalations from Gwen and her crew boosted my confidence. They believed me.

Our leader started to respond until I held a finger to her lips.

"The book is mine and will be until it decides otherwise. If there's nothing else, I'm leaving. This Coven lost the book, or so I've been told. A book with the power to kill people. So far I haven't figured out who lost it exactly, but I will. When I do—" I pointed at Gwen— "I will make sure they're held accountable. Just because I'm an apprentice, it doesn't mean I won't figure this out."

I broke the line of witches as I headed to the door. They knew stronger magic than me. If Gwen or someone else tried to stop me there was no way I'd be able to defend myself. I wasn't scared or worried. The memories within the library protected me. Amanda had been right. Our Coven was not one built on fear or threats. Like the picture in the hall, we were supposed to be light.

"And yet, you're called to protect Mort d'Evanoir."

Thanks, bird. I appreciate the uncanny timing once more.

Worrying about the crow's decree wouldn't help at the moment, so I ignored him as he continued to chatter in my head.

"Make your threats, Azami. I will see the book returned to its rightful owner. If I don't, then your fate will be that of the Hutchings family." Gwen thought she had the last word.

I'd make sure she didn't.

The Evanoir Coven revealed a new picture of reality. One I could choose not to be part of. I no longer questioned a connection between the book, Coven, and Mila's family. They were tied together. I just had to figure out who wove the threads of the tapestry.

CHAPTER 8

IN A PERFECT WORLD, I'D have driven my car and left as soon as I escaped the Council. Just my luck, since Tierney drove, I found myself stuck. If I didn't want to ask my mom for a ride back to the dorms, then I had to avoid the Council until Tierney decided she'd done enough ass-kissing and wanted to go home.

I tried to find my once-best friend, but no one knew where she was. She was still in the house; I just didn't know what part.

Alone with my thoughts, and a hefty amount of anger toward the Coven, I made my way to the garden tucked into an alcove about five hundred feet behind the house. A stone bench nestled in the middle of pink and yellow roses called my name. Lavender bushels filled in the space around the roses. The fragrant scents calmed my frayed nerves. Slowly, my heartbeat returned to normal. Thoughts of how to show Gwen she wasn't the all-powerful she believed to be dissipated with each inhale of the clean air.

We used lavender for many herbal tinctures. Oils for diffusers to help reduce anxiety and stress. Potions for insomniacs to ingest. Lotions for those who just wanted to smell good. It was the most common herb sold in the Coven store downtown. I quit counting how many bundles I'd collected over the years.

I closed my eyes and turned my face toward the sun. The heat wrapped around me like a tight hug. Comfort. Safety. Family. Those were things I should've felt every time I walked into the Coven house. It used to be that way. College changed us.

The book changed me even more. As I sat on the bench a desperate need to get home to *Mort d'Evanoir* pulsed through my body. My muscles ached to move. Anxiety tightened my chest.

"Hey." Mila chuckled.

I pinched my arm without opening my eyes. Mila wouldn't be at the Coven house. Her family wasn't allowed. There were wards to keep them out. I opened one eye to see if I'd been dreaming.

Mila sat next to me. Real. Not a dream. Her long black hair lay over her shoulders. The sun cast a halo around her. Or maybe it was my squinting. The deceptive innocence brought a smile to my lips. Somehow she'd managed to overcome Gwen's most powerful spell.

"You're late," I said.

"I'm sorry. That's not at all enough, but I am sorry. Something came up with my brother. I had to help him out." She took my hand in hers, lacing our fingers together. "But I'm free now if you want to get out of here."

"Your brother?" They'd been the two people we saw from the kitchen window. She didn't have to confirm it.

Mila had broken the wards, and she skipped our date to help her brother. The only missing piece was why they were at the house.

"Yeah, Dustin. He needed to...umm...talk to his girlfriend."

Katie. Was that where she'd gone? Skipped out of training to be with a Hutchings? I'd considered the same thing, but Mila bailed and took away that option.

"Did he kidnap her?"

She scowled off into the distance behind me. "Nope, no kidnapping involved. She willingly went with him."

I drew back at the intensity of her eyes. A simple question caused such an extreme reaction. The air around us turned frigid and I rubbed my arms. We were on a weakened pond of ice—one wrong move and I could've found myself drowning in frozen water.

"How did you get past the wards?" I tried to change the subject and bring back the side of Mila that didn't require walking on eggshells to prevent disaster.

"Dustin did it. Don't know how. Anyway, I owe you a

date. How about we get out of here?"

My attempt worked. Mila's smile warmed the chill around us, bringing the sun back from behind a gray cloud.

"*Do it.*" From above us, a crow cackled as it flew through the sky. "*Leave the Coven and spend time with the banished one.*"

His taunting words brought more excitement than I'd had all day. I didn't care about the herbs or how to mix salves. Seeing Mila behind the Coven wards, the flush of her cheeks, the heat sparking between us made me more alive than any potion or spell the Coven could've taught me.

"Amazing." I sighed.

Soft lips touched mine. I reached for Mila's face without opening my eyes. Our kiss lingered. I wasn't worried about begin caught. A bubble of hope that I would be caught began to form. If Gwen found us outside that would probably be the end of my apprenticeship.

For the first time, I didn't care.

"I'm sorry. I shouldn't have done that." Mila took my hand in hers and squeezed.

"Don't apologize. I'm glad you did."

Her brows furrowed. "What about the Coven? Your mom?"

"It's so stupid. Why should they have a say in who I date? I'm an adult. I can make my own decisions."

"Come on, Azami. My family is banished. We're not

even supposed to practice magic. I'm not just another girl you're dating."

She was right—and wrong.

"They've never even told us why your family is banished. So why should I care? Especially after Gwen's bullshit today."

Mila turned to face me. She pulled her leg onto the bench. Without releasing my hand, she rubbed her other hand up and down my back. The skin-to-skin contact of our hands started a tingle that magnified with her massage.

"Don't be petty. That's the opposite of being an adult. Let's go get some dinner and we can talk about whatever happened with Gwen."

I nodded. We rose from the bench at the same time. Mila had a point about being caught. I may have been upset with the Council, but I'd regret getting kicked out. Despite my recent lack of enthusiasm, being part of the Coven was something I'd worked for since I could walk.

A high-pitched scream rang out from the side of the house. The fear in the shrill noise turned my veins to ice.

Mila darted off toward the yell, her hand gripping mine until our fingers turned white. More than once I almost tripped over my feet, face planting both of us, but we managed to keep going.

Dustin knelt next to a girl laying on the ground, unmoving, one arm twisted at the elbow with her hand above her head. Her right heel touched her hip. Bits of bone poked through the skin around her knee.

It took a minute for me to figure out who the girl was. She wore a blue and white striped, off-shoulder short jumpsuit. Katie. My friend lay on the ground, dead.

The breath in my lungs evaporated. Every thought in my brain disappeared. Her chest didn't move. I couldn't do anything.

"Azami," Mila whispered in my ear. She pointed over my shoulder toward Katie's throat.

Blood dripped from a slice made from one side to the other. A tracing of lips in crimson lipstick, a possible clue, left on her right cheek. My body collapsed to the ground. In a rush, my lungs filled with oxygen only for my stomach to revolt and the little bit of food I'd eaten expelled itself from my throat.

Mila went to her brother's side. His body shook. The sounds of his wails muted the quick breaths from my lungs.

"What happened, Dustin?" Mila asked.

I squeezed my eyes closed, but the image of Katie's body crumpled on the ground wouldn't go away.

"She screamed and I came running. This is where I found her."

His words slowly took root in my thoughts. We'd heard Katie's scream. Dustin found her. Mila was with me.

"What are you doing here?" The acid in Tierney's words burned my skin, even though I knew they weren't directed at me. "Mila Hutchings, how did you get onto Coven property?"

Tierney spoke louder, breaking through the buzz of silence around us. My eyes stung from tears, I wiped the back of my hand across my mouth and searched for Mila. Except neither she nor Dustin were anywhere around.

"Where did she go?" someone asked from behind.

A quick peek over my shoulder revealed a growing crowd of members.

"She disappeared," another answered.

"That's impossible. Our wards are set to keep the Hutchings away from the house. Tierney, you must have been mistaken," this from Gwen.

"She was here. I don't know how she made it past the wards, but she did." The words burned with betrayal as I spoke.

I stood and turned to Tierney. On the outside, she appeared distraught. Bloodshot eyes, no doubt similar to mine, streaks of dried tears down her cheeks. Everything else about her, the way she fisted her hands on her hips, the lilt of her voice, her raised brows, they all said she didn't actually care about Katie.

"What are we going to do about Katie?" I asked. "We need to call the police."

Gwen examined the body, then faced me. "Yes. You're right, we should take care of this. We will figure out who did this to her after we clear all this away. This is a Coven concern, not the Evanoir Police. Do you understand?"

The monotone words offered no comfort to me or the rest of the Coven. I wanted to ask if we had some kind of ritual for honoring those who passed, but the question refused to form. I wanted to know why she refused to call the police. Instead of asking, I nodded my acceptance.

"Gwen, as Coven leader you should lead the ritual this evening so we can guide her body over," Amanda offered.

Behind me, sniffles and murmurs grew louder. Mila's name was spoken over and over. Gwen nodded at Amanda and the Council surrounded Katie's body, blocking it from view of everyone else.

I moved to join them, she was one of our core, but Gwen set her arm against my chest and pushed me back.

"You're not going to participate in any of the ritual tonight, and we don't need your help now. As an accomplice to this murder, you're not welcome."

The air rushed out of my lungs.

"But..."

"You admit to her being here. None of us would have harmed one of our own. Since you and Mila were the first ones seen next to Katie's body, what else would you expect me to believe?" Her voice projected across the crowd. "It's not surprising given the history of the Hutchings family. We must find them and bring justice for our young apprentice."

"No. She, we, didn't do this." I shook my head. "Mila

couldn't have done this. It's impossible."

Gwen crossed her arms. "How would you know Mila Hutchings didn't kill your fellow apprentice?"

Her gaze dared me to admit the truth. If I told everyone I was dating Mila, there'd be consequences. I broke a Coven law. But if I didn't, Mila would be hunted for a crime she didn't commit.

I swallowed hard before staring Gwen square in the eyes with my shoulders back. If I was going in, I'd go all in.

"We were together. That's how I know she didn't do it."

The Coven leader smiled and nodded.

"This is what I was afraid of. Mila has corrupted you. Not only did she break Coven wards, she convinced you to break Coven laws. I believe you and Mila worked together to take the life of our apprentice, Katie. There is no other explanation why she's gone and you were here before anyone else."

Fuck. My jaw clenched. I'd managed to get myself in deeper shit than I already was. Not only was Mila on the hook, but now Gwen named me as a killer too.

Mom had tears in her eyes. Silently, I begged her to help. With a grim pull of her lips, she lowered her head. Breathing became more and more difficult. My own mother didn't have my back.

"You're excused from training until further notice. Do not return to the Coven house. Goodbye, Azami."

"Go home, Azami. Let Mort d'Evanoir protect you."

I ran until my legs threatened to give out, until my lungs burned with starvation, until the tears from my eyes ran dry.

"Get in the car, Azami."

Mila's voice cut through the ringing in my ears. I didn't think, just walked to her car and climbed in. The air conditioning cooled my face but did nothing for the rage burning through my body.

CHAPTER 9

"I'M CLUELESS." A PIECE OF french fry threatened to fall out of my mouth.

Mila took a bite of cheeseburger. We ended up at Sandy's Diner after leaving the Coven house.

"You have so much more magic than I do. How did you disappear after we found Katie? Why did you leave? The Coven thinks you killed her. They think I helped." I put my head in my hands. "This is all going so wrong."

"We'll fix it. Nothing has happened that can't be undone." Mila wiped the corner of her lips with a napkin.

The french fry in my hand fell to the table with a thump. I stared at her with my mouth gaping.

"Katie's death can't be fixed, Mila. She's dead. There's no bringing her back."

Mila shrugged. "You don't know that for sure. What if there's a spell in the book that could raise her from the dead?"

"She's not wrong." The crow spoke. *"You're not home. I told you to go home."*

I needed food. Besides, I wasn't driving, Mila was. She didn't leave me much choice.

"Leave now. Go home. The book will show you the answers you seek."

"Do you really think Mort d'Evanoir has magic like that?" I asked Mila.

"I don't know, but it could. You'd have to read it to find out."

For the last week, I'd tried to read the book. The first time, I had a dream about Mila's aunt. After the second time I opened it, the vision of the woman came. After seeing Katie's gray, limp body, I was afraid to know what the book would show me next.

"Spending my Sunday thinking about all of this is going to be awful. Right now, I'm scared to go to sleep. What if the only thing I can see in my head is Katie's body? The lipstick on her cheek. The slice across her neck."

"Let's talk about something else." I started to argue, but Mila held up her hand. "Just long enough for you to settle down. Then I'll take you home. If you'd like, I'll stay the night. Help you get some sleep." Mila's smile had a hint of evil with the way she lifted her brows and tilted her head slightly to the side.

"How could you help me sleep?" I asked.

She winked. "There are ways."

"I'm not going to like this, am I?"

"Dunno. Guess we'll find out."

I sat my burger in its basket, wiped my hands, and rested them in my lap. One at a time I forced the images from the Coven into a box. Mila was right. I needed to relax. When thinking of her staying the night my lower body warmed. There was an infinite number of ways she could help me sleep. Thinking of them made my cheeks warm, no doubt giving away my current train of thought.

"Damn, Azami. You keep blushing like that and I'm not going to make it home with you. We'll have to stop at my place."

If *Mort d'Evanoir* wasn't in my sock drawer and the crow hadn't told me to go home, I'd have taken her up on the offer.

"We could go now. If that made things easier I mean." I tucked my chin to my chest.

She laughed a full belly, toss your head back laugh. Mila pushed her food to my side of the table then came over and sat next to me in the booth. Without asking, I laid my head on her shoulder.

"Kissing you is now one of my favorite things to do, and I haven't even had the pleasure that many times. Let's stay a little longer so I can savor the time before we burn the sheets off your bed." Mila chuckled.

"Tell me about your family." I lifted my head off her shoulder and took another bite of food. "I'm not ready to leave either."

Mila ate a couple of bites, too.

"Mm. What do you want to know? Dustin's my older brother. You already know him. I have two younger sisters."

More than anything, I wanted to know about magic within her family but wasn't sure how to ask.

"How did you learn magic?" I asked.

Mila tapped the table with her finger then drew a half-moon shape.

"Dad, mostly. And Aunt Monica. They didn't want to teach me much, just some basic stuff. I had to wait until I was eighteen to learn stuff like weaving memories together to change people's perceptions and teleportation. Lately, Dustin and I have been teaching ourselves."

Umm. Wow. The Coven hadn't told us about either of those things. The first time I'd seen teleportation performed was when Amanda did it at practice the week before.

"There are spells for weaving memories?" Something like that had to be dark magic. I couldn't imagine being able to manipulate people like that.

Mila shrugged. "Sure. There are spells for almost anything you can think of. Before you ask, no it isn't dark. Believe it or not, some of the worst spells don't involve dark or blood work at all."

"Interesting." I wiped the corner of my mouth. "How

did you teach yourself magic?"

"You're cute." Mila leaned down and whispered in my ear, "We've been breaking the Coven wards for months. I've spent a lot of time in your library."

We finished our dinner side by side. The realization of Mila's ability to get in and out of the Coven settled deep in my thoughts. She could've killed Katie and I would never know—except the idea of her being a killer didn't sit right in my gut. We'd been together. Katie had been with Dustin. Mila came for me. Dustin was with Katie when we found her.

Then they both disappeared, leaving me alone with the Coven.

Somehow I had to prove to everyone they were wrong. She wasn't a murderer and neither was I.

Mila pulled a pencil out of her pocket then grabbed a leftover napkin. I watched as she sketched a crescent moon with a crow.

"You designed that," I murmured.

Mila nodded. "It's nothing special. Just something I did during one of my classes."

"What's the moon mean?" I traced the shape with the tip of my finger.

"The Hutchings family believes the crescent moon brings protection."

"And my family believes the crow is a protector."

With her fingers under my chin, Mila tilted my face up.

"We protect each other, Z. That's why you dreamt about Aunt Monica. She was telling you to protect me."

I wanted the safety she promised more than anything. My breath quickened with need. I realized for the first time how much I missed the comfort of being protected, cared for. Dad gave that to Mom and me. After Dad died I felt the same thing within the Coven. Until now.

"Why was your family banished from the Coven?" Like word vomit, the question fell from my lips before I could stop it.

Mila put a bit of space between us, instantly making me regret the change in conversation. Except, we were tied together through Katie's death—like or not—and I needed to know everything.

"My great-grandma killed Gwen's great-grandma. Then, because she was being controlled by some dark magic, she went to the next closest coven, and wiped them out with one spell." Mila's monotone delivery of the truth did nothing for the rise of emotion within me.

Wow. She spoke as though what her great-grandmother did meant nothing to her. The woman used the worst kind of magic to kill not just the leader of the Evanoir Coven, but she wiped out another entire coven of witches.

"How...how does something like that happen?" I asked.

"To be honest, I don't know for sure. No one in my

family likes to talk about it. They hate the Evanoir Coven, don't want the responsibility of starting their own coven, and refuse to follow the rules of any other. We're in this vicious cycle of needing the energy from a coven, but too stubborn to find a way to make it work."

"But if your great-grandmother killed the Evanoir leader, then why would you hate the Coven?"

She shrugged. "I asked Aunt Monica one time. According to our family history, the two women had a feud between them."

I turned to face her. "Let me guess, there was a man involved."

Mila nodded and smiled.

"Of course there was. My great-grandfather, actually. Great-grandmother stole his heart and Gwen's family hated her for it. Years passed with nothing worse than words and poorly aimed spells once in a while. Then when they were both in their seventies, something happened and Great Grandma Hutchings finally had enough."

It was like a romance novel gone wrong. A true love triangle that ended in death years after the girl got the guy.

"Do you know what triggered Great-grandma Hutchings?"

After taking another bite of her hamburger, Mila answered.

"That's the thing—none of us know. Not the Graves family or Hutchings. Whatever the two women fought over was buried with their bodies"

"It doesn't seem fair that you and your family are still banished now that your great-grandmother has passed. She killed the leader, not you and not your dad."

"Aunt Monica believed the same thing. She fought with everything she could to get our family's name reinstated, but Gwen wouldn't do it. I think that had to do with Aunt Monica's love of men. Gwen was probably jealous or something ridiculous like that."

Growing up I'd always stayed away from Gwen. She tried to be the "nice Coven leader" but we didn't get along all that well. Even as a young child, I remembered disliking the way she made us do things we didn't want. The older I got, the more I resented how many restrictions she placed on apprentices. We were nothing more than slave labor for her and I hated it.

Now, more than ever, I despised the Evanoir Coven leader. I wasn't sure in that moment that I'd have cared if her name showed up in Mort d'Evanoir.

"You and Tierney are close?" she asked.

There were so many more questions I wanted to ask but decided to go with Mila's change in topic.

"We were growing up. A few years ago I had a serious crush on her. I pursued, she denied me. For a while we were amicable, friends but not the same as before. Lately though, she's been...weird."

"Hmph. Weird how?"

"Little things. Like she keeps showing up when I'm not expecting it and she's been a lot more demanding lately. Today she pretty much forced me to go to the Coven house with her. That's why I didn't have a car to get home."

The hamburger didn't do much in the way of distracting, nor did our conversation. Talking about Tierney made me recall the hint of deception in her wink when she told Gwen about Mila leaving. The way she put her hands on her waist and tilted her head with the rise of her eyebrows in a, "don't think I don't know what you did" stance.

"She's not happy about us." It wasn't a question, so much as an observation.

"No. It doesn't matter, though. Can we go?" I asked.

Yes. You need to get home. The crow's voice washed over me with a sense of comfort, bringing with it a wave of guilt. The last thing I should've found comfort in was the damn crow who led me to *Mort d'Evanoir*. I couldn't help but believe the book and Katie's death were somehow tied together.

"I've been thinking. Why do the people in *Mort d'Evanoir* die the way they do?" We'd made about half the drive to my place in silence.

Mila shrugged. "Haven't seen the book, so I can't say. What are you thinking?"

"It's just a guess, but what if they die by their greatest fear? Like my dad was afraid of being trampled. I don't know what Monica was afraid of."

"Me neither. That doesn't make much sense though. How would anyone know someone's greatest fear?"

She had a good point. I didn't even know my dad's fear, just assumed it was a possibility.

"There has to be a reason. The deaths aren't random." I shifted in my seat to face Mila. "If they were, the deaths wouldn't be so specific or accurate. The column would be more general. A date maybe. Or location."

"Have you read any more of the book?" Mila asked.

I shook my head.

"Z, you're going to have to read the end of the book to know if any new names show. If you don't, you'll never know if the magic has been activated."

"You're right, but what if I recognize a name?" My hands shook. The air in the car grew thin. It was so hard to breathe.

"Focus on me. You're not going to freak out on me now. I'm driving and pulling over isn't going to be easy on the freeway. Wait until we get home, then you can lose it. It's been a rough day, Z. Stay with me just a little longer."

Her voice broke through my anxiety, I tried to focus on her face, but the world spun. Images of Katie's body, Dustin kneeling beside her, the masked satisfaction on Tierney's face, my mom's disappointment swirled around my thoughts. With each one, my body pulled in on itself even more. My muscles tensed, then my entire body shook.

Cold. Fear. Sweaty palms. A ringing in my ears. Everything disappeared until the only sound in my head was Gwen's nasally voice telling me not to return to the Coven house.

I gave up and quit fighting.

"Fuck." Mila's curse came through as a distant whisper of thought.

CHAPTER 10

WHEN I WOKE, DAY HAD turned to night. The moon sat high in the sky. Soft fingers brushed down my cheek then pushed my hair behind my ear.

"Sleep well?" Mila pressed her lips against my temple.

"Yeah." She laid on her side next to me. "Did you sleep at all?"

Mila nodded and rubbed her eyes.

"This wasn't exactly what I had in mind for our first date, but I ended up in bed with you regardless."

I chuckled, but the dryness of my throat made it sound more like a growl than a laugh.

"My vote is a redo on the date. We call today a wash."

"Works for me. Hey, there's a crow outside your window. It's been there since we got back and has some noticeable features like the one at the park."

"White tuft on his head?" I asked.

"Yep." Mila nodded. "Kind of fluffy. Does it have a

120

name?"

"Hey crow, do you have a name?" I asked.

"Bennett." He tapped the glass with his beak.

Before sharing with Mila I pushed myself into a sitting position on the bed. The white crop top I'd worn to the house crept up, threatening to reveal more than I usually did on a first date. Then again, I didn't make it a habit of getting into bed on first dates either.

"He said his name is Bennett." I studied Mila while she processed the fact I talked to the bird.

She wore the same black T-shirt. Her jeans rode low on her waist, showing a sliver of dark, sun-tanned skin. Without asking, I reached out and brushed my fingers across her stomach. A spark of desire raced up my arm.

"You sure you want to do that?" Mila asked.

"Nope." I tucked my hand under my leg. Starting something right then was definitely a bad idea. In the best possible way.

Mila pushed up to sit next to me. She took my hand in hers then traced the lines of my palm.

"Soon, babe. You're exhausted, let's take it a little slow. With the Coven suspecting us of killing Katie it's going to be a long few days while we figure out what to do next. Any chance the bird can help us? Maybe he knows more about *Mort d'Evanoir* and can give us some clues."

It was worth a shot at least.

"When do the names appear in the book?" I asked

Bennett.

Two muffled caws came through the window, then I got his answer. *"When someone dies."*

"Before they die, while they're dying, or after?"

"All of the above. A name appears when the book adds it. Sometimes before, but you won't be able to stop the death. Once the name is in the book the magic is complete."

"So I could prevent it if the spell wasn't complete." There was a way to stop the book. If I read the book, then I'd figure out who was next and stop them from dying.

"No."

"Hold up. Don't forget I can't listen to whatever he's saying. By the way, the cawing is annoying AF," Mila said.

"He said a name appears when the book adds it. There's no set time. The magic is complete when the name shows up."

She shifted on the bed to face me. "So we can stop people from dying. That's easy enough."

I shook my head.

"Why not?" Mila demanded.

"Because you don't know who the wielder is."

"He said we don't know who the wielder is, so we can't stop them. I guess he can understand you too." An answer that did nothing to help us. I sighed.

Mila rolled off the bed then slid her tennis shoes on.

"You're leaving?" I asked as I tugged the covers up to

my chest.

"It's best." She bent over to get her bag off the floor. "If I stay I can't promise not to do something to make things worse. Besides, we have a path now. We find the wielder; we find the killer."

"Sure. Okay. Let me at least walk you out."

I rose off the bed, slid on my flip-flops, and headed to the door. Mila left the room before me, leading the way to the front door. The glow of the TV screen lit a path through the living room. Pippa laid on the couch, covered by the afghan my grandmother crocheted.

At the front door, Mila paused with her hand on the knob. I wrapped my arms around her waist and rest my head in the crook of her neck. Each second that passed made me want to drag her back to my room and fall asleep with her in my arms.

"I need to go, babe." Mila's words hitched.

"I know. I was just...you smell like fresh rain and sunflowers. It's hypnotizing."

"And your lips are tickling me. I'm going to go home and get some sleep so we can be ready to work tomorrow. We're going to New Orleans. Maybe if we get some space between us and the Coven we'll be able to think clearly."

"Yeah. Okay. Tomorrow."

Sleep screamed my name despite the headache budding behind my left eye. Bennett didn't say anything else after Mila left. As my head hit the pillow my phone buzzed with a text notification.

Sorry about today. We need to talk about what happened afterward. Meet me tomorrow.

Tierney.

I'm busy, sorry.

I hit send on the reply then fell into a fitful sleep.

CHAPTER 11

"PIP!" I YELLED FROM MY room.

Shirts flew through the air. Socks dropped to the ground. I searched under the bed, pulled every drawer out of my dresser. It was gone.

"Pippa," I shouted again.

"Bennett. Where are you?" I was seconds from begging.

The crow rapped his beak on the window.

The bedroom door flung open, hitting the wall with a bang.

"Where's the fire?" Pippa leaned against the door jamb, her hands in the pockets of her cutoff jean shorts.

"It's gone. I can't find it anywhere. Someone stole it."

"What's gone?" she asked.

I bit my tongue.

"Mutherfucther." The tip of my tongue pressed against the back of my teeth. Pain lanced through my mouth.

The day before I put the book in my drawer before going to training with Tierney. When I woke up there was no crow and no book.

"A book I had here in my room. Ouch."

Pippa tilted her head to the side. "Did you bite your tongue?"

I nodded.

"What's so important about this thing?" Pippa walked around the room picking up shirts, shorts, my bag, my purse, a towel, all in the name of finding my missing killer book.

My roommate wasn't a witch. She didn't even know I practiced spells or made potions and salves in my room. We'd been assigned by the university from day one. For the most part, we both stayed in our rooms and didn't bother each other. So far the arrangement worked.

I stood in the middle of the room and twisted back and forth hoping to catch a glimpse of the black leather cover. Without thinking, I chewed one of my nails to the quick. If I didn't find *Mort* soon, I wouldn't have any nails left.

"It's—special. A gift."

"So what can I help with? There's nothing in this mess." Pippa dropped a bra into the desk chair. "Not that you'd know even if it was. Don't you ever clean this place?"

She navigated back to the door by stepping over a few pairs of shoes, shoving some dirty tanks to the side with her toe, and hopping over my more-than-full mini trash can.

The fact that Mila managed to get me into bed the night before without injuring herself was a miracle. I'd have to apologize for the state of disaster she'd encountered.

I stood paralyzed in the middle of my room.

"This is so bad." The last word caught in the back of my throat. "Did you bring anyone over yesterday? Or did anyone stop by?"

Pippa didn't answer right away, which made me worry even more.

"Mac came over for a little while and that friend of yours, Tiny or Tierney, whatever her name is, she stopped by."

Tierney came over, and Pippa's boyfriend. Neither one of them would have taken the book—at least I didn't think Tierney would've. As an apprentice, she knew the power of the book but had no idea how to even open it.

"Did you let Tierney in?" I asked.

"Nah. She showed up right as I was leaving. I walked back out of the building with her."

"Thank you, Pip. I'm sure I just misplaced it somewhere." I jerked my messenger bag onto my shoulder. "If I don't get out of here I'll be late for class."

Pippa checked her phone as we both left my room. "Same. Have a good one, Azami."

We went our separate ways, me out the front door and

Pippa to her room for whatever she needed.

Bennett flew just above my right shoulder as I walked to the end of the street.

"You were supposed to keep Mort d'Evanoir *safe."*

I tripped over the concrete following his shrieking caw.

"You said it was your book." I snapped. "How do you not know where it is?"

Mila would know what to do. She text to meet me out front of the cafeteria. Coffee first then a road trip.

A crowd gathered at the entrance. Josh broke through the groups and ran toward me calling my name. He jumped into my arms and suffocated me with a hug. When I pushed him to arm's length, his tear-streaked face and bloodshot eyes grabbed my attention.

"Josh, what's going on?"

My voice cracked and my muscles tensed. Clouds covered the sun. The taste of blood I'd come to associate with dark magic coated my throat.

"Have you talked to Tierney this morning?" Josh's voice shook.

"She text me last night. What's going on? Why are your hands so cold?"

Our eyes didn't meet instead, he stared at someone, or something, over my shoulder. "She's dead, Az."

"Tierney?"

"No." His body wilted. Fresh tears washed away the

old tracks on his cheeks. He sucked in a breath, which led to a horrible coughing fit.

"Katie."

He nodded at my whisper. I realized I hadn't seen Josh after finding Katie. If he was in the crowd, I missed him. Gwen kicked me out before I had a chance to even check on him.

"I know, honey." I wrapped him in a hug. "It's going to be okay, Josh."

Hitched sobs added to the cacophony of noise.

"Did you see her yesterday after she left us?" he asked.

"No. Mila and I found her at the side of the house." I guided him into the cafeteria and through the line to get a coffee.

"I didn't either. I wasn't even there when she was discovered. I left after training. Why does Tierney think you and Mila had something to do with all of this? Why was Mila at the house?"

Questions I didn't want to answer. Josh was loyal to the Coven. If Tierney told him about the accusation, then he'd go with whatever they said.

Except he found me. He'd asked before assuming. The realization gave me a little hope that I wasn't alone.

"Mila and I are going to New Orleans. Come with us and I'll fill you in."

"Loved her, Az." He sniffed. "Now I can't tell her."

"You never told her?" I asked.

"She had a boyfriend. How was I supposed to tell her?"

I sipped my coffee and wished for Mila to show up sooner rather than later. I had no idea how to answer or help Josh.

"Hey, babe." Mila's eyes went wide as she stepped toward our table. "And Josh."

"Did you kill Katie?" He went straight for the kill.

Mila tensed then took a step back. Her upper lip twitched.

"What the absolute fuck?"

I put some distance between us with the punch in her voice. Quiet, but lethal.

He crossed his arms over his chest, from crying on my shoulder to accusing Mila of murder within a split second. I wanted to ask if his tears were even real. The little sparkle of hope disappeared as a seed of doubt was planted—Gwen or Tierney could have sent him to gather information. Catch us in some kind of lie that would prove we killed Katie.

"Josh, I think it's probably time for you to go. The Coven won't be happy you came to see me."

Mila nodded, but he didn't move. "As in now."

"By the way, how did you know where to find me?" I asked.

When Josh continued to refuse to look at me, the truth became clear. The Coven had sent him. All of this was a show, and I'd fallen for it.

He slid out of the booth we'd taken. "I thought I knew you. We were family. Then you met her." Josh hooked his thumb at Mila with tears in his eyes. "In just a few days, not even a month, we lost you. What happened? Why her? Tierney would've done anything for you."

I almost believed him when his voice hitched.

"Seriously, you motherfucking bag of greasy potato chips."

"Mila—" I placed my hand on her arm. "Josh is trying to do right by the Coven. I understand why. I don't agree, but I understand."

Josh gave a long sigh and nodded. He thought I was done.

"The problem is, he says they lost me, but that's not true. I haven't changed, the Coven has. Rather than ask me about when I found Katie, they assumed I killed her. You too, since you broke the wards. Josh is their puppet used for nothing more than to gaslight."

Mila took a sip of her coffee. I got up from the booth, tossed my bag over my shoulder, and pulled Mila to the door with me. Josh didn't deserve anything else. He'd done what he'd needed. It was time to part ways.

***

"You're quiet. Is Josh's visit bothering you still?" Mila asked about halfway through our ride to New Orleans.

I startled, lost in my thoughts.

"What? Josh? Goddess, no. I feel bad for the guy, to be

honest. He's doing the Coven's bidding and it's going to hurt him in the end. They don't even care about the fact that he loved Katie and what would they say if they knew she was dating Dustin? The Coven thinks I'm the only problem child, but none of us are innocent."

Mila laughed. The ease of her laughter lessened my worry.

"The only thing on my mind is the book. I um...well, it went...umm..."

"Spit it out, Z. What happened with *Mort?*"

A sharp sting hit me as I realized I'd chewed a hole in my cheek debating whether or not I should tell Mila what happened.

"It's gone."

My hands hit the dashboard with a bang when the car came to a screeching halt in the middle of the road. Steam poured from Mila's ears. Her face turned rose red, which was saying something considering her dark skin.

"You lost the book?" Mila's knuckles turned white as she gripped the steering wheel.

"I didn't lose it. Yesterday I put it in my drawer before I went to training. This morning it was gone."

"And you wait until now to say something?"

"When was I supposed to tell you? Josh showed up before you did and I've spent this whole ride trying to figure out what to say."

Trees turned to fields. Fields turned to pavement and

buildings. Neither of us spoke. We parked in front of a diner big enough for about ten people. My stomach growled.

"I hope we're eating here."

The scent of pancakes and syrup drifted through the open car windows. Pictures of steaming coffee cups and saucers of beignets decorated the tall glass front of the diner.

"Let's eat. Food will help us figure out what we need to do about Katie."

"And the book." Mila punched the unlock button.

A crow called from the top of the building. My crow. Bennett followed us to New Orleans.

"Bennett's here." I pointed to the rooftop. "Maybe he can offer some insight. Even if he was useless when it came to helping me earlier."

Since we'd made it in time for brunch, pancakes, sausage, eggs, French toast, bacon, and beignets covered the table. There was a week's worth of food set out before us.

"How are you handling everything, Z? The truth."

Somehow I knew she'd be pissed if I told her I hadn't processed everything yet. Finding *Mort d'Evanoir* missing had been more than enough distraction from thinking about everything that happened the day before.

"I don't know. I'm not even sure the reality has set in. After you left I just went to bed. The Coven doesn't want me back. I thought it would hit me harder if I ever got kicked out, but it's left me numb."

Katie's death was tied to the book. It had to be. The metallic taste, the weird way she'd died, there was no other explanation in my mind. If I wanted Gwen to see it wasn't me or Mila who killed her, I needed to figure out how it worked. After I told Gwen what happened and found the killer, things would be right and I could hold to my promise of helping Mila clear her family's name.

"So, what do we know about everything?" Mila asked around bites of bacon and pancake.

I took a drink of orange juice. This was what I needed, someone to ground me. Help me organize and keep focused on the goal.

"We didn't do it." At least I didn't think Mila had a hand in Katie's death.

A small part of me questioned that certainty though. First with her being at the Coven house with Dustin, then how she knew where to find me after I'd been kicked out of the house, and she was the last one with me the night before—a truth I didn't want to acknowledge, but couldn't deny forever.

"Right. Let's talk about the facts of yesterday and see if they help us. Tell me what happened, starting with when you woke up."

For the next few minutes, I replayed my day to Mila. We talked about how Tierney showed up and coerced me into going to the house with her. Then I told her about the kitchen with the strange desire that I wanted to cut out Katie's tongue. We talked about seeing her and Dustin walking across the property. I remembered how Katie disappeared right after that.

"How come you didn't say anything before?" Mila asked.

"We were talking, then going to get dinner, then Katie happened. Speaking of, what were you doing at the house anyway? I asked you yesterday, but you never answered."

With every second that passed, I wasn't sure if Mila was formulating an excuse or trying to break some horrible news to me. By the time she answered three shredded napkins made a pile of white paper snow in front of me.

"Dustin wanted to see Katie. She told him about y'alls training and he decided to surprise her. It was stupid."

That made sense. It didn't help with figuring out a suspect.

With a quick flick of her finger, Mila signaled our server. She grabbed the bill and paid before I had a chance. After brunch, we went to City Park to continue our conversation. Once we got there, Mila pulled a blanket out of her trunk then guided us a to a tree with enough branches and shade to cover us no matter where the sun was in the sky.

"What happened with the Council? I know you gave me a quick version yesterday, but maybe there's something we missed. A clue. Anything.”

I closed my eyes. All around the symphony of nature played. Birds chirped. Insects buzzed. Leaves bristled as a soft gust of wind blew through them. The warmth of the midday sun spread over us. I inhaled a breath of fresh air. A hint of sage from the botanical gardens near us filled my senses.

“They demanded the book be given to them. I refused. Mom and Amanda almost used magic against Gwen. I left. That’s pretty much it. Gwen threw out some threats, but if she really wants the book then she’s not going to hurt me.”

Mila lay down with her head in my lap. I ran my fingers through her hair, loving the touch of silk as each strand brushed my leg when it fell.

The day was perfect, but I didn’t get to enjoy it. Hatred began to creep its way into my emotional roller coaster. Whoever did this to Katie deserved to be punished.

“None of this is helping. We need to find the book and see if that will give us any answers. Do you have any idea where it might be?”

I shook my head.

“The last time I had it was yesterday morning. Tierney came over, you came over, and Pip’s boyfriend. Since he and Pip are clueless, that leaves you and Tierney who could have taken it.”

Mila closed her eyes and I held my breath. I didn’t think she’d just come and say she took it, but I needed her to say she didn't.

She reached up to run her finger across my lip.

"It wasn't me, babe. You'd have seen me carry it out, which leaves us with Tierney."

"But why would she take the book?"

"Power? Some sense of duty? To win you?"

I quit listening as she continued to toss out reasons, too focused on the idea of my once-best-friend taking the book so she could win me.

A hollowness grew in my chest. I'd lost Katie. Now Josh did whatever the Coven wanted to get information about me. Tierney had her own agenda. In one week everything had changed. I was no longer an apprentice of the Evanoir Coven, or at least I assumed I wasn't. Gwen had kicked me out after all.

Somehow, in that week, I'd found a book that foretold of death, finally talked to Mila, and lost my family.

Two things kicked off the change, the book, and Mila.

The more I worked everything out, the more it became apparent I needed to separate myself from Mila. I didn't want to. She was the only light in my suddenly dark world, but if I wanted any chance at solving the mystery, I needed to remove myself from everyone and everything. Consider a perspective from the outside.

"Let's go home, Mila. I need to get some studying done before tomorrow," I said.

Mila lifted off my lap.

"Did you come up with something?"

"Not yet." Telling her that she kept creeping up as a suspect didn't seem like a good idea. She knew more magic than I did.

I didn't think she'd do anything to me, but it was better to keep us out of that situation.

"We're halfway home and you've said all of three words. You figured out something at the park, what was it?"

I'd done a horrible job masking my emotions. Shutting down had always been my go-to and this was no exception.

"It's not a big deal. Yesterday is just settling in. The calm of the park let me get lost in my head. Probably not a good idea right now." I reached across the console and took Mila's hand in mine.

If she came back to me after all of this was done, then we were meant to be together. At least that's what I told myself when I played the conversation we needed to have over and over in my thoughts.

"You're lying, but given all the shit you've been through, I'll let it slide."

The smile I offered barely curved upward. When we pulled into the dorm parking lot, I didn't rush to get out. It'd be easier to do this in the car rather than at my front door.

"Listen, I think it'd be best if maybe we didn't see each other right now," I blurted out the words in a single breath.

"Why?" She drew the word out. Mila's eyes widened. "You think I had something to do with Katie's death."

"No." Mila arched one brow at me. "I don't know. In my gut, I know you didn't kill Katie. My head keeps arguing with my gut. You were there yesterday when Katie met up with Dustin, then you came to me. You were with me last night, then *Mort d'Evanoir* went missing. You never cared to even say hello to me before I found *Mort*. These could be coincidences, but at the same time I'd be an idiot to not at least consider other explanations." I didn't want to see the truth of my words or the disappointment of my accusation in her eyes.

"Right. You did think this through."

"I'm sorry," I whispered.

Mila put two fingers beneath my chin and lifted my head until our eyes locked.

"Do not apologize. Be confident. You've put together a puzzle, whether I agree or not, it doesn't matter. But hear this, Azami. We're not going to stop seeing each other. I made a promise, and I vow to keep my promise. You take a day or two and sort things out in your head. At the very least, consider keeping me around just so you can see that I didn't do it, or prevent it from happening again if I did do it."

She pressed her lips to mine in a quick, but sweet, non-judgmental kiss.

"Okay," I said.

"Good night, Azami. Get some sleep and call me when you're ready to talk."

I climbed out of the car. Mila drove off, while I stood on the sidewalk and watched. She'd been sure enough of herself that she refused to walk away—even offered to stick around so I could see that she didn't kill if I was convinced she had.

Someone who'd killed Katie wouldn't make that offer.

<h1 style="text-align:center">CHAPTER 12</h1>

I'D SPENT THE WEEK TRYING to find the book, without any success. No one at the Coven would talk to me. Friday night, I broke down and went to Evanoir to visit my mom.

After clearing the table of leftover pot roast and potatoes, I moved to Mom's study. Mom left the room and came back with an old shoebox decorated with permanent marker and glitter. The box contained a book of spells she'd put together and some pictures she'd had from her time as an apprentice. The notebook, more like a journal, was not as big as a normal piece of paper, but too big to be pocket size. She'd put colored tabs at the start of each section. On the first page of each tab was a description of what she'd kept in that section.

"This must have taken forever to organize," I said.

"Not really. Monica and I worked on it together. The hard part was finding the information. We spent many nights huddled in a corner of the Coven library with a flashlight reading spell books." Mom sat next to me with a steaming cup of tea.

September in Louisiana wasn't exactly hot tea time of the year, but Mom loved it year round.

"Who is Monica?"

For a few minutes, Mom didn't say anything. I turned to the tab labeled "Death."

"That section was a special request. Monica Hutchings was my best friend."

My head jerked up at the mention of Monica's last name. The same Monica I'd dreamed about; Mila's aunt and my mom were friends.

"You were friends with a Hutchings?"

Mom nodded.

"But how? That's forbidden. How did you get her into the Coven library?"

I closed the book.

Mom swirled her finger around the top of her mug.

"Your grandmother raised me to question everything and doubt everyone. I took that further and did the opposite of everything I was told. Mostly. Grandma's switch across my rear was unpleasant enough I knew my limits."

We both chuckled. I knew the sting of Grandma's switch. At eighty-five her threats of bending me over her knee weren't ignored.

"Anyway, I had a few classes with Monica in high school. We became good friends and the Coven's rule about her family pissed me off. It didn't make any sense. So I ignored it."

Hmm. I wondered if she knew the truth behind the family banishment.

"What happened with the Coven? I mean, how did they react?"

"I won't tell you who you can and can't be friends with, sweetheart. You're smart and I trust you. But be careful. My decisions almost caused irreversible damage to our family. If your grandmother hadn't stepped in, I don't want to think about what could have happened." Mom sighed.

As expected, the Coven wasn't fond of Mom's friendship.

"You survived. Why haven't you talked about Monica before? If you were so against the Coven rules, then why haven't you told me to ignore them before now?" I asked.

"Because I wanted to protect you from my mistakes."

"Are you saying being friends with Monica was a mistake?"

Mom shook her head.

"No. Not at all. Talking about her reminds me of all the things we did. Some of them were mistakes. I was young and stupid and I didn't want you to have the same reputation I did. And if I'm honest, I wanted to prove to Grandma that she didn't waste her time bailing me out for all the rules I broke. I needed her to be proud of the way I raised you."

"Is she? Proud of you, I mean? With everything going on."

The last time I talked to my grandma was my high school graduation. It wasn't that we weren't close, but she moved three hours outside of Evanoir my freshman year. Going to see her took an entire weekend, and wasn't a trip we made often.

Mom picked at her fingernails when she answered my questions.

"She doesn't know as far as I'm aware. Until we get it all figured out, there's no reason to worry her."

I cleared my throat. When I came over to see her, my sole purpose was to ask about the book, but now that I was there, *Mort d'Evanoir* didn't seem as important.

"Do you really think I had a hand in Katie's death?"

When she shook her head I let out a long sigh. At least my mom hadn't given up hope.

"I don't think you did it, but I think it has something to do with *Mort d'Evanoir*—a book that's in your possession."

My relief came a little too quick. I lowered my chin to my chest. Mom rubbed my back.

"Sweetheart, that book is evil. Our Coven has tried to find it for years, but it found you and I don't like that at all. The worst part is I'm your mom and I can't do anything to help you."

No, she couldn't help. No one could, especially since the book was gone.

Mom's study was my favorite room in the house. A collage of pictures and souvenirs decorated the walls. Each one from a country she visited before I was born. Except for the wall behind her desk. That one was empty, saved for the trip she and I would take someday.

Across from where we sat was the Paris wall. She said that trip was when she fell in love with my dad. A mix of photos of them together and sites they explored made a heart in the center of the wall. Paintings, shadow boxes of gifts they bought each other, and pages from love letters Dad mailed home for her to read later hung in organized chaos around the heart.

"What was that spell you were going to do to Gwen last Saturday?"

"A bad idea." She studied the inside of her teacup with far more interest than necessary.

I needed to know more. She'd done something Amanda said could get her in trouble. It didn't make sense that she'd protect me like that when she wanted the Coven to have the book as much as Gwen did.

"You were going to hurt Gwen, weren't you?"

Mom nodded. "Yes. Thankfully, Amanda stopped me."

"But why?"

"Two weeks before I was to be recommended for full

Coven membership, I made one of the dumbest decisions in my life. You see, our family is related to the Graves family. Gwen is my cousin."

My jaw dropped. "Why did I not know this?"

If we were related to Gwen and Mila's family had killed Gwen's great-grandma, then that meant they killed my relative as well. Not that I held a grudge. It was decades ago.

"Our families agreed when the Coven formed that it would not be openly discussed. Rivka and Marguerite, your however many greats grandmother, were cousins, but they didn't always see eye to eye. In truth, we could have been the line of Coven leaders, but Marguerite refused. She didn't want the responsibility, so she agreed that there would be no disputes about which family was the rightful heir to the Coven leader title."

Marguerite sounded lazy, or at the very least, like someone who didn't care about other people. She had an opportunity to lead and protect a family and she chose not to. Then again, I'd probably turn it down too. The fear of someone in my family getting hurt was too great to take on a role like 'leader.'

Of the founding families, I took note that two of them were not fond of Gwen's family. These ripples in the formation of the Evanoir Coven began to turn more suspicion towards Gwen—or at least her ridiculous rules. I asked myself if she wanted *Mort d'Evanoir* because of the potential power it would give her. Did she want to exact revenge against the families who had wronged her relative so many years ago?

"What does that have to do with yesterday?"

"Back to my original story. Right before my acceptance, Gwen wanted to spend a little more time before our final test, but the rule was we had to study together or not at all. Because we weren't full members yet, we still weren't supposed to practice magic alone. I'd already started celebrating and had a few drinks. One spell led to another and before I knew what had happened, I lit a building on fire. It was an accident; I was practicing a spell to light a candle without fire. Gwen, being Gwen, ran to the Council the next day and told them what happened." Mom pointed her finger at my chest. "Do not do what I did. No one was hurt, but it was still stupid."

I held my hands in the air in surrender. "No worries, Mom."

"You say that now. Anyway, your grandma managed to talk the Council out of denying me full membership. Somehow, she got them to agree that it was just a stupid mistake and I would never do something like that again. It was part of my probation to start teaching the apprentices."

Wow. I'd never expected Mom to admit that she almost burned down a building. I propped my elbows on the desk, waiting for more of the story. This was far better than going to class.

"Wait. I thought we were assigned our roles based on what our parents did, which would mean you weren't supposed to be a teacher."

Mom nodded. "That's right. Your assignment is a result of my punishment. Grandma was the Coven historian. She kept records of everything that happened during her time on the Council. Our family has always been the historians. If you cared to, you could appeal to the Council."

I didn't want to appeal, but I did want to know more about our former role. Maybe Grandma would have some insight into *Mort*. Although, Mom said she hadn't filled her in on what was going on, which meant I couldn't exactly call her up and start asking questions. Not without spilling some tea of my own.

"Is that why you were quick to cast against Gwen?"

"That was more about revenge than anything else. I'm sorry, it was a childish thing to do. I was protecting you, but I do want the Coven to have *Mort*. When she started mouthing off I took the opportunity to protect you and get back at her. It was not a shining moment for me. Azami, I'm not happy about what happened. I'm proud of you for not backing down, but you need to get rid of that book."

Mom finished her tea and I lay my head on the back of the chair with my eyes closed. It'd been a long week and I felt no closer to figuring out the clues than I had on

Sunday. The ache in my chest from Mila's absence grew every day. Even then, as I relaxed in Mom's office, I wanted to text Mila and tell her everything I learned. But I couldn't. Because no matter how hard I tried, I couldn't get rid of the sense. that she somehow had a place in all of this.

The arm of the chair buzzed when I received a text. I glanced down to see who it was from. Tierney, of course: the last person I expected.

T: There's something you need to know about your precious book.

Me: What?

T: We'll talk in person. Tomorrow afternoon. My last class is over at three. I'll meet you at the alley by three-thirty.

Before I agreed to meet Tierney, I needed one more answer from Mom.

"It was five against one at the house and none of you even tried to take the book from me. Why is that?"

She stood then paced between our chairs and her desk.

"It's the book. The Council asked the same questions of each other yesterday. None of us even considered taking it, which was odd. We don't have any other explanation than that."

I nodded. It didn't make sense to me why the book would be the reason they didn't take it from me. Of course, I hadn't had it with me, but they didn't even ask if I'd brought it to the house. They only told me to return it to them.

"All right. I'm going to head out. Thank you for dinner."

Mom walked with me to the front door. "You're my daughter, Azami. No matter what happens at the house, please don't ever think I'll put the Coven before you. I love you and will always protect you."

Her promise gave me the strength to face Tierney. On my way home I sent her a text to meet me at my place. There was no reason to wait.

Not your place. Meet me at the alley if you want your book back.

I wanted the book and wasn't in the mood to argue, so I told her I'd see her there in thirty.

Tierney's family owned the alley. A few years ago they redecorated the whole thing in a modern-retro design. Each lane had a mural painted by local graffiti artists. Computerized scoreboards were mounted on the ceiling. If a lane wasn't in use they could turn on whatever sports game people wanted to watch. The lanes were polished and smooth. For a retro touch, they replaced the uncomfortable, beige plastic benches with clear plastic chairs and custom memory foam cushions covered by a burgundy and gold fabric.

"Did I do something to upset you?" I asked before the door to the alley closed.

She sat at the bar along the back wall. It was the only

piece of furniture left from the original building and stretched the entire length, front to back. Our parents used to let us run to the middle of the bar then slide head-first across the top to the end. They stopped letting us play slip and slide when Katie almost went off the edge.

"I'm surprised you don't know the answer to that already."

"Not sure how I'm supposed to know. You haven't talked to me in a week."

"Mila."

One word. She thought that explained everything.

"Call me stupid, but I don't get it. How does our friendship dissolve so quickly over one person?"

"She killed Katie. Her family is nothing good. I've tried to get close to you, even wanted to ask you on a date, but then she showed up. Since the two of you started talking it's like I don't exist. Now do you get it?"

Oh yeah. I understood. Her jealousy was stronger than I'd realized. She failed to recall that she was the one who denied me first.

"Right. Do you remember during our sophomore year of high school I asked you to the Winter Dance?" Tierney shook her head. "I asked you to the dance. You said going with me wouldn't help with your status. For you to say I'm the one who treats you like you don't exist is wrong. The fact that you don't remember me asking you out and you didn't notice how Katie conveniently didn't invite me places lately tells me everything I need to know."

Tierney stared at me, her mouth gaping.

"You're hung up on a sophomore dance? I didn't even know you meant it as a date. I thought you wanted to go as friends. We're in college now, that was high school. You chose Mila over our Coven. She killed Katie and you stand behind her."

"What do you want to tell me about *Mort d'Evanoir*?" It was time to move on so I could go home before the rift between us grew even bigger.

My Coven sister, who no longer acted like family, stood on her stool and leaned over the bar. From behind she pulled out a rectangle wrapped in leather. It was similar in size to the book. Tierney shredded my heart from my chest without a single ounce of emotion. I hadn't wanted her to be involved. We had our differences, and even though I should've hated her, I still loved her.

"Here. Take it home. Don't open that here. I don't want anything to do with the abhorrent magic inside it. I wish you'd just give up on Mila. This would have been so much easier."

I didn't give her the satisfaction of reacting. Instead, I took the book from her and left. There was no need to turn back. Tierney had been loud and clear about her opinions.

As soon as I got home, I ran upstairs to my place and straight to my room where I shut and locked the door. The last thing I needed was for Pip to come in and ask what was going on.

Carefully, I pulled back the leather cover. Beneath the leather wasn't my book.

CHAPTER 13

WRAPPED IN THE LEATHER WAS was a book, but
it wasn't *Mort d'Evanoir*. Someone had wrapped up a
leather-bound book filled with empty pages. Well, all
except the first page.

The first time I read the letter my knees went weak and
I sat on my bed. The second time my hands shook and tears
dripped from the corner of my eyes. The third time rage
snuffed out the hurt.

Azami,

*This is not what you expected, just as life doesn't
always provide us with what we want or expect. Mort
d'Evanoir is too dangerous to be in your possession. So
I've taken it. You may ask yourself how, but that's not the
question you need to answer. Someday you'll figure it out,
but I caution you from spending too much time on the
mystery just now.*

Instead, consider what you'll do to help Tierney. Another Coven apprentice. Will she die as Katie did? Will someone find her with a perfect red kiss on her cheek in the morning? Or will you get to the farmhouse in time to save her?

By the time you read this, I'm sure it will be well into the night. Choose, Azami. Drive to the house and save Tierney or tuck into bed and resume your search for the book tomorrow.

Your decision will weigh heavily on the minds of those who matter.

I didn't hesitate. The choice was easy; I'd go for Tierney. No matter where we stood at the moment, she was family by choice if not blood, and I would save her. The screen on my phone lit to reveal it was already after midnight. I had a thirty-minute drive back to Evanoir, then at least a fifteen-minute walk through the woods to the field. On my way out of town, I stopped for an energy shot, two energy drinks, and some snacks to keep me awake.

In Evanoir I pulled into a three-car parking lot at the edge of the forest. With flashlight in hand, I climbed out of the car, locked the doors, then headed into the trees. Bennett followed, singing his crow song as I trudged through the tree limbs and leaves littering the ground.

"Did you like being protector of *Mort d'Evanoir?*" I asked.

"No. I should've been the wielder, not the lowly protector."

"You want to kill people?"

The bird flew up and down in the rays of the flashlight.

"I want the power over people. To right the wrongs done to me."

"The people that wronged you, are they the same ones that made you a bird?"

If he was going to fly with me, then I was going to take advantage of the moment. At least with Bennett there, I could fill the silence of the woods with my questions. He could tell me more about how he became a talking bird protector.

"Yes. It's their fault even if it wasn't their magic. But they're dead. The only way to get what I want is to kill the heirs."

Wow.

"It is the book who's behind it all."

Bennett screeched one loud caw then two short ones before flying away and leaving me to my thoughts.

He was wrong. The book couldn't command death.

I crossed the border from woods to field and looked across the black of night to where I remembered the old gray, weathered farmhouse sat. Coven families owned the property around the field. At one time, the house was the gathering place.

"Bennett, where are you?"

I'd lost track of the crow near the edge of the woods.

"Eating."

An image of worms falling out of his mouth flashed through my mind. I gagged.

"Gross. Is someone living in the house?"

"No."

A light flickered from a window on the second floor. He was wrong. I pulled my backpack off and clutched it to my chest.

"Are you sure?"

The wooden door didn't creak when I pushed it open. Inside, I found a light switch against the wall. The entry came into view, illuminated by a crystal chandelier hanging from the highest point of the ceiling. The floors had been polished, marble replaced wood. The cobwebs brushed away. The staircases on either side were refinished. The house appeared brand new.

"Wow."

Steps sounded from above. I froze in place, my hands in fists ready to fight just in case.

"Hello," I called out. I'd seen a light outside, but it didn't seem like anyone was in the house.

Everything went silent. No noises from outside. No more footsteps.

Halfway up the stairs, I called out again. "Is anyone here?"

No answer, so I continued up to the second floor. Last

time the staircases were crumbling slats of wood, some of them missing completely. Three steps from the top I recited a simple revealing spell that was supposed to show anything or anyone hidden behind walls and doors.

"Hello?" I tried one more time after I finished the cast.

The spell didn't show me anything. Whoever was inside the house had blocked magic other than theirs.

A light at the end of the hall came on. "Who's down there?"

The floor creaked beneath my feet. No one spoke. The rooms stayed silent as I passed each one. Four total. The closer I got to the room with the light, the harder I squeezed the backpack against my chest. Last room on the right. I moved against the wall and came to a stop next to a half-open door. A woman recited an incantation over and over. I didn't recognize the language or the spell. There was no metallic taste, no hint of dark magic. But the voice didn't sound like anyone from the Coven.

I tiptoed back up the hall, down the stairs, and to the front door. That wasn't Tierney. She wasn't in the house. The letter was wrong and I had to go.

"Hey. What are you doing in my house?" a lady yelled at me.

I reached for the doorknob, ready to run.

One agonizing inch at a time I turned to see who was in the house with me. Addison Clarke, Tierney's mom, stood in the middle of the balcony wearing a floor-length ivory shift dress. Her hair had been pinned up on the sides. Tierney was a younger version of her mom.

"Mrs. Clarke," I gasped her name.

"Azami. Why are you here?"

I needed a quick excuse, too afraid to tell her about the letter. Surely, she wouldn't have sent something like that for her own daughter. Except, as part of the Coven it made sense. How else would the author of the letter have known details about Katie's death?

"Just went for a walk and found this place. Thought I'd check it out," I said.

"Well, we bought the house a couple of weeks ago. It's private property now. I'd expect you not to visit without an invite."

"I apologize. It won't happen again."

Mrs. Clarke made her way down the stairs. Her shift flowed over the steps like the dresses women wore in old black and white movies, or a ghost with a haunting destination in mind.

"Thank you," she said with a finality I shouldn't have questioned.

"Where's Tierney?" I asked.

"She's here, safe." Mrs. Clarke gave me a smile with no warmth at all.

There was no invitation to stay and no further insight on Tierney.

"Good. Well, I'll go ahead and go. I'm sorry for

bothering you."

"Azami, why did you come to my house this late at night? Are you searching for something?" She tilted her head to the side.

I searched my brain for a quick response that wouldn't let on to the real reason I'd shown up at the farmhouse after midnight.

"This is where I found Mort. I thought maybe if I came back, I could learn more about it."

"So you have the book with you now?"

Crap on a cracker. Trying to stay as close to the truth as possible didn't work as well as it should've. The palms of my hands turned sweaty. My mouth went dry. I absolutely could not tell Addison that I'd lost Mort. Even if she was the one who left me the note, I couldn't admit the truth.

I shook my head.

"Speak up," she said.

"No. I don't have *Mort d'Evanoir* with me. That's not exactly a book anyone should carry everywhere they go. The dark magic in that book could be deadly in the wrong hands."

Shut up. Shut up. Shut up. The words kept coming no matter how many times I told my brain to quit spitting them out.

Mrs. Clarke made her way down the steps to where I stood near the front door.

"If that's how what you truly believe then why do you keep the book from the Coven? Are you worried *we* are the wrong hands?

Her words dripped with a mixture of curiosity and accusation. A creepy-crawly sensation worked its way up my spine. The instructions in the letter were to go to the farmhouse to save Tierney. It never said I had to find her to save her, just show up, which I did. When Addison stepped closer I yanked open the door and crossed over onto the porch—at least being outside she wouldn't be able to keep me from leaving.

"Of course not. The book chose me, so I guess it just makes sense that I need to keep it until we figure out a way to destroy the magic." Yes, that was a good answer.

The worst thing I could've said was I wanted to defy the Coven. I wanted to finally do something they didn't dictate or control.

"Or you mean to say, destroy it after you finish using it. Admittedly, I am glad you chose Tierney tonight. It would've been such a disappointment otherwise."

The wind shifted directions and the metallic taste of magic returned. The air filled with the scent of burning wood. Long fingers of fire grabbed the side of the house and pulled around the front. The wood didn't catch even with flames burning blue and white. The hottest it could be, yet the house stood strong.

The flames rose higher.

"How dare you try and burn down our home." Mrs. Clarke rushed past me to the front of the house and began weaving a spell.

"No. Not again. I didn't, this isn't me." The tase of blood wasn't strong. Just a hint.

I didn't wait any longer. Mrs. Clarke would extinguish the flames. With a prayer to the goddess, I took off to the trees. It was time to go home. Tomorrow, I'd find *Mort d'Evanoir* and make sure no one had the chance to take it again.

CHAPTER 14

SATURDAY MORNING I WOKE TO the sight of Mila leaning against the dresser. She didn't say hi, didn't respond to my comment about not seeing her. Her eyelids lowered over her eyes. I couldn't help but notice how the tie of her black tank top accentuated her waistline. Or how the jean shorts showed off her legs. I loved that her bright pink toes stood out against her black flip flops. She was light and dark. As I made my way back up her body, stopping at her hands, I noticed a package. Not any package. A rectangle shape wrapped in the same bandana I used for *Mort d'Evanoir.*

I sucked in a breath. The events of the night before rushed back to me.

"Please don't tell me..." Each word trembled more than the last. I covered my eyes with my arm, afraid to get out of bed. "That's not what I think it is. Is it?"

No. No. No. Tierney hinted that the Hutchings had the

163

book. Or I decided that they might have had it. I couldn't remember.

"Z, you have to listen to me. Please don't jump to conclusions."

"No." I shook my head. "I'm keeping an open mind. I'm listening."

I bit the inside of my lip to keep from blurting out the truth. Every thought in my mind contradicted the words I spoke. She had the book. She was the only one who knew where I kept *Mort d'Evanoir* and now she stood in my room with it in her hands.

Mila unwrapped the item she brought. As expected, the book in her hands had the tell-tale brown leather cover. The gold-embossed lettering. *Mort d'Evanoir.*

"I didn't take this." She placed her hand on the cover.

I'd spent the last week trying to figure out where to even start searching for the book.

"How long have you had it?" I asked.

"This morning I woke up and it was on my bedside table. I swear. I did *not* take the book from you." She enunciated each word while keeping eye contact with me. "Z, I didn't take the book from you. Are you comprehending my words?"

Truth shone in her gaze. I wanted to believe her. Needed to believe her. But how could I? The evidence went against everything she said.

"You don't believe me." Mila sighed. "Okay. Along

with the book, there was a letter."

"A letter?" I asked.

She nodded.

"What did it say?"

She handed me a folded piece of paper. I unfolded it one corner at a time.

"Does it say who had the book?" I smoothed out the creases in the paper.

Mila shook her head.

Taking my time, I read the letter.

Mila,

You made a deal with Azami, which she will do her best to keep. But she won't succeed. I will ensure that she fails. However, I have a task that if you succeed in completing, will ensure you find the banishment of your family lifted.

It's a simple task. Return this book to Azami and end your relationship. You and your family will be allowed to apply to become members of the Evanoir Coven once more, so long as you never interact with Azami again. Consider it a restraining order of sorts. As soon as I see the book returned, I'll go to the Council and discuss the removal of the banishment.

The choice is yours.

The handwriting was the same as my letter. They knew

of our deal, which I hadn't told anyone about. They were right about my failing to uphold my end of the deal. Too many things pointed away from Mila. She hadn't stolen the book.

"Are you going—" I started but the words stuck in my throat "—to do what they said?"

"No." Mila rushed to the side of my bed but stopped short of sitting down. "I talked to my family. They agree. Whoever put this in our house is playing some sort of game. They had the book, why not keep it? We don't understand why they're willing to lift our banishment just so I'll break up with you."

Yeah, I didn't get that part either. What was so special about our relationship that it was worth removing the banishment?

"I'm lost, Mila. The pieces don't fit."

"Are you convincing yourself I set this up? Do you still think I stole the book?"

"I don't know. Some of it seems like you are, but you can't make a promise to restore your family's name or go to the Council. Only someone within the Coven can do that."

A scream scratched at my throat. I wanted to throw the book in a fire. Let it burn to ashes.

"Azami, what can I say to make you see the truth?"

Our hands found each other, and I laced our fingers together. Her touch calmed my thoughts. Warmth flowed from her skin to mine. Her light pushed away the darkness in my soul.

"I believe you. I hope one day I don't regret it, but I believe you."

Mila let out a long breath. The muscles in her arm relaxed.

"I'll do everything I can to keep you from regretting it."

A rapid beating on the window pulled our attention outside. Bennett perched on his normal spot on the sill.

"Today will bring trouble to you and yours. Protect Mort d'Evanoir *so it is not lost again."*

Mila and I reached for the book at the same time. I started to pick it up only for the leather to slip through my fingers. It landed open on the floor between us. I bent down to get it and gasped. A new name appeared at the top of the empty page.

Katie Guidry   Sliced clean through her throat.

It killed Katie. The wielder had their first victim.

"Tell me I'm not seeing what I think I'm seeing." Mila choked.

"You are," I said.

Beneath Katie's name a letter "O" appeared. Then another and another until it spelled Olivia Jennings. I slammed the book shut. None of us needed to see how she died.

"Do you know Olivia?" Mila asked. Her voice barely a whisper.

My whole body trembled. The room became so cold my teeth chattered. Voices around me grew distant like I was in a tunnel of some sort. That awful metallic taste returned. I tried to move, but my arms and legs were stuck.

Panic settled in for a long stay as my room faded away to be replaced by the partly cloudy, gray sky outside. I wasn't on the floor anymore but standing on a brick building. My arms lifted then I was falling. No matter how hard I tried I couldn't catch my breath. When I hit the ground everything went black.

My eyes opened and I watched as Mila leaned over me. She shook my arms, but I didn't feel her. My muscles twitched. My chest hurt like it had been crushed. I couldn't talk. Couldn't scream for help. All I could do was wish for whatever was happening to end.

Finally, my body stopped shaking. Warm hands rubbed up and down my arms. My vision shifted and I was back in my room.

"Azami, talk to me."

I tried to tell her I was okay, but the words wouldn't form. My mouth couldn't open. I tried to move, but some kind of weight sat on my arms and legs making it impossible. A soft touch to my lips cleared away the weights. Mila hovered over me with a plea in her eyes. I ached to pull her close. She leaned down and the softness of a moment ago returned. She was kissing me. A quick one, but it felt like it lasted a lifetime. I squeezed her hand in mine.

"Don't let go," I whispered.

"The book lives. It's happy." The joy in the crow's voice brought another round of chills.

How could death make someone happy?

"What just happened?" I asked.

"I was hoping you could tell me," Mila answered.

"I don't know." I tried to get the metallic taste out of my mouth, but couldn't. "One minute we were reading and the next I was falling from the top of a building."

"Is there..." Mila pointed to her mouth.

"Dark magic?" I asked.

She nodded.

"Bennett." I made sure to reach out through my thoughts, not ready to share the full experience with Mila. Part of me wanted to keep it to myself a bit longer. Whether it was control or the thrill of having something no one else did, I wasn't sure. *"What just happened?"*

"Mort d'Evanoir *shared its power with you."* Bennett cawed outside the window.

"I didn't see anything." Unless he meant falling from a building.

"Ahh. Silly child. The book doesn't do as you expect."

"Who died?" I asked even though I wasn't sure I wanted to know the answer.

"Only you can know that. The book doesn't tell me the names of the lives it takes," Bennett said. *"Not anymore.*

That power is for you alone."

"Z, tell me what's going on," Mila insisted.

"I don't know. We need to find Olivia to see if there is a connection to anyone else we know. Whatever the reason for her death, *Mort d'Evanoir* has noted it and Bennett says I've now seen the power of the magic."

If we were going hunting, then I needed to put on some clothes.

It didn't take long to find the woman in my vision. According to the obituaries, she died two days before. It didn't say how she died, so we decided I needed to read *Mort d'Evanoir* once more. Olivia died when she fell from a building.

CHAPTER 15

MILA AND I SAT ON the bed with our heads together. In the last twenty-four hours, we'd made zero progress finding a connection between anyone we knew and the sixty-year-old, Olivia Jennings.

"There's a new name." I traced the letters one at a time. "The sister of one of the guys in my class. She died of a heart attack."

"The wielder's at work again. Do you feel anything?" Mila asked.

I shook my head.

"Azami." Tierney came into my room Sunday morning, unannounced.

"Who let you in?" I snapped.

Tierney held up a key. One that I hadn't given her, and I was pretty sure Pippa hadn't either.

"I let myself in."

"With a key you stole?" I asked.

The only good thing about the surprise visit was I didn't have to worry about whether or not Tierney was alive. I'd made it to the farmhouse in time to save her, but I wasn't sure if she knew anything about the letter or my visit to her house.

"You'll get over it. The Coven wants to talk to you." She considered the two of us. "Both of you."

"What about?" Mila asked.

"The Council has determined you and your family are the cause of the *Mort d'Evanoir* murders."

Wow.

"How could they determine her family did this? A single death does not warrant some kind of serial killer title. Besides, we already knew the Coven suspected Mila. Gwen made that clear a week ago." I clenched my fist.

"There's something else I wanted to talk to you about. You seem to be the only one who can read that book. Fortunately, Pam made the argument of you being the protector and not the wielder. Gwen knew the difference, even if the rest of us didn't."

"So what, now you're on the Council?" Mila asked.

"You're not even a full member. How could you be on the Council?" I followed.

Tierney smirked.

"Nah. Mom told me everything. If you want to get out from all of this, you need to destroy *Mort d'Evanoir*. Since you refuse to give the book to the Coven, the only other option is to burn it."

"Mort d'Evanoir *cannot be destroyed*," Bennett said.

"*Everything can be destroyed. Some things are harder than others. I'll find a way.*"

First, I needed to know where *Mort d'Evanoir* came from.

"*Bennett, where can I find the history of* Mort?"

If he told me, I wouldn't have to waste time researching. I didn't get my hopes up though.

"*There is no history. Why would I help the one who wishes to destroy my book and me?*" He sang from the tree outside my window.

The bird was ridiculous. Of course, there was a history. Books that killed people didn't appear out of nowhere without a background of some sort. My family had been the historians and the Coven kept records of everything that happened. I needed to get Tierney out of my home then talk to Mila about breaking into the Coven house one more time.

Mila stood in front of Tierney. With one hand on her shoulder, she turned my Coven sister toward the door.

"Thanks for stopping by, but it's time for you to go. Leave the key on the kitchen counter on your way out."

I relaxed on the bed with a smile stretching my lips. It was nice to see Mila handle Tierney for me.

"*I don't want to destroy you. Just* Mort d'Evanoir." I returned to my conversation with Bennett after the click of the door following Tierney's exit.

"You do not pay attention, Azami Durand. I am Mort d'Evanoir."

"What?" I whipped my head around to the tree. "You're killing these people. I'm the protector, so if you're killing then that would make you the wielder."

"No. Mort d'Evanoir does not kill without direction. I merely record the deaths as they happen."

If the book was nothing more than a record, Bennett was a delusional bird on top of everything else. I'd been naïve to think he was helpful at all. All he did was send me in a circle of confusion.

"It is not just a record. It is control. It is death."

The branches rattled. Control. Death. Whoever used *Mort* controlled the death of others.

"But why a book? Why not just kill them? It was the same thing," I whispered as I began to pace a path between my desk and bed.

"Because the best way to get away with murder is to leave as little evidence as possible. The killer is never found. By pouring magic into a book that can do things like slice someone's throat without so much as a fingerprint the wielder isn't caught." A sad smile stretched my lips when Mila answered.

"How do you know that?" I asked.

"I talked to my mom. It seems my family helped bring the book to life."

It made sense. Mom and Monica. Gwen and me. Mila's great-grandmother and Gwen's. The Hutchings may have been outcasts, but it wasn't always that way.

"We need to destroy *Mort d'Evanoir*."

"That's impossible, Z. The magic is impenetrable."

Why did everyone keep telling me it couldn't be done?

"Nothing is impossible. Difficult, yes. Tricky, sure. But I will find a way. Even if I have to do it on my own. *Mort d'Evanoir* chose me. That means something."

"You're crazy." Mila smiled her perfect smile. The circles under her eyes lightened slightly. "You don't have to do it alone. I'll help. Come over, stay the night. I think Mom would love to meet you."

I nodded. I wasn't alone.

CHAPTER 16

I FOLLOWED MILA TO HER house. She lived on the northern outskirts of Evanoir, about fifteen minutes from Romilly. Their house was small, considering the size of her family. The cottage sat at the end of a cul-de-sac with light yellow paint that matched a few of the other houses on the street. The bright, turquoise front door stood out like a beacon. I parked out front in the street while Mila went out back.

Inside white walls and cream furniture gave it a clean, open decor.

"Your house is so light."

"Thanks. Mom does all the decorating; we just do the cleaning. And dirty it up."

I laughed. "I know the feeling. There's only one of me, though."

"Come on. Mom's in the kitchen."

We walked through the living room into the kitchen.

There weren't many walls, so we could see the back door from the front door. Mrs. Hutchings stood at the stove cooking. Steam from the pot she stirred carried scents of garlic, thyme, and shrimp through the space.

"Mom, meet Azami." Mila waved her arms from side to side. "Azami, meet Mom."

"Hello, Mrs. Hutchings. It's nice to meet you." I held out my hand.

"Call me Tracy." She shook my hand then returned her attention to the stove.

"Is that gumbo?" I asked.

"Sure is."

"Smells delicious."

I took a glass of water Mila offered.

"You don't have to suck up to her. She'll like you regardless."

"Mila. Don't be rude," her mom chastised.

I stuck my tongue out at Mila.

"I'm not sucking up. It really does smell good. I love gumbo."

"By the way, Z is going to crash here tonight. We've got some research to do before class tomorrow."

Mila took my empty hand and pulled me toward the back door.

"We're going outside, Mom."

Tracy waved her hand, her back to us while she added more seasoning to the pot.

I blew out a puff of air once outside. So many questions and few answers ran through my thoughts. We needed to figure out who wielded the book, how to destroy the book, how to clear the Hutchings name, and how to get the Coven away from this idea that Mila and I killed Katie.

"Where do we start, Mila? I imagine this is what it's like to fall in a damp well and I'm too deep to find my way out."

I tilted my chin toward the crystal blue sky. There were no birds. No clouds. Just sun. I wanted to lean back and soak in the rays rather than deal with the fire I'd found myself in the middle of.

"That's part of the problem. I don't know. If I had more information about the book and how it came into existence, I could probably find something useful."

The same idea had crossed my mind at home. An image of the stack of books Amanda had in the library flashed in my mind.

"I need to go to the Coven library. They have a ton of books about our history. What do you wanna bet there's something about *Mort d'Evanoir* in one of them?"

Mila narrowed her eyes and pursed her lips. "How are you going to get into the library?"

The library was at the back, near the exit for the greenhouse. Rather than a traditional security system, the house had wards to keep out unwanted guests. As long as I didn't do something stupid and break the wards, I could go in the back door unnoticed.

"With you. Didn't you say you and Dustin figured out how to break the wards? We can do the same thing for me. Very few members spend time at the house on Sunday, and if they do, they aren't in the library. I'm pretty sure we could get in through the back door. They don't lock the doors since the wards keep out intruders."

"We?" Mila questioned. "Let's say I drive and wait for you outside. Keep an eye out in case someone shows up."

"It would be faster if we both went in," I said.

"Only if we don't run into any problems," Mila argued.

I sighed. My selfishness and fear were getting in the way of finding what I needed. "Okay. You go as a lookout."

We agreed to wait until later that evening. Mila said she needed to talk to Dustin before she told me how to break the wards.

"Are there any more names today?" she asked.

"I haven't checked." I pulled the book out and unwrapped it.

We held our breath while I turned to the last page. A name started to appear. Marigold S.

"Bennett," I called. "Stop. Don't do this again."

The last name didn't appear beyond S. Hmm. I'd made him stop. Maybe being the protector could do some good.

"You don't control the magic. If it does not complete, then the spell was not completed," Bennett replied.

"Who controls the magic, Bennett?"

A caw came from the side of the yard. Mila's eyes grew big. She shook her head and jumped up from her chair, knocking it over in the process.

"My parents will flip if they find out Bennett's here." She fast-walked to the side of the house. "They believe crows to be harbingers of death."

"Bennett, you have to leave." I followed her to the fence.

"The book is here. I must stay."

Behind me, the back door clicked open then closed. Dustin passed us with a slingshot in hand.

Mila's back straightened as she sucked in a breath.

"No, Dustin. You can't," Mila growled.

He lifted his arm, pulled back the rubber strip, and launched a rock at the tree. Leaves rustled. Branches cracked. A splat rang out. My lungs failed to pull in air. The blood in my veins froze. I tried to pull myself over the fence, but I was too short.

"Is he dead? Did you kill him?" I snarled the last word. My hand clutched my chest. "Is the crow dead?"

"Let's hope so." Dustin held his hand out to me. "You must be Azami. I'm Mila's brother. I tried to kill that stupid bird at the Coven house too. He flew away that time."

"Why? Why did you kill him? How did you even know he was out here? That crow didn't do anything to hurt you."

Telepathically I searched for Bennett. *"Are you okay? Talk to me."*

"His obnoxious noises kept interrupting my activities upstairs. We don't like crows. If he'd been scared, he would have flown away. Hell, it was just a rock. Not my fault the bird was too stupid to move this time."

"Bennett," I tried again.

Still no response. The tree was quiet. No rustling limbs. No squawking birds. Empty. Dustin had killed Bennett.

Mila's face paled. She knew what her brother had done. Tried to stop him even, but he never missed a step. Ready. Aim. Fire. Dead.

Dustin fist punched the air. "Dead. Good. Mom said dinner will be ready in a couple of hours."

I shook my head. "You killed Bennett and you don't even care. Have you murdered puppies too? Maybe a kitten here or there."

"It was just a dumb bird. Why are you acting like it was your best friend?" His eyes narrowed and he moved his gaze back and forth between me and the tree where Bennett had been moments ago.

"Because he was. Bennett brought me to *Mort d'Evanoir*. He was the one helping me figure out how to stop its magic."

Dustin reeled back when I mentioned the name of the book. The muscles in his arms quivered and he clasped his hands together. Interesting.

"Well, next time tell your bird friends to stay off

private property."

He walked back inside the house without another word. I didn't know what to say.

"I'm so sorry, Z. I should've told you about my family's thoughts on crows. You could have warned Bennett."

"I told him to leave. He said he couldn't since the book was here."

"That doesn't make sense." Mila leaned with her back against the fence.

"Sure it does." I furrowed my brows. "He was the protector."

"No. You're the protector. That's not what I mean though. If he had to be where the book was, then he knew who stole it. Either he lied about not knowing who the thief was, or he lied about being here because you brought *Mort d'Evanoir* here."

"Let's go to the library. Forget talking to your brother. I need you to get me inside now."

I didn't wait for Mila to follow. Since my car was out front, I'd go alone if I needed to. Mila knew how to break the wards, but I knew the Coven house like it was my own. I'd find a way to break in.

***

The house was empty when we arrived. Mila drove around the block to park a few streets away. We agreed it would be better if her car wasn't in view. To stay out of sight, but still have a view of the back of the house where I'd go in, Mila found an empty bench at the neighborhood park where she quickly taught me the spell to disable the wards long enough for me to get into the library. I'd have to do it again in order to leave undetected. The Coven house sat at the front of twenty-five acres of land. A neighborhood had built up over the years in the open fields on all sides.

I gave her a quick kiss before walking to the house. The back door was unlocked, so I didn't have any trouble getting in after casting Mila's spell. If someone came in, I wanted to hear the noise of them moving around before they discovered me, so I left the lights off. I'd have more time to leave without getting caught.

The library's back wall had three stained glass windows at the top and four full-length windows along the bottom of the wall. These offered more than enough setting sunlight for me to search.

Each shelf was labeled by subject matter. I searched for our history. Halfway down the eight rows, I found the section I wanted. I wasn't sure how far back to go.

The Coven banished the Hutchings family in nineteen fifteen according to our classes. I searched for the eighteen-ninety to nineteen-twenty time frame. It didn't take long to find since the years were printed on the spine of each book. Unfortunately, five huge volumes covered the thirty-year span. It was too risky to read them in the library, so I stuffed my satchel and eased back to the front of the library. So far I'd made it in and found what I needed without any trouble.

My phone rang as I turned the knob of the door to leave.

I yanked my phone out of my bag, my heart raced so hard I thought it might jump out of my chest. How stupid could I've been? Of all the things to forget. My fingers shook and I came too close for comfort to dropping my phone. After a couple of attempts, I declined the call and silenced the ringer. I stood still, listening for any sign of a fellow witch or apprentice in the hall. Once no one had shown up, I turned the knob slowly then peeked through a crack in the door. All clear. It was time to return to Mila. I'd done it.

At the street corner, I still hadn't run into anyone. I started to celebrate but bumped into a brick wall in the form of Josh's chest. He grabbed my arms to keep me from falling on my butt.

"Azami? What are you doing here? They told me about Mila. I'm sorry."

"Who? What about Mila?" I asked.

The letter she got said we had to break up, but I wasn't sure how Josh knew about that.

"Yeah. It sucks. Katie was my love, but she didn't know it. You and Mila were starting something serious, but now she's gone."

I searched for Mila, but she wasn't at the park anymore. Josh followed my search. If I was going to get back to Mila without him knowing I needed to be more cautious.

"Right. Yeah. It's...hard."

"So what are you doing here? Gwen told us you weren't allowed back until this stuff with Katie was finished."

Stuff with Katie. For someone who claimed to love her as much as he did, the nonchalance of his tone caught me off-guard. This had to be another setup like the cafeteria, which meant I needed to do better at playing along.

"I know." I glanced all around, hoping he caught on. "Please don't tell Gwen you found me here. It's just... I thought I could practice until we got back to training."

Josh squinted and tilted his head to the side.

"You've never taken books from the house before. What gives? Besides, if you wanted to train I'm sure your mom would help you."

Was he testing Mom too? I didn't need to study. If I learned the background of a spell before trying to perform it, the wielding came naturally. Josh knew that as much as anyone.

"I just thought it might be good to keep learning. Teach myself while we wait to get back into classes. I don't want to get too far behind, and with Mom being part of the Council it doesn't seem right to ask her to help me. Gwen might see that as going behind her back or something."

A car similar to Mila's stopped at a stop sign a few streets away. Smart girl. She must have seen Josh and went for our escape. If I wasn't able to make it out with certainty, then I hoped he couldn't either.

"Are you still seeing her? You can be honest with me. Was the breakup all a cover-up to appease the Council?" he asked.

The last thing I wanted was to stand around and chat, but I couldn't walk away. If I did, then Josh would know something was up.

"We're not together right now. There was no cover-up. Just curious, why does the Council care whether we're dating or not? They've accused both of us of killing Katie. I'm not even supposed to be on the property."

Mila turned right, away from us. I was going to have to find another way back to her place. Josh stepped in front of me, blocking my view of the street. When he crossed his arms over his chest I couldn't help but wonder if he'd done it on purpose.

"So you don't think she killed Katie? You think the Coven is wrong?" he asked.

Josh was staying strong in his belief that someone killed Katie. I didn't blame him for trying to find the answers he needed. I was doing the same thing.

"What are you doing here anyway?" I deflected his question.

"Gwen asked me to get some stuff for her."

My brows furrowed.

"Since when do you run errands for Gwen? I thought

you had a theory that she was in on Katie's death."

Josh hadn't actually said anything about Gwen killing Katie, but it was worth throwing it out there to see his reaction, which supported the Coven leader—just as I suspected.

"Why would I think our leader had something to do with her death? That's ridiculous. As far as what I'm doing, it's Mom and Gwen. They need me to get some ingredients for a spell they're making."

Nope. I didn't buy his story, but I couldn't put my finger on the reason. Maybe it was the way his eyes shifted from left to right. Or how he kept wringing out his hands.

"What kind of spell? I mean, what do they need it for? I'd like to learn. Can I come back with you?" I shouldn't have asked since Mila waited around the corner for me. This was not going well. It was exactly what we didn't want to happen.

"Umm. I don't think...well, they...I mean..."

"Right. Well, I need to get home. Forget I asked and forget you and I ran into each other." I batted my eyelashes and clasped my hands in front of my chest. "Please."

Josh sighed. He didn't seem to notice my complete one-eighty. I headed down the street toward home.

"Wait, Azami," Josh called out.

"What?" I turned on the ball of my foot.

"Do you need a ride home? Your car isn't here."

The one detail Mila and I hadn't discussed. My brain

misfired trying to come up with a believable answer.

Note to self. I was no good at sleuthing.

"Umm, no. I'm good. Mom's meeting me at the park and we're going to dinner."

I crossed my fingers hoping he'd buy my reason and wouldn't offer to stay with me until she arrived. If he'd paid close enough attention he'd have asked how I got to the house.

"All right. Well, I'll see you tomorrow, I guess."

"Yep. Have a good one." I waved while walking toward the park.

Mila met me less than five minutes later just out of view from the house and I released a sigh of relief. I climbed in the car and threw my bag in the back.

"Did he follow?" I asked.

Not that it mattered. If he had, our cover was blown and the Coven would no doubt wait at my place until I got home. They'd been known to send someone over when we missed training to check on us—or so they said. Lately, I figured it had more to do with control than concern.

"No. He went inside right after you left. Did he say why he was there?"

"Yeah. He said something about getting stuff for his mom and Gwen. That doesn't make sense though."

"Why is that odd?" Mila asked.

I shrugged. "I dunno. Just something about the way he acted. Also, he was sorry for you and me. He asked if we were still together or if we'd broken up. Do you think the letter you got with the book came from the Coven? I mean, why else would he ask that?"

"Did he want anything else?" She made a left turn toward her house.

It didn't take long to get back to Mila's house. We didn't get out of the car right away and Mila didn't answer my question.

"Tell me something, Z. Why do you care about me, my family, and the Coven? What are we to you?"

"Because what the Coven is doing is wrong. I know we didn't kill Katie. Part of me wonders if Gwen or one of the Council is the wielder. The list of people who have knowledge of *Mort d'Evanoir* is so short, but we have no clues."

"That's it? Because you disagree with the Coven?"

What did she want me to say? Of course, it was because of them.

"Mila, I know we haven't been dating long, just a couple of weeks, but I feel like I've known you forever. Your family deserves better than the way you've been treated. I can't be part of a Coven that blindly judges people."

She nodded. "But why?"

"Nothing. I get nothing from it except knowing I helped a family who's been treated wrongly."

"Let's go inside to read. I need to repay your kindness." Mila smirked as she climbed out of the car.

I brought back five books. Even though it was late, we decided to hang out on the back porch. I wanted the fresh air and Mila wanted to keep some distance between the books and her family for some reason she didn't mention. The first book named *Mort d'Evanoir,* but there weren't any details until book four.

"So this says your family was banished for using dark magic to their advantage. It also says there was another person exiled from the Coven, but it doesn't give their name."

Mila pulled my chair closer to her. Her mom brought gumbo to us, which was the only break we'd had. We were running out of time.

"Mom and Dad have never mentioned anyone else. We could ask them."

"That's a good idea. They probably know what we're going to find. I think with their insight and whatever is in here, I can put the pieces together."

Tracy and Mr. Hutchings were in the living room watching TV.

"Mom, do you think you could tell Z what you know about *Mort d'Evanoir?*"

"Will it help?" Mr. Hutchings asked.

"Yes, sir. I think it will. The Coven doesn't have a lot of information about it. They don't mention it by name at all."

"No, I would imagine they don't. That's what happens when the Coven leader breaks her own rules and uses another family as a scapegoat."

Mila sat on the couch with her legs in a crisscross.

"You never told me that."

"No, honey, we haven't. There was no need. We don't have a reason or desire to care. Our family has nothing to prove. Since the day of the banishment we've known we did nothing wrong, but have paid the price for others. We didn't want you kids to have a biased opinion based on something your great-great uncle went through. Unlike the Coven and their training, which makes sure everyone is taught to stay as far away from us as they can." Tracy tsked. "I always hoped one of you would try to befriend our children, like your mom and Monica. It wasn't their fault the Witches of Evanoir outcast our family."

I scooted to the edge of the couch.

Mr. Hutchings rubbed his chin.

"Let's see. It was my great uncle, so that would be your great-great uncle's Coven Council."

I did the math. Four leaders ago. For the first time, the Coven's practice of memorizing leaders came in handy. Gwen, Maurine, April, Cassandra.

"You mean Cassandra Graves. She was from Salem. Are you saying she had something to do with *Mort d'Evanoir?*"

"No. I'm telling you she created the book. When the magic became too powerful for her to handle she had to cover up her mistake."

"I thought you said Great Grandma was the reason for our family banishment. She killed Gwen's great grandma."

"That's where the details are unclear. As the story goes, Cassandra fell in love with your great-great uncle. When he turned her down, repeatedly I might add, her love for him transformed into hate. After losing control of the magic in the book, she funneled all that rage into destroying our family. Some say her banishment decree included something like 'May your family endure the pain you have caused for all of eternity.' After a few years, the Hutchings were allowed back into the Coven. Then your great grandmother happened and we've been out ever since."

Incredible. Love gone wrong and magic abuse resulted in a book that could kill people when wielded by the right person.

"Why haven't you told me that part of the story?" Mila asked.

"It's like your mother said, we don't care about the Coven. There's no reason we're trying to hide from you. The Hutchings family tells the story as a legend. It's been years since all of this happened. We haven't been part of a coven for long enough that we no longer care. We have the freedom to practice how we want. When we want. No rules. No questions."

He spoke the words, but they lacked conviction. If they didn't care, then why stay in a town full of people that didn't like them? I didn't believe Mr. Hutchings was as indifferent as he said. On the flip side, I ached for the freedom they had. While my Coven family had once consumed my life, the last year being away from them had me wanting more. More opportunity. More friends. More...everything.

"Can you tell me how the wielder is chosen? Do they find the book and then use a spell?"

Mila's dad relaxed in his recliner. "There is a thought that the wielder knows the spell as soon as they see the book. Instinct passed down from one generation to the next."

That meant one of Mila's family could be the wielder. Or Mila herself.

"All right, ladies. It's late and we have to be up early for work. Good night." Tracy pulled her husband from his recliner and the couple left the living room.

Mr. Hutchings' additions to the story helped me begin to unravel the mystery of *Mort d'Evanoir*. I knew how Gwen's family connected to the book. I still didn't know why she cared so much about it. Like Mila's dad said, that was a long time ago.

It would be rude to argue or ask Mr. Hutchings if we could talk longer. They let me stay without question. Since I was still a stranger in their home the least I could do was respect their rules.

Mila shared a room with her two younger sisters while

her brother Dustin had a room to himself. I offered to sleep on the floor in the living room, but her parents said they trusted us to be on our best behavior. I would, of course. It was nice to have their trust. For tonight they let the younger girls have a campout in the playroom.

"It must be nice to practice magic without someone looming over your shoulder all the time. We aren't supposed to do any magic, no matter how simple, until we finish our training."

I crawled into the sleeping bag on the floor. It'd been a long day of information to process. We didn't talk about anything else.

Monday morning came way too soon. I wasn't ready for class. Mila's bed had been made by the time I woke up. The clang of pots and pans floated into the bedroom. I needed to get moving.

Mila and her family sat around the kitchen table, passing plates of bacon and pancakes around. Dustin shoved a piece of bacon in his mouth.

"Sit and eat," he said around the pork dangling out the corner of his mouth.

Shay, the second youngest, pat the chair between her and Mila. "Sit here."

I slid into the chair and took a pancake from the offered plate.

Breakfast flew by. Before I knew it, it was time to go. After throwing on clean clothes and finger-brushing my hair, I turned off the light in Mila's bedroom then headed for the front room. Just outside her room, two voices made me pause.

"I'll tell her. Promise." Mila's voice drifted down the hall outside the bathroom.

I slunk around the corner and waited for them to finish their conversation. Mom taught me not to eavesdrop, but they were talking about me.

"She can't stay tonight." Mrs. Hutchings' words held more than a hint of finality.

The eggs and bacon threatened to make a second showing. My foot banged against the baseboard. I'd wanted to do something so they knew I was coming, but hurting myself wasn't exactly the plan.

"Z, is that you?"

I limped to Mila who stood at the end of the hall.

"Yeah. I'm going to head out. I need to catch up on homework this morning."

"Oh. Okay. Well, I guess I'll see you later." She leaned forward for a kiss, but I shifted at the last second and hugged her.

Kissing Mila felt wrong. Not just because of where we were. Whatever the reason, Mrs. Hutchings didn't want me around anymore. I couldn't kiss her daughter knowing that. I hated the confusion in Mila's eyes. It would be okay.

"Thanks for letting me stay, Mrs. Hutchings. I appreciate it." I waved goodbye to Mila and her mom.

CHAPTER 17

I MANAGED TO MAKE IT to the end of the day without running into Mila or Josh. The last thing I wanted was to face questions from Mila about my exit that morning or Josh about why I was at the house this weekend. My luck ran out after my last class. Mila and Josh both stood at my car, one on each side, waiting with lips pursed, eyebrows furrowed, and pink cheeks. If I had to guess, they'd already gone a couple of rounds with each other. Guess it was my turn.

"Z," Mila started.

"Azami," Josh said at the same time.

I held my hands up to both of them. We were going to do this my way.

I turned to Mila. "You first."

To Josh, I said, "I'll come find you later." He hesitated so I added, "I promise. If I don't come find you then you have my permission to wait at my place until I get there.

Go relax in the main hall or something."

He relented and left Mila and me alone.

Mila sighed. "You heard my mom and me this morning, didn't you?"

"Yeah. Not everything; just the point where you promised to tell me something and she said I couldn't stay any longer."

"I was afraid of that."

I brushed my finger down her cheek. Our relationship, if that's what it was, wouldn't last past today. My chest constricted. I'd never experienced heartbreak, and if the pain was normal, then I didn't want to ever again.

"She has a point. I have *Mort d'Evanoir*. The Coven wants it and they're already after your family. Like I said yesterday, I wouldn't want me around either."

"It's more than that, Z. The...umm..."

"Spit it out, Mila. The suspense isn't helping either of us."

I put my things in the backseat of my car, hoping the distance would make talking easier for Mila.

"The Coven didn't accuse me of the *Mort d'Evanoir* murders," she said.

"I know."

She turned me around to face her.

"Azami, listen to me."

"I'm listening."

I put my bag on the floor. I didn't want to listen. The

distance was as much for me as for her. If she could get out what she needed to say, we could go on our way and start to figure out how to get through this. If I denied whatever she had to say long enough it wouldn't be true. At least, that's what I tried to convince myself to believe.

"The Coven didn't accuse me of Katie's murder."

It took several seconds to process her words.

"What? But Tierney said…"

"I know. Tierney lied—and so did I."

"You? Why?" My words came out lower than a whisper.

She… More denial. Mila's lies led to other truths I refused to face. I took *Mort d'Evanoir* to prove I couldn't be controlled. If my own girlfriend lied to keep something from me or to manipulate a situation, then taking the damn book was pointless. I shook my head and stepped further away.

"There was a second page to my letter. It went into detail about how the Coven never thought I had anything to do with Katie's death. There were awful things said about my inability to do magic, but none of that matters." Mila lowered her chin to her chest. "They only blame you, Z. They want to strip you of all magical abilities and said the only way to prevent it was to convince you to get rid of *Mort* before I broke up with you."

Why me? I'd been trying to help Mila's family prove their innocence, but there was nothing to prove. I was back to square one.

"But you refused to do what they asked. Or was that a lie too?"

"Dad says they shouldn't be able to take anything from us, but he doesn't trust Gwen. Her family has always been vindictive." Mila answered. "I want to figure out another way. We just need to..." She studied the floor with determination, but not before I watched a tear fall from the corner of her eye.

"He was checking on me. Those questions yesterday were to see if we'd split yet."

Mila nodded.

"And you didn't want to be seen by them so they thought it was real."

She nodded again.

"I see. That's what you two were arguing about before I showed up this morning."

The third nod. Putting together this corner of the puzzle was getting easy. Only, I didn't like the way the puzzle was forming. At all. My toes curled against the rubber of my flip-flops. As I replayed the conversation with Josh in my head a sour taste formed at the back of my tongue. Manipulated. Played. Naïve. Controlled. Name the word that described being used by someone for their own agenda and that was me at the moment.

"What do I do now?"

"Mom wants us to take a break. At least until all this is

figured out."

Did we have any other choice? Josh waited outside for me. If he thought we were still together, I'd signed my magic away. If we agreed to stop seeing each other, the Coven might back off of the Hutchings family. That was our original deal, after all. She'd help me with *Mort d'Evanoir* and I'd do everything I could to help clear her family's name.

Falling for Mila had never been part of anything. Sure, she'd been the one to ask me on my first date. When her family's future came into question, I didn't blame her for putting them first. Even if it did make me hurt like I'd been kicked in the chest by some Jujitsu master.

Gwen would always have a vendetta against her family, it seemed, but if the Council questioned their decision it would at least buy me time to find the real killer and the reason they focused on me.

"Do you think that will help?" I rubbed the pain where my soul should've been if the Coven hadn't metaphorically removed it piece by piece with each run-in I'd had with Tierney or Josh.

It took Mila a few minutes to answer. "Yeah. I wish I didn't, but I do."

"I don't like it either. Now I'm on my own to destroy the book and find the wielder." I wanted to hug her. Get one last kiss.

"We're going to figure this out. I promise." She

brushed her finger down the side of my cheek.

"Yeah. You should go before I do something like kiss you. That would really piss them off." A chuckle caught in my throat.

I wanted one last touch. One more moment of her arms around me. I didn't know how long it would take before we could try again, and that was the worst part. If I could have that, then I could focus on getting what I needed in order to have Mila as mine again.

Mila laughed. I got my kiss, even if it was a small one on the cheek. More than ever, I hated the Coven. Hated what they were doing.

My blood boiled with rage at the whole situation. Without thinking I began forming signs with my fingers. The words to the spell played through my thoughts. It was a new cast to me, one I'd never even seen in a book. Magic to curse a person of my choice. The metallic taste began at the back of my throat and rose until it coated my tongue.

It took effort, but I forced my fingers to form a fist. If they weren't making the signs, the spell wouldn't complete. Losing Mila had done this to me. Made me want to cause the same pain I experienced.

"Mila." My voice hitched. Her name a whisper on the wind.

She came back without hesitation. It'd been easy for her to say we should separate, which hurt worse than breaking things off for now.

"Z, what's wrong? Your eyes are bloodshot."

"Help," I choked out then held my fists in the air.

One by one she opened uncurled my fingers, then smoothed her palm over mine.

"Tell me what just happened."

I shook my head and bit my lip. "It's embarrassing."

Mila took my face between her hands. She pressed her lips to mine once more. The fury that had overwhelmed me moments ago lessened, but the truth kept it from fading completely. I needed her more than anything. She would keep the darkness of *Mort d'Evanoir* away. The Coven made sure I didn't get her. To hell with them. If having the book didn't help me find a way to break the strings, I'd figure another way.

"Z, let me help you one more time."

Sadness rolled through my veins. My knees hitched and unshed tears burned my eyes. I bit my lip in an attempt to keep my emotions in check. She really was leaving. But I couldn't tell Mila what had just happened. If I did, she'd change her mind; decide to stick around, and tell the Coven to jump off a cliff.

Her family would lose. We'd lose each other. No matter what, I refused to allow that outcome.

"Could you do me a favor?" I asked instead.

"Anything" she replied.

"Promise when this is through we'll find each other again." Her assurance would give me the fuel to keep going.

"I promise," she whispered as she turned her back and left me once more.

When she walked away the second time I didn't stop her. I had one more person to talk to before I could go home. He sat inside, waiting.

"Josh." I didn't sit down when I joined him at the table. The conversation was meant to be a short one.

"Azami, I'm sorry."

The lump in my throat made it difficult to talk. I squeezed my eyes closed to push back the tears that threatened.

"For what?"

"Everything. Mila. All of it. I know how you're feeling."

Wow. I couldn't believe he apologized, even knowing the only reason he wanted to talk was to make sure I broke up with her. Rage settled in deep within my bones once more. The tears dried and heat filled my body. I rolled back my shoulders and held my head high.

"Incredible. You're waiting to see if I broke up with my girlfriend, then you apologize. We both know you don't care, so cut the crap. Run back to Gwen and tell her Mila broke things off. That should make her happy."

Josh shrugged. At least he'd dropped the games.

"Good. I'm supposed to tell you—"

"No." I interrupted him. "You're not going to *tell* me anything else. I'm not bringing the book to Gwen. Apparently, I'm to destroy it. She can threaten me, she can banish me from the Coven, but she will not intimidate me. Nor will her lackey, meaning you, bully me into something I don't want to do. You're a weak little boy. I felt sorry for you after Katie. Guess I should have known better."

Once I started, the words exploded from within a dark place. I wanted to hurt him. Not with words or emotionally. A burning desire to physically hurt him grew until I could no longer resist. My fingers twisted into different shapes, another spell pushed at the back of my thoughts, begging to be spoken. Once more, I didn't recognize it, but I knew it was a bad one.

"Az, you have to know this is for your own good. Gwen, the Coven, we're protecting you. *Mort d'Evanoir* has changed you. Look at yourself. I can see how angry you are. This is why the Hutchings were kicked out. They changed too."

"Answer one question for me." I had every intention of proving him wrong of all accusations.

A book didn't change me. The Coven did. My own mother had a hand in my change since she was as restrictive as everyone else. I was a witch, damn it, and I was going to become the practitioner I was meant to be.

"Sure." His lack of worry over my question made me even more upset.

"Why is Gwen so concerned with Mila and I breaking up? I mean, what's so big that she had to threaten my girlfriend?"

Everything had a connection except her insistence about us. That was the one piece I had yet to put together.

"Mila is a Hutchings. It's against the law to date her."

I digested his response. More than once, I'd considered the same reason. If Coven laws were the reason it made sense to harass me, not her.

"If that were true, then Gwen would threaten me for breaking it, not Mila. There's another answer. What is it?"

"Maybe she just doesn't like Mila. I mean, the girl isn't exactly a shining star. Have you seen the way she dresses? Not to mention she's talked you into performing dark magic, which is another rule broken. I'm still pretty sure she killed Katie."

Fire lit beneath my skin. Josh took another step toward me. I placed my hands on his chest, magic ignited beneath them, lighting them up until they glowed white.

"She did not encourage me or talk me into performing any magic. I've done everything without coercion. As far as the way she dresses, way to stoop to a new, petty low."

I crooked my fingers into his pecs and shoved. He flew across the room. I watched with a certain satisfaction as he landed with a grunt then fell onto his back. Rage continued to cloud my vision. I should have gone to him. Called for help. But I didn't.

"Stay away from me and stay away from Mila. You know as well as I do that she didn't kill Katie. I don't know what Gwen's done to you, but you're acting like a totally different person."

He was right. The book had changed me, but not by some dark magic spell. Since I'd found *Mort d'Evanoir* I'd seen people were not who they said they were.

***

By the time I got home, my anger with Josh and Gwen faded, only to be replaced once more by heartbreak.

Pippa met me at the door. Her eyes rose in question, but I shook my head. Right then was not the time to break the news she lived with a witch.

"Going out with Mac. You want to come?" she asked.

"No thank you. Have fun," I said.

She left with a smile on her face. At least one of us would have a good night. Once the rush of tears started, I couldn't stop them. Hard, wracking sobs stole my breath. I cried until my eyes ran dry.

CHAPTER 18

TUESDAY GREETED ME WITH A migraine, puffy eyes, and dehydration. So I skipped my morning classes. By the afternoon, I'd become so engrossed in recalling everything I knew about Katie and *Mort d'Evanoir*, that I skipped those classes too. I sat at my desk with a list of questions.

Figure out who killed Katie. Why her?

Figure out why Gwen wants Mort d'Evanoir so badly. Does she know how to use it?

Why me? What am I protecting?

How does Mort d'Evanoir work?

If I could solve the question of how *Mort d'Evanoir* killed people, or what the magic wielder had to do for a name to end up in the book, the other questions would be easier to solve.

Thanks to Dustin killing my bird, I couldn't talk to Bennett, not that he'd been much help. The Hutchings family wasn't an option—Mila's mom made that clear. If I had no other option, Mila would've come to help, but I didn't want to put her in that position.

I tried to recall Bennett's cryptic comments. He'd said he was tied to *Mort d'Evanoir* and it would be destroyed if he died. If that were true, then his death should have done something to the book. Except I had no way of knowing if that were true. Without having an idea of who cast the spells, it wasn't like I could ask if they'd had problems killing anyone recently. But the book hadn't disappeared. I could still read the names even though there weren't any new ones, which could mean the wielder hadn't killed anyone lately. So I was pretty sure that bit of information had been a lie.

A memory smacked me in the forehead. There was a partial name written. The letters started but never finished. I hadn't opened the book since Mila's house. I grabbed *Mort d'Evanoir* and opened it to the list of recent names.

The half-written name was still there and a new one below it. Martha Sanderson. She died from internal bleeding due to poisoning.

Martha Sanderson was a retired librarian. I remembered going with Mom to the library for story time with Ms. Sanderson. She always sat in an old rocking chair at the top of a purple and blue circle carpet. We gathered in front of her and listened to her read books. I couldn't name the stories she told, but I recalled how she loved to use different voices for the characters. My favorites were Dr. Seuss stories. He was still my favorite author.

"Why did you take Ms. Sanderson?" I asked the book not expecting a response.

It was a book, not a person. The scratch of pencil on paper sounded next to me. A sentence formed on the page in my notebook where I'd written my list of questions.

It was her time to go.

I leaped off the bed.

The wielder decides the victim. I give them the experience of the person's death of my choosing. The wielder's pain and resulting death of their chosen person gives me power in return.

Holy crap buckets. *Mort d'Evanoir* talked to me. I tried another question.

"Why are you telling me this now?"

Bennett is gone. You must know about the book to properly protect it. I will answer what questions you may have. Do not expect every question to be answered in the way you wish.

I shook my head. Only a crazy person would protect an item that gained power by inflicting pain and death.

"I don't want to protect you. You shouldn't exist."

There is only one way to break our connection.

"We don't have a connection. Or bond. Or anything close."

You know that is not true. If it were, I would not be able to speak as we are now. You would not see the names as they are written. You would have left me at the house.

Not for the first time, I regretted ever walking out of the farmhouse with the book in hand. Now there was another price to pay. Would I have anything left to give when this was over?

"Who is the wielder?"

I cannot tell you the name. When you decide to face the truth you know, you will have the answer you seek.

"How did Bennett become your protector? Was he human once?"

Yes. Bennett did not choose. He was an offering to break the bond with another. I accepted.

Oh.

"But he was a crow."

Ahh, yes. Punishment for when he tried to kill himself.

"Can you be destroyed?"

Yes, there is a way and a price. If I am destroyed, the Witches of Evanoir will cease to exist. Your protection of me results in my protection of you. As my protector, you cannot die unless I deem it so.

Whoa. All witches. How was that even possible? What kind of magic did Cassandra weave into this book? I wasn't protecting the book, but the Coven. The last thing I wanted was the responsibility of saving the lives of every witch in Evanoir.

Gwen and the Council threatened to take my magic ability. If they did that, then I would be unable to protect them. They'd known I'd been chosen, but how many of the Council knew I was protecting them as well as the book? If I had to guess, only one and she was determined to gain possession of *Mort d'Evanoir*.

"All witches? But what if a witch moved to Evanoir?"

My creator wanted to ensure the punishment for destroying me was enough of a deterrent. Should I be destroyed, the spell connecting us will be broken and a ward placed around the town. No witch shall pass through the ward. They would not understand, of course, but the result would remain the same.

"The woman in my vision at school. She tried to burn you. What was her betrayal?"

That was her betrayal. She was a wielder and did not like the death following her request, so she attempted to destroy me. Fire will not work. I was born in the flame; I cannot die by the same fate.

I stared at the words on the paper. It took reading everything four times to believe I was carrying on a conversation with a book. Even then, I wondered if I would remember anything the next day. Was it all a dream? Had I fallen asleep at my desk and this was my imagination?

On a whim, I pinched my arm until the skin broke and blood dripped onto the desk. Definitely not a dream. I had two choices: 1. Keep asking questions and hope for answers to help me figure things out. 2. Ditch the book alongside the road and never think about it again.

"Why did you deem Bennett's death as necessary? Did he do something that I need to know about, so I don't repeat it?"

His time was done. You are the new protector. Bennett had aspirations beyond his means. He could not become the wielder. He did not have the power needed to control me.

The metallic taste of dark magic returned. I ran out of my room, afraid I'd experience the next death just like I had last time. I slammed the door shut behind me. My heart raced as I tried to get away.

I soon found myself behind the wheel of my car headed toward home.

My feet led me to the old farmhouse. Mrs. Clarke told me not to return, but it didn't seem to matter. Since leaving with *Mort d'Evanoir* the first time, the puppet strings had tethered me to the house. My hand hovered over the doorknob. I couldn't go in unless I'd been invited. My stomach revolted. I rushed to the edge of the porch, leaned over, and puked up what little I had inside. Thankfully, lunch was hours before and there wasn't a whole lot left to force its way out.

Mrs. Clarke found me crumpled in a ball on her front porch. I didn't know how long I'd been there, but the sun had set and locusts sang their nighttime songs. A crow cawed in the distance. It wasn't as comforting as it had been before. Bennett. A sacrifice for a book of death. No, the sound made me shudder. Family guide or not, crows would never give me peace the way they had before.

"Azami." She helped me stand, then with an arm draped over my shoulder, led me inside. "Come on. I can help you."

The warm cup of tea she placed in my hands helped stop the shivering.

"Thank you," I murmured.

"What brings you here?"

I used the tea as my excuse not to answer right away. I couldn't exactly tell her *Mort d'Evanoir* told me the truth of being a protector. No doubt she knew about the Coven's orders for Mila.

"It's been a rough day, so I decided to go for a drive and ended up here."

"I know about you and Mila."

That wasn't a surprise. She was part of the Coven. Not to mention, Tierney would have found out from Josh. Despite expecting her to say something, the exchange left me wanting to scream. My Coven had no secrets among us—and not in a way I was at all comfortable with.

"As I anticipated," I murmured around the rim of my teacup.

"She misses you. Tierney, I mean."

I stared at Mrs. Clarke.

"I wish that was true. If she missed me, then she wouldn't have let things end the way they did last week."

Mrs. Clarke lowered her gaze to the sofa table in front of us. I crossed one leg over the other, then switched it back. The warm tea wasn't soothing. Each forced swallow left my throat dry and itchy. I began to wonder if it had been messed with, or if it was an instinctual warning to get the hell out of the house.

"My dear, there are things you do not understand."

I stood, ready to return home. When I took *Mort d'Evanoir* from the house, I hadn't understood anything. Right then, I accepted that taking the book was more than I'd ever bargained for.

"Thank you for the tea. I should go home before it gets too late."

"Can you give me five minutes?" she asked.

"Sure."

I was certain I wouldn't have been able to leave if she didn't want me to. The door clicked shut behind Mrs. Clarke. The time alone gave me a chance to check out the redecorated room.

The last two times I'd visited I didn't explore. Mrs. Clarke brought me to a sitting room at the front of the house. A clean settee bench sat in the middle of the room. It was big enough for three or four people. To the left of the bench was a cushioned armchair with matching footstool. The room didn't have any lights. Instead, two full-length windows provided enough moonlight to see. I settled back onto the settee. A few more minutes passed before I realized the tell-tell sign of dark magic wasn't around.

I glanced at the clock on the wall. Seven o'clock. It'd been stupid to run out of the house without my phone, but that was the last thing on my mind. Emergencies would have to wait.

One question weighed heavier than everything else fighting for attention in my head. I had to make an offering to *Mort* to break the bond. I had to make someone agree to protect a book with magical abilities to kill. Bennett had tricked me into taking the book because he wanted to become the wielder. The thought of sacrifices and forced bonds made me sick to my stomach again.

What if there was a way to protect the book and keep another from wielding the magic? I had to figure out who the spell caster was first.

Mort d'Evanoir said I already knew. That didn't make sense though. The only possibilities I had were Tierney, Josh, Gwen, or the Hutchings. I didn't think it would be anyone else within the Coven since they wouldn't want to cross Gwen.

Josh was a long shot. I had no reason to suspect him other than something was up and I didn't know what. He'd only been added to the list since the day before, maybe a little because I was pissed at him.

"Hey." Tierney came into the room.

"Hey."

We stared at each other in silence. What was I supposed to say?

"So, Mom said I should come talk to you. I heard about Mila. I'm sorry."

I rolled my eyes and vowed to myself never to apologize to someone following a death. Not that Mila had died, but we broke up, and all the "I'm sorries" grated on my nerves.

"You aren't sorry. It's what you wanted. I mean, you said Mila was the problem. Now she's out of the picture. I'd expect that makes you happy."

Tierney dropped down next to me. She started to place her hand on my thigh, but I scooted away.

"I'm sorry, Azami. I didn't actually want you to break up. She seemed to make you happy. At least for the day that I saw you two together."

"That's not what you said."

She cleared her throat. "I'm jealous. There, I said it. Does that make you happy?"

I cocked an eyebrow and stood to put more distance between us. The conversation did not sit right, making me nauseous. It was either that or the damn tea. Tierney's attention to our breakup and no mention of her life being in peril, or me saving it, led me to believe she was clueless about the letter I received.

"No. Not really."

"That's why Mom sent me in here. She wants us to mend our friendship and figures if I tell you the truth it will help. Do you want to know how I found *Mort d'Evanoir* so I could return it to you?"

Once more, I realized Tierney wasn't as connected as she thought. No one told her the book she turned over to me wasn't *Mort*. Regardless, at some point, she'd had the book in her possession, which meant answers. These were the reasons I needed to be in the house at that moment. It wasn't to repair our relationship or find a familiar tie with my Coven sister.

No. I'd found my way here to learn more about the truth of Evanoir coven and its connection to *Mort d'Evanoir*. So I took advantage of the opportunity.

"Actually, yes."

Tierney stood and began to pace.

"I stole it. Well, not exactly."

I leaned against the wall near the door and crossed my arms over my chest.

"You're all over the place. I can't keep up. Considering I didn't willingly give it to you, then you stole it." I nodded for her to continue.

"Well, yes. I used my key to get into your place."

The key I didn't give her. "You used a key that you copied without permission, broke into my house, and took a book that wasn't yours."

"Yeah. That sums it up." Tierney stopped pacing and

lowered her chin to her chest. She picked at the edge of her nails.

For a moment, as short as it was, I felt sorry for her. I wanted to ask how she lost it but refrained. A small part of me still hoped Tierney was innocent. The flame of that hope weakened with her confession of how she got into my place.

"Did you read the book? Or learn anything about it?" I asked. If nothing else, maybe I could learn more from her.

Our friendship, however, was beyond repair.

"No. Gwen says only the protector and wielder can read the book, but even the wielder's access is limited."

"The wielder decides the type of death. If they have limited access to the information inside how would they know who dies? Or if anyone dies?" I asked a question I knew the answer to. I was wrong of course, the wielder chose the person, not the way.

"*Mort d'Evanoir* communicates through magic. The spellcaster can talk to *Mort d'Evanoir*, make requests, or stop a death in the process."

For what it was worth, the one who made *Mort d'Evanoir* had thought of everything.

"So I can read who dies, but the wielder cannot." I didn't agree with her explanation.

Since I still didn't know who the wielder was, I couldn't call her out in a lie. For someone to go to such extremes in spelling a book, they wouldn't leave anything to assumption. The one who cast the curse would need to confirm the deed had been done. Otherwise, too many questions would be left unanswered.

"Gwen thinks Mila is the caster. That's why she's worked so hard to split you up. Since Gwen's family and Mila's family are archenemies, it makes sense that she would want *Mort d'Evanoir* in her possession."

Tierney may have been right about Gwen's assumption. I bounced on my toes. The reveal meant Gwen wasn't the spell caster and neither was Tierney. Her mention of Gwen's desire to have the book prompted a memory from the night I became its protector. Bennett said Gwen wanted to bring death, so if she wasn't the wielder then she wanted to be and a person could orchestrate unbelievable events when they wanted something bad enough. Like killing Coven members and framing others.

"When did you talk to Gwen about everything?" I asked.

"I was there when Katie died. I've stayed in touch with our Coven leader the whole time. As an apprentice who associated with Katie daily, it's my duty to make sure I do whatever I can to find the one who murdered her."

She meant to say me. At least that's what Gwen told Mila. I still wasn't sure how much Tierney knew. Even though I took her off my list of possible wielders, her mom wasn't. The letter that brought me back to the farmhouse had to have come from Addison. She knew why I'd shown up.

"So what are you doing to find the killer?" I asked.

We stood toe to toe. Tierney placed the palm of her hand against my cheek. Her touch was too intimate, something I'd expect from Mila, not her. I stepped back into the wall. There was nowhere to go.

"You're where you need to be, Azami. I messed up before, I see that now. Let me help you." Tierney's eyes spoke more truth than her words.

She wasn't done with her games. But I was done playing them.

"I'm going home."

Tierney shook her head. "Not until Mom releases you."

Nope. I recited a spell I'd found in Mom's journal. Tierney gasped as she was tossed across the room. She landed on the floor with a thud. I turned the knob of the door, thankful when it opened. The spell had worked. One day I'd thank Mom.

CHAPTER 19

WEDNESDAY WAS THE SECOND DAY I skipped classes. If I didn't solve the Katie murder soon, I'd be in trouble with my professors. But concentrating during their hour-long lectures in dark lecture halls was out of the question until I figured this out and cleared my name. I sat at the kitchen counter studying my list while my roommate made breakfast. My plan to get to work right after I ate would be better if I prepared. I made new notes under each item.

Figure out who killed Katie. Why her?

Tierney gave me a lot of answers, but not that one. Katie's death somehow tied to *Mort d'Evanoir* and the only way I'd figure out why was to learn who.

~~*Figure out why Gwen wants Mort. Does she know how to use it?*~~

After recalling what Bennett told me the first night, I no longer wondered why she wanted Mort. It didn't matter if she knew how to use the book. She wasn't the wielder, and would never become one if I could prevent it. With the number of details Tierney shared about *Mort d'Evanoir* it was a safe bet Gwen knew exactly what to do with the book.

Why me?

The answer for that was solely my benefit. I'd accepted the role of protector. Maybe I'd been chosen, but not like those books where it was the person's destiny. There was a way out, but I wasn't sure I could take it. Besides, the amount of guilt I'd be plagued with if a new protector failed and we all died was enormous. It was almost easier to keep the book, even if I didn't want it. With Mom's connection to Monica and me to Mila, I had a pretty good idea fate intended our families to stay intertwined throughout time. *Mort d' Evanoir* said I chose the book, but I wasn't certain about that.

~~*How does Mort work?*~~

Mr. Hutchings gave me the starting point I needed. The book and others helped me fill in the blanks. I'd learned enough for the moment. Now I could talk to the book whenever I had more questions.

To move forward, I needed to mark more items off my list. After breakfast, I made a call.

"Mom, we need to talk. I need to know why Gwen wants Mort."

"To destroy it. I've told you that." Her exasperated reply put me on edge.

Well, yeah, but that wasn't true. Gwen had everyone convinced it seemed. I couldn't be the only one who distrusted her. What I really needed to know what her ulterior motives. If Gwen wasn't the wielder, or couldn't be, then she had other plans in order to accomplish her goal of destroying someone.

"I don't think that's it. I think she wants to take control of it."

"Sweetie, sometimes we try so hard to see things a certain way. Even if it's wrong, we believe it's right."

Pots and pans clanged in the background, which reminded me I hadn't left the kitchen table. I gathered my things and moved to my room. Our walls were thin, but if Pippa turned on the TV then hopefully she wouldn't hear our conversation.

"What if I'm not wrong? Do you think you can set up a meeting with the three of us?"

"Sure. I'll call Gwen and find out if she has some time today."

Perfect. We said our goodbyes and I told Mom to text me when she had everything ready.

Next up...I needed to talk to *Mort*.

"How does someone take control of you?"

I stared at my open notebook, waiting for an answer.

The only way one can receive the power to use Mort d'Evanoir *is if the previous wielder is dead.*

"How is the protector chosen?"

They are those with extreme magical abilities. The magic comes to them without trying. Remember the protector is not chosen, however. They choose to accept the book when offered.

Great. I didn't have some grand excuse for being chosen. I'd done this to myself. But I didn't know of any special skills. Everyone in training was as good as me. Lately, I'd been able to perform some new magic, like the spell I used against Josh and the one at Tierney's house. A few of the Council thought having visions was magic as well. They called it freeform magic because there weren't any spells; it just happened to those who opened their mind. Maybe my visions of the woman and the deaths were enhanced magical abilities.

"Can I stop the wielder from completing spells to kill someone?"

No.

"How come there are people left in Evanoir? If someone always has the power to use you, wouldn't we all be dead?"

There hasn't been a wielder for fifty years. If I have no wielder, then I do not have power.

That didn't make sense. My dad's name was in the book. He died sixteen years ago, not fifty.

"Why are there names less than fifty years old if there hasn't been a wielder?"

Mort d'Evanoir *was created in part by the souls of all*

those in Evanoir. For this reason, the book records all deaths because each one ensures the continued life of the book. It provides the protector with a history. When no wielder gives power to the book, deaths still occur, but they are in a natural order with no intentional connection to the person.

So the book wasn't all bad, except when a person fed it power through the need to kill. I had to find the wielder and stop them before Gwen found them and killed another person. My stomach sank at the possibility of Mila, or anyone in her family, being the wielder. I didn't want to imagine my leader killing my girlfriend. Just the idea brought tears to my eyes. My chest burned with fear. Nothing else mattered beyond finding the wielder. A plan began to form and I needed to know how easy it was for one to take control if I was going to put it into place.

"If I gave *Mort d'Evanoir* to someone else, would they know if they could wield magic while the current wielder still lived?"

I hoped the book understood my question. I wasn't even sure I did.

One who can wield the magic needed senses the pull when they are near the book. The power calls to them.

"How do they make *Mort d'Evanoir* theirs to control?"

It's a choice, like that of the protector. The difference between wielder and protector is the bond. A wielder must offer a blood sacrifice to prove the desire for power and willingness to kill.

A wielder wasn't a nice person. Proof of a desire to kill. That sounded like a check-off list for a psychopathic serial killer.

I had the answers I needed to put my plan into action.

Mom: Head on over. Gwen has some time now.

Mom's text came at the perfect time. I quickly closed my notebook and safely tucked *Mort d'Evanoir* into my backpack.

As soon as I got to Mom's she began lecturing on what I could and couldn't do when we met with Gwen.

"Azami, you will not speak to Gwen about the Mort Murders unless she asks. Is that understood?"

I nodded. It wasn't like her to set ground rules. Her voice didn't even sound like her. It was comparable to talking to an AI. At times, talking to Tierney had been similar the night before. In the sitting room, she gave all the right answers, or no answer at all. She acted like she cared. That was the problem. Tierney deserved a Tony Award for her performance.

Gwen had a hand in the weird behavior. I had no proof, but somehow she'd manipulated magic to ensure the Coven did exactly as she directed. They would follow her orders, making it easier to select a sacrifice for the blood bond.

***

Gwen's home was within walking distance from the Coven

house. Her family built it over one hundred years ago. Mom said even though Gwen had three sisters and two brothers, she got the house because she was a leader and the oldest.

The Coven leader met us at the front door. I stood behind and to the left of Mom so I could watch Gwen's body language. Her smile started small and grew when Mom said I wanted to talk to her about *Mort d'Evanoir*. I could've gone to her house by myself, but the plan worked better if Mom was there to speak for the Council.

"Of course." Gwen ushered us inside.

"Thank you." Mom smiled.

The inside of the house made me motion sick. Flowers and pinks and pastels covered every inch of the walls and furniture. Brass fixtures broke up the floral décor but didn't help.

"You've redecorated recently," Mom said when we walked into the dining room.

Gwen had set the table with three place settings. In the middle was a silver tray complete with a sugar bowl, creamer pot, tea bags, and a teapot of hot water. I hated tea, but the elders of the Coven drank it when they got together. To me, it was preppy and unnecessary. This wasn't England and Gwen wasn't the Queen. Even though she liked to think of herself as one.

Mom sat to the right of the head of the table. I almost took the head seat just to see what they'd say. Instead, I sat in the chair on the left. For my plan to work I needed to play nice. The three of us prepared our cups of tea. I had to wait for Gwen to start the conversation. If I wasn't yielding to her, she'd doubt my sincerity in what I had to offer. Or I assumed she would. We were in her house after all. Besides, Mom would not tolerate disrespect even if I was twenty-one years old and an adult.

"So, your mom said you wanted to talk," Gwen finally said.

I nodded. "Yes, ma'am."

"What is it you'd like to discuss?" Her pinky stuck out when she raised her cup to her lips.

I wanted to pour the whole kettle of hot water into her lap. This was a joke. Gwen sat in front of us sipping Earl Gray in a navy blue, custom-made pantsuit. Her hair had been colored and her makeup was flawless. The outside, a show of good and kind. Inside, I was pretty sure Gwen was a killer. She wanted to bond with *Mort d'Evanoir*, use its power, and revel in the pain of her victims. I had to act a part to show everyone the truth about our precious Coven leader.

I reached into my backpack and pulled out the book, still wrapped in my bandana.

"*Mort d'Evanoir*." I pushed the book toward Gwen.

Mom choked on her tea. Gwen clapped her hands together. When she realized her mistake she gently placed her hands in her lap and wiped her face of emotion.

"I see. Is there something specific I can tell you about the book my ancestors spent more than a century protecting?"

Half-truths were worse than lies in my opinion. Bennett had protected the book. He'd been offered as a sacrifice. Her family brought the horrendous book to life. Filled it with the darkest magic they could, then blamed Mila's family.

"Sort of. Did you have someone named Bennett in your family?"

Gwen tapped her chin.

"Yes, I believe we did. He was my mother Lorna's cousin."

I bit the inside of my cheek so hard a drop of blood landed on my tongue. The Graves family had sacrificed one of their own to the book. What kind of family did that? Then again, Cassandra brought a book of death to life. The sacrifice of a family member wasn't all that unimaginable when I took the time to consider the source.

"There was a crow in the house where I found *Mort d'Evanoir*. He said his name was Bennett."

Mom's eyes went wide. She made the connection, which I needed if I was going to convince her Gwen wasn't a good person.

"That is an interesting coincidence. Not to rush you, but I don't understand what this has to do with the book."

I shrugged. "I don't know. Nothing, I suppose."

"Have you come to return *Mort d'Evanoir* to my family, where it belongs?"

One day I'd have to ask Gwen how she played with words the way she did. The emphasis on "where it belongs" was not missed. I wondered if Mom caught on that Gwen referenced her family and not the Coven.

"I am, but what do you plan to do with it?"

Gwen gifted us the smile where she showed too many teeth and her lips stretched so thin the skin at the corners of her mouth were cracked.

"Destroy it, of course. A book like that, with its dark magic, is too dangerous. We must terminate it to prevent it from ending up in the wrong hands."

Terminate. An interesting choice of words given the book talked to me. So far Gwen was falling for my plan. I just needed a few more answers.

"I read *Mort d'Evanoir* can't be destroyed. That's what our history books said." I propped my chin on my fist, curious what she'd say next.

Mort d'Evanoir told me it could be destroyed, but no one knew how and of course the consequences. At least I was pretty sure they didn't.

"When did you read that?" she asked.

"A couple of weeks ago I borrowed some books from the library. That's what they said."

"Ahh. Well, the information is not quite accurate. There's a way to destroy it."

She told the truth. It'd be a lie if I said I wasn't surprised.

"Can you tell me how? I would like to help if I can, since I found the book. It only seems right that I help get rid of it."

"Oh. That's a great idea, Azami," Mom chimed in. "You could see the Council in action. The apprentices don't usually get that kind of experience."

Gwen's cup rattled when she placed it on the saucer. I sat a little straighter in my chair. I couldn't wait to see how she wiggled her way out of the predicament I put her in.

"I don't think that's a good idea. We must use dark magic to break the bond between the wielder and the book. As a rule, we cannot perform such magic, but I believe this is a reasonable exception."

Not quite true. If one classified murder as executing dark magic spells, the bond could be broken. But that wasn't destroying the book. The problem—I didn't know if Gwen played a game or didn't have the knowledge of how to destroy the actual book.

Mom set down her teacup and spoke to Gwen. "If dark magic is to be used, the Council will vote. You need a unanimous decision. We must all be present while you perform the magic as well. These are your rules. Why would you ignore them?"

Gwen whipped her head around to me. I smiled.

"I...well...this is a delicate situation, Isabelle. Perhaps

you would understand if I made a few executive decisions as Coven leader.”

“No, Gwen, I don’t believe I would. The Evanoir Coven takes the use of dark magic very seriously. If you choose to override our laws under the reasoning of being Coven leader, then I would have to recommend a vote to elect a new leader.”

Under the table, I fist-bumped Mom. She’d put Gwen in a position she couldn’t get out of unless she wanted to lose her title of leader.

Would she choose magic or family? Her family founded the Evanoir Coven, but ten years ago, a revision in the bylaws removed the clause that the leader must be of the Graves bloodline. Gwen initiated the change. Mom said at the time Gwen hadn’t planned on having kids. The Council agreed there should be a more democratic selection process for leadership. After all, the leader led training for apprentices and was often the face of the Coven within our community.

Gwen had done some good things to bring us in line with more modern beliefs. In fact, before *Mort d’Evanoir*, I wouldn’t have doubted her either. Ever since the book came around, I’d uncovered a far more sinister side of our leader.

“Then we shall take this to the Council. It would be best if you left the book here until a decision is reached.”

Gwen reached for Mort, but Mom placed her hand on

top of Gwen's arm to stop her.

"No. We'll take this home with us. Azami will retain possession of it until the Council meeting. She'll also attend the meeting and witness the vote."

Mom's voice turned stern. She may not have agreed with me having the book in the first place, but she was particular about rules and setting an example. The last thing she'd allow was for Gwen to break them.

"I could help find the wielder while we wait for the meeting," I volunteered.

Since no one had died since the librarian, at least that we knew of, I wasn't sure she'd share even if she did know the wielder.

"What of the accusations toward Mila and the Hutchings family?" Mom asked.

Gwen tsked. I'd managed to forget about their threats to her family.

"There are some questions of whether or not the Hutchings are responsible for the death of Apprentice Katie. While I still believe it true, the Council believes we should consider all possibilities, including Azami."

I tried not to let my disappointment and shock show. The hope I held disappeared at the mention of my name. She still suspected me and Mom hadn't said a word. It seemed finding the wielder was even more important. Not only did I need to prove them wrong about Mila and her family, but myself as well.

Mom and I left shortly after.

"Did you intend to give *Mort d'Evanoir* to Gwen?" Mom asked once we were away from the coven leader's home.

I could lie and tell her yes, or I could tell the truth. A lie took more work to make it believable.

"No."

"So that was a setup. What were you trying to do?"

I stared out the window and fidgeted with the seatbelt. If I told her everything she could prevent me from doing anything else. I took a deep breath.

"Get her to admit to wanting *Mort d'Evanoir*, but not to destroy it. Also, I was hoping she knew who the wielder was. That's the key to proving my innocence, something you don't seem to believe."

Mom tapped her steering wheel.

"Why didn't you tell me before we got to Gwen's? I could have helped."

"Can I ask you a question?" I didn't look at Mom. She still didn't acknowledge my innocence. The one person I needed to believe I wasn't a killer, and she refused.

"Of course." She took my hand in hers as we drove home.

"Last night, did you talk to anyone from the Coven?"

I counted to twenty before she answered. There was more to Mom's disregard for my innocence than I first realized. Knowing Addison spelled the room the night before to lock me in made a new theory take shape.

"Addison called to tell me you were at their house. We talked about other Coven stuff, that's it."

Mrs. Clarke had called Mom, which was my fear. I needed more information before I revealed my suspicions to Mom.

"Why isn't Mrs. Clarke on the Council?" I turned to watch her reaction.

One thing I'd learned recently was how loud body language spoke. Words meant nothing in comparison to a person's physical voice.

"The Clarke family is one of the newer families in the Evanoir Coven. To be a Council member you must be at least second generation. Addison is not eligible, but Tierney will be when Gwen's time as leader comes to an end."

Mom didn't falter. She kept her eyes on the road but glanced my way a couple of times. Nothing out of the ordinary.

"I see."

The Clarke family fit right in, or so I thought. If Tierney was eligible to be on the Council, it would make sense for Addison to do everything she could to place her daughter in a position to obtain leadership.

"Do they have more experience in magic than we do? Does Mrs. Clarke practice different magic than us?"

Mom surprised me when she pulled into the Chinese

food place I loved. Today was turning out to be a great day. Much better than the last few weeks.

"I can't say for sure. I wasn't part of the review committee when they requested to become members. Amanda mentioned in the past she thought they might. Why do you ask?"

"You have to promise not to get mad at me without considering what I have to say a possibility."

Mom nodded and we followed the hostess to a table near the back of the restaurant. I crossed my fingers and my toes that she wasn't lying.

"I think Mrs. Clarke is doing some kind of spell that makes everyone agree with Gwen no matter what."

"You mean brainwashing or hypnotizing us."

"Basically. This morning you weren't acting like yourself, almost like someone or something was controlling you. You told me not to bring up the book when we met with Gwen unless she did. You said she intended to destroy it."

She sat silent. My muscles tightened and the neck of my T-shirt constricted around my throat. Our server came to the table and took our order, delaying our conversation even further. Telling Mom my theories probably wasn't the best choice given her current opinions of me, but I didn't have anyone else to talk to since Mila stuck to our breakup. I found a book, decided to break free of the Coven's ropes, lost the people I thought were my family, and had been accused of murder. Nothing was going the way I'd hoped. Cutting ties from the Coven was supposed to be my ticket to adulthood.

The server left and Mom picked up right where we left off.

"Addison asked about how you were and I told her you were upset. I don't know why I told her that. Did something happen last night? What do you mean I gave you directions today?"

"Mila and I broke up yesterday. I don't want to go into the details, but it's directly related to Mort and our Coven." My voice hitched at the end.

"Honey, why didn't you say something? I can't say I'm surprised. If she's anything like her aunt, then you two must get along really well."

The rolled-up napkin became my comfort right then. Mom didn't know about Mila. She didn't know about our conversation that morning. Her avoidance of my questions about Katie's death wasn't normal. A bud of hope blossomed that she was in the dark about my accusation as well.

"Mom, do you really think I killed Katie?" I held my breath and waited for her to answer.

She gasped. "Why would you ask me that? How could you possibly think I believe you to be a person who could..." She looked to her right, squeezed her eyes closed, then wiped them with the back of her hand. "No. I don't think you killed Katie."

I reached across the table to touch her arm.

"Please don't cry." I swallowed around the lump in my throat. "I...it's...you turned your back on me the day it happened. Today I mentioned it a couple of times and you ignore me. Can you blame me for needing to ask again?"

Mom shook her head.

"You may be right about Addison. I'll talk to Amanda and see what she thinks. If she and Gwen are manipulating our members there is a much larger problem to handle."

"I'm sorry, Mom."

Her eyes went wide and she squeezed my wrist with her free hand.

"Azami, you don't ever have to apologize for questioning me. I'm glad you did. You may be twenty-one, but you'll always be my little girl. I love you, Azami. Don't ever doubt that."

I nodded.

Mom's phone rang. She held the screen up for me to see.

Addison Clarke.

She had no reason to call. I wasn't at her house. She wasn't a Council member. As far as I knew, she and Mom weren't good friends. Mom accepted the call and put it on speaker before placing her phone on the table. She held a finger to her lips. I stayed quiet.

"Hello, Addison. How are you?" Mom answered.

"Hey, Isabelle. I'm good. How is Azami today? Tierney said she still seemed upset last night."

I chuckled silently. Upset wasn't the word I'd use. The words to ask how Tierney's ass felt were on the tip of my tongue, but I held back.

"Oh, she's okay. She came over this morning, so we spent some time together."

"That's good. I know they're young, but our girls need a break every once in a while."

Mom's brows rose.

"Yeah. I'm sorry, but did you need something? I'm kind of busy."

I smiled. My mom was smooth when she wanted to be.

"Of course. Yes." The sugary sweet tone of Addison's voice shifted to a darker, cold one. "You met with Gwen today. You agree that *Mort d'Evanoir* must be destroyed. The Council does not need to convene; Gwen can handle it on her own."

Addison's words were the same pitch, same speed. Monotone at best. Nothing she said had been a question. She'd woven a spell into the orders. Whatever she did had no effect on me. Was this *Mort*'s protection? If that were true, I'd be grateful for the book—for the first, and probably last, time ever.

Mom's eyes turned glossy. She gave a nod with each order. Thankfully, I'd recorded the conversation at Gwen's. I just hoped it would be enough to break her out of the trance she'd been put in.

I waited until we got home to play the recording. That gave some time for the spell to wear off and we were at home where no one else would overhear.

"Hey, Mom, before I go home could you listen to this?"

"Certainly, sweetheart."

I had to lie. She needed to hear for herself Gwen talk about destroying the book and going behind the Council's backs. The distance Addison could work her magic from was unknown, just as the way to break her spell.

As I played the recording I watched for a change. Ever since the call with Mrs. Clarke, she'd returned to AI Mom. If she didn't snap out of it quick, I was afraid she'd do something like order me to give Gwen *Mort d'Evanoir* for safekeeping.

"When did you get this?" she asked when it was done.

I clenched my fist at my side. My plan to replay our conversation and jolt Mom back to reality failed. A headache started behind my right eye. I tugged the phone out of Mom's hands. Every time I thought I made progress I took two steps backward.

"Never mind. Don't worry about it." I started for the door. "Love you, Mom. I'll call you later."

I slammed the front door a bit too hard on my way out. Mom called my name, but I didn't go back. Somehow, I had to break Addison's spell. There was no one else to help me. No one else believed I was innocent.

Tears blurred my vision the entire drive back to my dorm. When I got there, I sat in the car for another forty-five minutes counting my breaths and forcing myself to calm down. If Pippa saw my bloodshot eyes and tear-streaked cheeks she'd ask questions.

I screamed into the empty car until my throat was raw and my voice scratchy. My crow wasn't even there to irritate me. Life was truly lonely if I missed a talking bird. It seemed my options were running out to solve the murder, get my girlfriend back, and save my Coven from *Mort d'Evanoir*.

Maybe it was time to pack up my car and move away from everyone. Start fresh.

CHAPTER 20

EVERY HOUR ON THE HOUR I video chatted Mom, hoping she'd remember our visit with the Coven leader. It took three hours for that to happen. On the last play through, she jumped up from the couch, ranting about how Gwen was abusing her power.

Since I knew she was back to normal, I ended our call and told her I had things to do. My thumb hovered over Mila's name. It hadn't been twenty-four hours since we split and I missed her so much I considered going to her house to see her. But I couldn't. That would ruin everything. The sooner I found the killer, the sooner Mila and I could get back together. She and Mom were the reasons I decided running away wouldn't work.

Mort d'Evanoir was open on my desk. There hadn't been any new names, but I had a sixth sense one would show soon. I tapped my pencil on the desk. How was I supposed to find a killer with very few clues? Gwen wasn't the wielder. She'd confirmed that when she continued her attempt at manipulation to get the book in her hands.

Tierney didn't kill anyone, but I wasn't sure Addison hadn't.

Josh was on my list, more because I didn't want to overlook anyone than because I actually thought he could've killed Katie. Josh's change in behavior could have been the same as Mom's—a spell from Addison. He still talked to Tierney, so she had access to him. He wouldn't have willingly killed Katie.

Since I didn't really know anyone other than Mila in her family, I didn't see how it could've been any of them. Dustin killed Bennett without a second thought, but that didn't make him the wielder of the book. I'd only met him twice, though, so I hadn't ruled him out completely.

I stood from my desk and paced in front of the bed.

"You said I would know the wielder when I was ready. I'm ready now, yet I still don't know who it is. Why doesn't the protector find out right away?"

The scratching of pencil to paper surprised me and I tripped over my own foot.

It was never said to be easy. The protector is not meant to know the wielder in case there is conflict.

I sighed. I wanted the bond between wielder and book severed. Of course, once I discovered the wielder I'd have a bigger problem. The only way I knew to break the bond was death. Could I kill the one who gained power from a book I protected?

Simply...no.

I needed Mila. So far she'd been the only person I had to talk to about Mort and actually figure things out. But I couldn't talk to her. There was no chance I'd put her family at greater risk, even if I didn't understand why Gwen wanted us apart.

Since talking to her wasn't an option, I did the next best thing. I grabbed the book, my keys, and my journal. If we couldn't talk in person, maybe we could talk through magic like we had before.

"I'm going to the park be back later," I said to Pippa as I reached for the front door.

"Go get some lovin'. You need a lot of TLC right now."

She had no idea how true that statement was.

***

The bench I'd come to call mine sat empty. Mom's journal landed on the table with a thump. As I flipped through the pages, reading the spells for the third, sometimes fourth time, the sun tinted the sky orange with a hint of pink. My favorite time of night was when the sky turned into a rainbow hue of pinks, purples, and orange with blue and white mixed in. The palette was a calming finish to any day.

"How's it going?"

I slammed the book shut and came eye to eye with Josh who'd taken a seat across from me.

"Fine. As you can see, Mila isn't here. So you can go

244

now."

Josh had no reason to show up and I had no desire to talk to another lackey.

"Azami, I'm sorry about that. You were right."

His apology gave me pause. He'd become adept at spewing those two words lately.

"About?" I asked.

Josh huffed. As he stared over my shoulder I watched him chew his lower lip. A tick he'd had for as long as we'd known each other. When he was stressed he chewed on anything—his lip, his nails, a pencil.

In those few minutes, it hit me how much I missed him and Tierney, too. Lonely was my word of the day.

"Gwen told me after the memorial service that Mila was *Mort d'Evanoir's* wielder. She said Mila killed Katie. I didn't want to believe her, but I didn't have a reason not to. I mean, she's the Coven leader."

Wow. I shouldn't have been surprised. We'd talked about Gwen influencing him, but there'd been a part of me that dismissed the possibility. Josh was too smart for that. Or so I thought.

"And now?" I wasn't sure I wanted his answer.

"Even though I don't want to believe Gwen, I think Mila is the wielder. Ever since Gwen gave me the idea I've been doing my own investigation."

His admission stole the breath from my lungs.

"She took the book from you, Azami. I followed her

from your house and she had it in her hands."

I shook my head. "Mila didn't take it. Somehow it ended up in her room, but she didn't take the book."

"You're not listening to me. She left your house with the book. Neither you, nor your roommate were home."

He was wrong. Tierney admitted to coming in the house and taking it. Whatever Josh had seen, he was wrong.

"How can you say that when I was using the book right before it disappeared? I had it the day before and when I woke up, it was gone. That was the same day Katie died. You and I were with her. You can't be in two places at once."

My skin tingled. The taste of blood returned. I searched for anyone else, but Josh and I were the only two in the area. Instead of making things right between us, Josh was building a stronger divide. Nothing he said made sense. He had to expect I wouldn't believe him.

"Fine. I made up the stuff about the book, but I'm telling you, Mila is the wielder. I know it, not because of Gwen, but I've seen her do magic. She knows way too many dark magic spells. Death magic, even. She's the killer. Your ex-girlfriend killed Katie. Why can't you see that?"

I stood up and leaned over the table until my face was inches from Josh.

"Enough. You know she didn't kill Katie, just like I know she didn't kill Katie. I'm done with your lies and stories. Our friendship is over. Goodbye."

Josh stood. A tear fell down his cheek. We used to be friends. I wanted to trust him, had even hoped we could mend the rift between us. But this was the last straw. I'd officially lost another one of my childhood friends all because our leader decided to manipulate his emotions. Regardless of whether Gwen wielded *Mort d'Evanoir*, she was guilty of tearing our Coven apart. I'd prove it to the Council and have her removed.

"You'll see. The Hutchings family is as bad as we've all suspected. You've got blinders on because of some absurd crush. But you'll see I'm not wrong."

He left without another word, leaving me alone once more. My chest constricted and my throat dried up. I wanted to cry, but the tears refused to form. A few minutes passed and the metallic taste of dark magic lingered in my mouth.

I opened Mom's book again in search of a spell that could help me communicate with someone at a distance. I couldn't see Mila in person, but she needed to know Josh was watching her. I didn't want him to hurt her.

It didn't take long to find one that could work. After reading the words a couple of times, I closed my eyes and focused my breathing. It had to come from within my soul, nothing could distract me. The air around me stilled. The birds stopped singing. The smell of fresh-cut grass filled my senses on my last deep breath. Carefully, I repeated the lines from the book:

Je demande le portail pour se connecter

Je demande le pouvoir de parler

Je les demande au nom de la protection

Nothing happened, so I tried again:

Give me the portal to connect

Give me the power to speak

I ask for these in the name of protection

Minutes passed and still, nothing happened. There was a note beside the spell. Two phrases I didn't recognize. In one last attempt, I added those to the spell.

Clé de vie

Je demande le portail pour se connecter

Je demande le pouvoir de parler

Je les demande au nom de la protection

Clé de la mort

At the end of the spell, I ran my hands over the table. A splinter pierced my skin. A drop of blood landed on the dirt beneath the table. Leaves lifted off the ground, swirling into the air. Overhead, the sky darkened to an eerie black. Crows and owls sang a song that sent chills up my spine. The metallic taste filled my mouth stronger than any time before.

What had that spell been? Those words...they could have been death magic. Or when my finger bled. My mind raced with the possibilities. A sharp burst of adrenaline rushed through my veins at the same time. It was like that blast from going down a twenty-foot hill on a roller coaster. I wanted more, but I was scared of what I'd done. I opened my mouth to scream, but nothing came out. Instead, a voice entered my thoughts.

"So you've joined the other side of magic. I didn't think we'd see you this soon." It was a male. His voice was familiar, but I couldn't think of where I recognized it from.

Slowly an image formed in my mind. A male at least a foot taller than my five-feet-one-inches. He was skinny, almost too skinny. His collar bones stuck out against his chest. The blue of his eyes matched Mila's. The blurry image focused until I recognized him.

Dustin. Mila's brother.

"Why are you here?" I asked. I'd hoped to talk to Mila, not her brother.

"My sister can't travel through a portal like the one you opened. I can, so I volunteered to come talk to you."

Travel through a portal? All I'd wanted to do was talk to her telepathically. Leave it to me to screw up a spell so badly.

Dustin laughed. "You didn't screw up the spell. You enhanced it. This is why you bonded with *Mort d'Evanoir*. Your magic strengthens spells, brings a new dimension. It's incredible."

He was wrong. I didn't have the ability to enhance spells, or do what he said. That was impossible. Except...I'd sent Josh sailing across the school lawn. I'd unbound the book without knowing it. The visions.

"Did I use blood magic to open the portal?" I asked.

"Yep. How does it feel? Intense, isn't it?" Dustin walked close enough I could've reached out and touched him.

I raised my hand and paused. He wasn't wrong, the magic heated my body. Sparks of energy bounced around my nerves, the sensation was strange but exciting. Like touching the tip of a battery to my tongue. Performing blood magic was against everything we'd been taught, but I didn't want to stop; I wanted to see what else I could do.

"Don't get sucked in, Z. Blood magic is dangerous," Mila spoke.

Not only had I formed a portal, but I could communicate with Mila.

"Wait. If you can talk to me, then why did your brother come?"

"Dustin loves trying new things. He's an adventurer. When we noticed you opened the portal he jumped at the chance to walk through. I can talk to you, but not see you. What were you trying to do, Z?"

Right. The whole point of this spell. "I wanted to warn you about Josh."

"Josh?" she asked.

I nodded. Dustin laughed.

"He's watching you. Thinks you killed his precious friend, Katie." Dustin pointed to me. "You could tell him.

She shouldn't have cheated on me."

My mouth fell open.

"Did you...kill Katie?" I asked.

"Maybe I did. Or maybe Mila did. I mean, anyone can wield the magic of *Mort d'Evanoir* if they know how. Considering our family helped bring the book to life, wouldn't you say we had the knowledge?"

No. That was obvious. The wielder wouldn't be so upfront about the book. Mila would never have killed Katie. At least I didn't think she would. Maybe I was wrong, especially if it meant ending her brother's hurt.

"Z, I didn't do it." Truth and desperation rang through Mila's voice.

I wanted to believe her. Once again I considered going to her house to check on her, make sure everything was okay.

"I swear, it wasn't me. Dustin is just trying to get you to react." The plea in her voice pulled at my heartstrings.

"So it's Dustin? He's the wielder." I bowed my head and said a silent prayer that it wasn't Dustin either. None of my research gave me ways to break the bond between wielder and book without death.

"Is that what you think? Tell me, Azami. If it's me, you know what you must do to sever the ties." Dustin turned away from me, presumably talking to Mila. "She would have to kill me, Mila. How would you handle that?"

Killing my ex-girlfriend's brother wasn't on the list of

things I thought I could do.

"Why do you think it's Dustin? Because you think it has to be one of us? Seriously, Z, have you always thought it was my family? Is that why you agreed to date me? So you could investigate my family?"

It didn't make sense to blame her for the quick change of tone. I would've protected my brother, too. At the same time, I couldn't dismiss the possibility. He walked through a portal to talk to me. He knew of blood magic and Katie's death. More than anyone, Dustin had motive.

The words I needed to say stuck in my throat. Years of pining over her and I'd lost all that time because of a misguided rule within the Coven. My supposed best friends had turned on me. Even Katie.

None of this made any sense. Her brother. Mila. My life. Numbness stilled my muscles. Air escaped my lungs. Nothing worked. I would die before I killed Mila or her brother, and yet, she doubted me just as I'd doubted her.

"You have no idea the crush I've had on you. I've never liked someone the way I like you, Mila. If it weren't for the stupid rules, I might've had the courage to do something about it. Until now, all I wanted was to please my mom and the Coven. Prove to them that I was worthy of being a witch of the Evanoir Coven."

"You didn't answer my question. Do you think my brother is the killer?"

Heaviness weighed down my shoulders until I rested

my head on the table in the park. The softness of the wood dug into my skin. The answer in my gut was not what Mila wanted. But everything lined up. Katie and Dustin's secret relationship. His understanding of the rush of blood magic. He'd been at the Coven house when I sensed the dark magic. Dustin killed Bennett.

Even though I didn't have all the answers, I knew he was the wielder. My next words were going to end my relationship with Mila. There'd be no chance for us to reconcile. I sucked in a deep breath.

"Yes. I think he's the wielder. I can't prove it, but my heart and soul tell me he is."

Dustin laughed. I'd forgotten he was with us. I should've held my opinion to myself and come up with a different answer for Mila.

"Such an accusation without any proof. A rookie mistake, really. Let's say I am the wielder. How do you think figuring it out will change things for me? Maybe I would lie low for a while. Make you second guess yourself."

There were two ways to take the conversation. Admit I screwed up, or roll with it. If he admitted to being the wielder it could help me save my relationship with Mila. Then again, he could make things irreparable. Dustin had already proven himself smart enough for that given I'd forgotten about him—twice.

"Or, rather than play it off like you know nothing, you could tell us how you're so well-versed in blood magic.

When did you first experience the high of casting a blood spell?" I asked.

"Don't you know, the Hutchings family only practices dark magic. We learn all the nasty spells first, then when we get bored, we dabble in the boring recipes your Coven loves so much. I've been working blood magic since I was a toddler."

Yep. It backfired. If I pushed further it would only make things worse. I gave a long sigh.

"Mila, please..." I didn't finish. What did I ask? Please forgive me for accusing her brother of being a murderer. Right. As if that was something she'd be okay with.

"I guess we were right to end things between us. At least now I know the truth. Two weeks and I thought I could fall in love with you. It was all a lie. Goodbye, Azami."

The setting sun brought the rising moon. The portal I'd opened slammed shut with Mila's final words. My chest ached. Tears flowed through the slats of the table. It made no sense that I'd hurt so much over a girl I'd only started to get to know. Mila made everything brighter, more vibrant. Even with the shadow of *Mort d'Evanoir*, the little time we spent gave me the courage to step outside the box I'd put myself in.

At eight forty-five, the alarm on my phone yanked me back to reality. Somehow, I made it to my car and drove home, surrounded by the fog of loss. If I was right, I had to have proof. I couldn't kill Dustin on a gut feeling.

But my proof would have to wait until the next day.

CHAPTER 21

AFTER MAKING IT BACK HOME from the park, I'd fallen asleep while researching Dustin and *Mort d' Evanoir*.

"I told you to take care of Mila. Destroying her brother is not taking care of her. You can do better than this, Azami." Aunt Monica's voice jolted me awake.

I sat straight up in bed, my hand pressed to my chest, panting. The sun shone through my window. I glanced at the clock, it was two in the afternoon. She was right. I wasn't taking care of Mila. I had to fix things.

A faint knock came from outside my door. I listened as Pippa spoke to the visitor. A couple of minutes passed before the familiar sound of footsteps reached my room.

Mila stepped inside and I coughed on a breath.

"What are you doing here?" I snapped.

I hadn't meant to sound ungrateful, but the pain of the night before hadn't lessened. My night and morning had been spent searching for some kind of evidence that Dustin was the wielder. *Mort d'Evanoir* refused to tell me and everything else I had was a coincidence. Just because he knew dark magic and had dated Katie it didn't mean he was a killer.

"I needed to see you."

"You said goodbye last night." My voice hitched as new tears formed at the corner of my eyes.

She sat on my bed. Her foot bounced up and down and her gaze floated around the room, never stopping in one place.

Mila nodded. "I know. This is important. Like life and death kind of important."

She sucked her upper lip between her teeth. I wanted to tell her to stop. It was either that or let her keep going and then kiss away the pain. That was a dream that would never come true.

"What's going on?"

I sat next to her and started to place my hand on her knee to stop it from bouncing but froze. She probably wouldn't have appreciated my affection.

"My brother, Dustin, is a murderer. You were right."

The only response I had was to nod.

"I'm sorry, Mila. How did you find out?" I asked.

The space between us grew as Mila stood from the bed. Across the room, she leaned against my desk and crossed her arms over her chest. My foot tapped a staccato rhythm against the wood floor. Sweat pooled in the palm of my hands. I hated that her brother turned out to be the wielder. It could have been anyone.

She didn't respond right away. I watched as her throat moved up and down each time she swallowed.

"Mila, babe, talk to me. We can still figure everything out together. Things don't have to be done between us."

"Check the book."

"I just did. It hasn't recorded a new name."

She shook her head. I caught a tear on the tip of my finger as it fell off her cheek.

"Martha Sanderson."

I stared at my ex-girlfriend with a slack jaw. There was no way for her to know Ms. Sanderson's name was in the book. I hadn't told anyone about the latest addition.

"How?"

"It's so awful, Z."

We sat side-by-side, our breathing syncing. My pulse racing. Mila had the evidence I needed to break the bond between the wielder and the book. I still didn't want it to be Dustin, but I had no control over that. He'd formed the bond. I had to release it or more people would die. It wasn't like I could destroy the book.

"I'm here. You can tell me. I *need* you to tell me."

"Yesterday after I got home, I went to his room to talk. I hated myself for allowing us to break up. I was mad at you for going along with it and not fighting harder for us. Then

I realized I loved you. Anyway, there was a lot going on in my head and I needed to talk to someone."

Mila loved me. I think my heart quit beating for a second or ten. I wanted to ask more questions about that, but I'd have to wait. Her admission of knowing before I'd talked to them didn't get past me. But she loved me. We definitely had a chance.

"Was he there?" I prompted her to continue.

"Yeah. When I called his name he didn't respond, so I pushed open the door slightly. I didn't want to believe you yesterday, but I needed to know for myself that it wasn't true. So, as quiet as I could, I peeked in on him. Dustin sat on the floor in the middle of the room, chanting. In front of him was a piece of paper. I watched her name appear from nothing."

Just like it did when Mort answered my questions. Dustin Hutchings cast spells to initiate a death. He paid *Mort d'Evanoir* in blood. He'd killed Bennett. I knew why he chose Katie, a surprise to say the least.

"Oh. Mila." I didn't know what else to say. What kind of comfort did I offer knowing everything wouldn't be okay?

"When you told me last night you suspected him, I shouldn't have said the things I did. Your admission made it all real. He's my brother, Z. Shouldn't I have known he had the ability to kill? Maybe I could've stopped him."

I shook my head. "No. Why would you have ever

guessed he was a killer? No sister would. Even if you thought it was a possibility what could you have done?"

"Nothing, I guess. If it weren't for you I wouldn't have believed it anyway. Are you going to turn him over to the Coven?"

"No." I wrapped my arm around her waist to hug her closer. "The Coven cannot find out about him."

Gwen would kill Dustin without a second thought. I'd hoped her confession of love would give us a spark to work with in the future. If that was true, I couldn't let the rift between her family and the Coven grow deeper.

"He can't keep killing people, Z. That's not right."

No. He couldn't.

"The power gained using the book is addictive. The magic feeding *Mort d'Evanoir* is more than dark magic. It's blood magic. The user forms a bond with the book."

Mila joined me on the bed again.

"Great. So we break the bond and get my brother help." Her gaze filled with hope. A hope I had to banish.

I wished it was that easy.

"The only way to break the bond is death."

Mila backed away until she almost fell off the bed. The color drained from her face. An emptiness filled her eyes.

"You're going to kill my brother? There has to be another way. Where can we start the research? I won't accept death, even if it means he continues to use the book. My brother will not die. We can destroy the book. That would sever the connection."

I shook my head.

"No. If I destroy the book then all witches in Evanoir die. The book was made with the souls of the Evanoir Coven, which means your family, too. You were still part of the Coven at that time."

Mila held up her hands when I took a step toward her. I didn't want Dustin to die, but I wouldn't give others' lives to save his. If the bond remained there was no limit to the number of people who could die over the years. No way could I live with those deaths on my soul.

"I'm not going to kill him." I vowed to myself that no matter what, Dustin would not die because he was a wielder of *Mort d'Evanoir*. "But the blood bond cannot continue. You can't help me with this, Mila. You're too close. I have to find a resolution on my own. Until then, I'm going to have to leave town. If I'm here with the book, he can continue."

"Stay away. Don't come closer. Of course you'll kill him. You have to. You can't let a killer keep killing. That's what you just said, and I don't want you to leave. My brother will just find another way."

"Mila..."

My ex-girlfriend ran out of my room. I followed her, but she made it to the front door before I was out of my bedroom. I stood at the door, watched her back out of the lot, wiping her tears at the same time. My knees refused to hold me up. I'd lost her again. I wanted to go on a real date, keep falling in love with her. That possibility disappeared with Mila when she turned the corner. I couldn't blame her. I ran too. Home to Mom.

Mom's arms wrapped around me before the door closed behind us and she guided me to the couch. This time I didn't cry. My entire world crumbled to dust. I had no tears. No pain. Nothing. I had absolutely nothing.

At that moment I gained an understanding of needing to experience something, even if it was pain. I couldn't kill someone for the opportunity, but I could almost see how it became possible. The ache of losing her could only be replaced by another emotion. Someone else needed to hurt as much as I did at that moment. Dark thoughts filled my mind. There was no sadness. A burning desire to shed my feelings burned through my veins.

"Mila's older brother, Dustin, is the one wielding the magic of *Mort d'Evanoir*." Even my words fell flat.

"How do we help?" Mom asked.

"I don't know. The only way to break his bond with the book is to kill him. Mila thinks that's what I'm going to do."

Mom gasped.

"She's in shock, sweetheart. Once she has time to process this truth about her brother, she'll realize you wouldn't kill him."

"Maybe. The problem is, I don't know of another solution. If he's able to cast spells he can control *Mort d'Evanoir.*"

I don't know how long we stayed on the couch. Eventually, I laid with my head in Mom's lap. The repetition of her fingers brushing my hair lulled me to sleep.

My dream started with Dustin sitting in the middle of a bedroom. His hands moved in ways similar to Amanda's.

"Where did you learn magic?" I asked.

Dustin startled. His arms fell to his sides.

"Azami, nice to see you again."

"Umm, you too." I searched my surroundings for some kind of evidence of reality or a dream.

The white walls reflected light from an unknown source, nearly blinding me. The floor was covered in a blue and red gingham rug. Nothing screamed reality. This had to be a dream, or vision of some sort.

"Your precious Coven leader, Gwen, taught me."

I bit back a laugh. The most unlikely of people. How bad would it burn to know her student controlled the book she so desperately wanted?

"You said you learned when you were little." One of his answers was a lie.

"Nope. Just wanted to get a reaction out of you and my sister. A disappointment, really."

I tilted my chin to the left. "What was a disappointment?"

"The way you didn't argue or question me. You gave

up too easy." His crooked grin didn't ease the headache blooming out of frustration.

Real or fake. Truth or lies. Dead or alive. I rubbed the back of my neck. All I wanted was answers. Not more questions. Dustin didn't seem to mind when I sat next to him and reached for the cards laid out in front of us.

"How did you find *Mort d'Evanoir*?"

He leaned back on his hands and laughed.

"I sensed its power after you and Mila started talking. The mark of the book was all over Mila when she came home the weekend after classes started."

How was that possible? I sat on my hands to hide the trembling. A tingling sensation started in my chest.

"The mark?" I asked.

"Yes. *Mort d'Evanoir* leaves its mark on all those powerful enough to wield the magic within. Even though it called to her, she never would've acknowledged it."

"But you did?"

He nodded. "Of course. I've used magic to probe for the book ever since Gwen told me about it. The family gave it to Gwen's sister for safe-keeping, but she lost it. They've searched for years, which is why she's tried so hard to get it from you. Gwen doesn't want to admit her family lost one of the most powerful magical objects in existence."

"You tried to get the book from me a couple of times, didn't you? That was you outside my window."

Dustin performed another series of hand gestures. I

reached for a piece of paper on his left and he slapped my hand away.

"I'd appreciate it if you didn't interrupt my zen," he snarled.

"Are you weaving another death spell?" I asked.

He huffed. "I'm trying, but you keep breaking my focus with your questions. What does all of this matter anyway? It's not like you're going to stop me. The protector can't destroy the book and since you're my sister's girlfriend, you won't kill me."

Dustin thought he had everything figured out. His assumption was right and wrong. I couldn't destroy the book or kill him, but that didn't mean I wouldn't do everything in my power to stop him, especially since he was already working on the death of the next person.

"How did you bond with it if you never got it?'

"Didn't need to touch it. I knew the bonding spell. That night outside your window was all I needed."

It seemed too easy. A book as powerful as *Mort d'Evanoir* should've had a more difficult bonding ritual.

"How is it so easy?" I asked.

"The only easy part was casting the spell outside your window. The blood bond was not easy at all. Now can we be done? I'd like to keep going."

There were more things I wanted to know, but I expected he'd boot me out of his head soon.

"I have a favor to ask," I said.

For the first time since my dream-vision started, he quit moving his hands through the air.

"What?"

"Please hold off on another death. At least until I smooth things over with your sister. We aren't exactly on good terms."

The request had been a Hail Mary play, but if he cared for Mila like I thought he did, then I had a chance.

"Fine. I can't figure out the right weave for this one anyway. I'll give you a week."

A week wasn't long, but I'd make it work. Hopefully, I'd come up with a solution in the next day or two. The room around us became fuzzy. Mom caught a tangle in my hair sending a bite of pain to the base of my neck.

"Thank you," I whispered.

When I opened my eyes I stared at a bookcase full of witch and coven artifacts. On the top shelf was a book: *Myths and Legends of Witchcraft*. I'd seen the book a million and one times, but never bothered to read it.

"Mom, what's in that myth book?"

"Nothing, really. I found it in the Coven library. We were clearing it out and this one had been tossed aside. I asked a few people about it, but no one had read it. I brought it home and haven't taken it back."

The book didn't stand out in any way. There weren't any spotlights or glittering signs saying "Read Me." I rolled off Mom's lap to get the book. As I held it in my hands it fell open. The words *Mort d'Evanoir* were written in bold, black ink. How had no one read this?

"There's a chapter titled after the book."

Mom joined me in front of the shelf.

"I don't remember ever seeing that in there. Interesting."

The first five pages of the chapter didn't give me anything new. Same story as what I already knew. On the last page, I found a theory that could be the answer I needed.

The power of Mort d'Evanoir *comes from death. While legend says the wielder must die to break the bond, some believe it's more about removing the thirst for power and urge to kill. Remove these, break the bond.*

"That's it!" I shouted.

"What's it?"

"Dustin doesn't have to die. We need to remove the thirst for power and urge to kill. Like a twelve-step program or something to stop addiction."

Mom moved around the living room. "How are we supposed to do that?"

There had to be a way. It was so easy; I couldn't believe I hadn't thought of it sooner. Then again, nothing easy ever worked as expected.

"I have an idea, but it's going to mean a change to the leadership and Council. We're also going to have to offer an ultimatum to one of the members. Banishment or assistance."

There were a few more details, like confirming my suspicions about Addison and Gwen, but I was pretty sure it could work.

"Follow me to the kitchen. I need a drink of water," Mom said.

I dragged myself behind her. We finally had a way to make everything right and Mom worried about getting a drink of water.

"Mom, have you talked to Addison since we left the Chinese place?"

"No. I've been in and out of my office today with my phone turned off."

I studied her eyes. They were clear. She hadn't demanded I go to the Coven with the Dustin news. I crossed my fingers that what I had to say would stay between us and she'd come out of the Addison trance completely.

"First, I propose we confirm Addison's ability to hypnotize and then use it to brainwash Dustin. We just need to change the way he thinks. Replace his need for pain and desire to kill with a less violent solution."

"That sounds reasonable but difficult. If Gwen has Addison under her thumb, it won't work. You need to be sure of this, Azami. What you're proposing is no different than what we believe she's been doing to the Coven all along. How can we threaten banishment and then ask her to do the same for us?"

I climbed onto one of the kitchen barstools. Mom was right. My proposal wasn't fair. I needed to rethink my approach.

"I know. It's just, the other option is death. If I have to pick the best of the worst, I'd rather him not die." Later, I'd do some self-reflecting on how easy it was to be okay with brainwashing when it benefitted me. "We need a Council meeting. Gwen has to be voted out as a leader and removed from the Coven. While I was asleep I had a dream about Dustin. He told me Gwen taught him magic."

"There's nothing wrong with that."

I shook my head.

"Yes, there is. Dustin is a Hutchings. If we're forbidden from socializing with Mila, then the same should be said for her brother. That's minor, though. A technicality. Dustin is the wielder of *Mort d'Evanoir*. That means he performs dark magic. Gwen taught him."

Mom squealed. She actually squealed. The joy took me by surprise. The last thing I felt was happiness. Relief for finding a potential solution, sure. Worry that it would work out the way I hoped, definitely. But nothing good.

"Combine that with our meeting earlier. I don't see how the Council could let her remain. The Evanoir Coven was not founded on hunger for power or disregard of our laws."

She hugged me so tight I couldn't breathe.

"Azami, sweetheart, you're a genius."

"Not really, but thanks. The final step is giving Addison the ultimatum. She chooses the Coven and helps with Dustin, or she and Tierney leave."

"As relieved as I am that we have tangible information to take to the Council about Gwen, your plan for Addison is not one I will take to the group. For what it's worth, telling everyone Gwen trained Dustin is hearsay. You'd need him to share his own experience with the Council."

I could call Mila, tell her my plan, and see if she could get her brother to come to the Coven house for a meeting. Then again, I wasn't sure she'd answer my calls or go along with the plan. I had to convince her it was the best option.

"So I'll call Mila and ask her to bring him. She supports her brother and doesn't want him to die, I don't see why she wouldn't be willing."

Mom sighed and walked over to the stove where she sat a teapot of water on the burner.

"This may not work, Azami. You accepted your role with *Mort d'Evanoir*. If it comes down to it, you must take responsibility and remove Dustin from the equation. Can you do what it will take?"

My shoulders dropped. My plan had to work. Everything we knew, the life of our Coven was at risk if it didn't.

"No, Mom. I can't."

CHAPTER 22

ONCE I ADMITTED I WOULDN'T be able to kill Dustin, Mom agreed to come with me to talk to Addison. The proposal would have to be altered, but we'd make that decision later. Dark magic no longer surrounded the farm home in the inner circle of woods.

Neither Mom nor I understood why Mrs. Clarke agreed to hypnotize the Coven members. We weren't even sure she'd used magic on them, but I was about to find out.

I knocked on the now white, wooden door. It didn't creak when Tierney pulled it open.

"Azami. What are you doing here?" she asked.

Mrs. Clarke joined her at the door. "Can we help you?"

"May I please come in? There's something we need to discuss." I shoved my hands in the pockets of my shorts.

Tierney and Mrs. Clarke glanced at the messenger bag hanging against my hip. I'd brought *Mort d'Evanoir* with me and held it close. In truth, I'd hoped it would intimidate them so they'd talk rather than hide behind whatever secrets or power they thought they held.

What I needed to say had to be done quickly. I'd left a message for Josh to come out to the house in half an hour. If this was going to work, I had to do some manipulation of my own. Josh trusted Tierney, so hopefully, he'd agree if she did.

"I should call the Coven." Mrs. Clarke stepped back.

She began to shut the door in our face, but Mom's hand shot out from behind me to push the door open wider. Tierney and Addison's eyes went wide.

"No. This is between us. What I have to tell you does not leave the house."

No one said a word until we reached the sitting room they'd had me in last time. Mrs. Clarke closed the door then whispered a spell I assumed was a ward to keep the conversation private.

"All right. We can talk freely now," she said when she sat in the plush, oversized armchair across from the settee where Tierney and I sat. Mom stood guard at the door with her arms crossed over her chest.

"I know you're hypnotizing the coven to do what Gwen wants." I jumped right in. There was no point in sugar-coating the reason we'd gone to their house.

The faster I ripped off the band-aid, the sooner we could get to my plan. All Addison had to do was admit to her actions, then we'd move forward.

"What the hell, Azami? You come into our house and accuse Mom of hypnotizing members. As if you have evidence and can prove it." Tierney's outburst didn't surprise me. She played right into what I needed.

"Actually," I held up a finger when she started to talk again. "I didn't say which one of you was hypnotizing anyone. You just gave your mom away."

She shook her head. "No. Your attention was on Mom when you said it. That implies you meant her. I didn't give anything away."

Mrs. Clarke shushed us both.

"Tierney, it's okay." Her voice was calm, quiet. Not so much resigned, but accepting of the truth.

Now that the truth was out, I sat still. In awe at her power. She was far more powerful than anyone else in the Coven.

"You're right, Azami. I have been hypnotizing Coven members. I'm honestly surprised it took this long for someone to figure it out."

Whoa. I hadn't expected that twist. If she'd been doing it for the entire time she'd been a member of the Coven, how many things had she coerced people into doing for Gwen?

While my mind wanted to go off on a tangent of all the things Mrs. Clarke could've done to our Coven, I focused on the reason behind my entire plan. To save Dustin and hopefully get Mila back.

"Why?" Tierney asked.

I turned to my former best friend. Her lower lip quivered even though she tried to keep it from showing. The single word shook. This was more of a surprise to her than it was to me. I couldn't imagine what she felt at that moment. She rubbed her hands up and down over the top of her jean shorts.

"How?" Tierney turned to me when she asked her second question.

All of us knew the question wasn't for me, but her mom. Our gazes locked. Silently, I promised to be there for her. We had our differences, but once everything came to light I hoped we could find our way back to friendship. Eventually, even bring Mila into the fold. She wouldn't replace Katie but bring a new perspective.

Mrs. Clarke cleared her throat. She adjusted in the chair, sitting up taller with her shoulders squared. Her body language spoke of confidence, not guilt or remorse.

"I did what I had to do for our family. Gwen is not the right person to lead the Evanoir Coven. Her intentions have never been pure. When we arrived, I knew right away this Coven needed our help."

That didn't make sense. How could Mrs. Clarke have sensed something was wrong but do Gwen's bidding anyway? I started to ask, but she held up a finger to silence me.

"Your question is legitimate. My answer is not one you

are old enough to understand."

Tierney huffed.

"Give it up, Mom. You honestly think Azami can't understand? Or better yet, me, your own daughter, won't get it. If you knew the Coven needed our help, then why didn't you do something?"

Mrs. Clarke moved her chair to sit directly in front of Tierney. She placed her hand on her daughter's knee and held her gaze. In that moment I felt like an outsider, a third wheel. To be polite, I should have left, except I wanted the answer as much as Tierney.

"Because I have. I've spent years grooming you to take over. I've set Gwen up to take the fall for all of the manipulations. When she's done as Coven leader, you will take her place."

"You did what?" Tierney asked.

Her mom lowered her lids.

Gwen was worse than I ever expected, but Addison outdid Gwen. To my surprise, Tierney didn't react at all. She didn't swallow hard or push her mom away. Tears didn't come. Her breathing didn't change. My best friend sat perfectly still as though we were talking about the weather. Mrs. Clarke showed more emotion than her own daughter. It didn't fit, but I couldn't put my finger on the reason why.

"Mrs. Clarke, I have a question."

She lowered her chin in my direction. "Go ahead."

"You said the Coven needed your help. What skills do you, or your family, have that would help us? Besides the hypnotism, of course."

She crossed one leg over the other with her hands rested on her knees. I'd never noticed how proper Mrs. Clarke was. Tierney didn't have the same mannerisms at all. In some ways, I envied her. Then again, it had to be tiresome to be so perfect.

"Tierney and I have learned to read auras. We can see how you're feeling and manipulate your emotions to improve or intensify them. I've not been hypnotizing as much as manipulating."

Without thinking, I pulled away from Tierney. How many times had she manipulated my emotions?

"No. I've never manipulated you, Azami." The quick reply came from Tierney.

I gave a half-hearted sigh of relief. She wasn't telling the whole truth.

"Is that true or is it more like you tried to manipulate me, but couldn't? That's what the thing at the bar and then here was all about. You wanted me to fall in line. It didn't work, though." I turned to Mrs. Clarke. "Why? Is it the same reason your manipulation of my mom after we went to Gwen's didn't affect me at all?"

The lady with the perfect posture shrugged. Turned out she did have flaws.

"Honestly, I don't know why our magic has no effect

on you. I have a theory, but you won't like it."

Oh, I had theories too. She was right, I wouldn't like her if it was the same as mine. That didn't matter though. If we were going to fix the Coven, the secrets had to stop. Fixing the Coven came second to getting Mila back though.

"I have some weird dark magic blood or something that blocks your spells."

"Yes, something like that."

I had no idea what to say to her confirmation. Admittedly, it had helped me see the problems within the coven, but I wasn't a fan of having a tie to dark magic. Sure, it didn't have to always be bad, but that was the general consensus.

"Why, Addison? Why are you so intent on having Tierney lead our Coven?" Mom spoke for the first time.

Tierney's mom shrugged. "Power. The reason for all the things we do."

"Power isn't the answer for all of us. What power do you think she'll gain? There is no power as Coven leader."

This time Addison laughed a full-belly laugh. Mom left her post at the door and came to my side.

"If you believe that, you're more naïve than I thought. I was right to set it up for Tierney to take over. You won't be in the Coven by then, so your opinion won't matter."

"Excuse me..." I chimed.

"Tell me, Azami. Why did you come here the first time?"

I gulped. With all the accusations, no one had asked me about when I actually obtained the book.

"Our family familiar," I answered.

Addison nodded.

"That's right. You followed a bird. I suppose it forced you to take *Mort d'Evanoir* when it was revealed to you."

If I lied, then I'd be no more innocent than the two people we'd just accused of wrongdoings.

"No. He didn't. I chose to take it myself."

"Why?"

The question I didn't want to answer but I knew she'd ask. Give and take, just like I'd had to do with Mila in the beginning.

"I wanted to break away from the hold the Coven has on us. This was something I wasn't supposed to do, so I did it anyway."

Mom took a minute to pull a chair closer to us. I wasn't sure where she got it from, but when she sat down it wasn't at my side. She was in front of me. I wasn't sure if the shine in her eyes was unshed tears or a reflection of the sun. Either way, more than anything, I wanted to know how she felt about my revelation.

"Mom..."

"Do you regret what you did?" she asked.

Addison leaned back in her chair with her hands clasped in her lap. Tierney snickered. They'd flipped the script on me. We'd come to talk to them about manipulating our Coven and somehow the focus was now on me.

"We found the wielder of the book." I picked up the book from where I'd kept it next to me. I could do the same they'd done.

"Who is it?" Tierney asked. Her eyes lit up in eagerness. I swore for a second she actually bounced in her seat. "Was it Mila?"

Mom cleared her throat. Later, I'd apologize and answer her question. Right then, I ground my teeth together. It was not the time to get into an argument about her automatic conclusion that it was Mila. Even if she wasn't too far off. Nor was I ready to ask why she seemed...happy.

"No. It's her brother, Dustin."

"And what do you plan to do with this information?" Mrs. Clarke asked.

"That's why we're here. Mom and I have a proposal. One I think you'll want to consider."

"I see. I suppose next you will tell me this proposal comes with conditions."

Of course she'd expect that.

"There are, but they're not bad. We want you to stay in the Coven. But you'll be placed on a probationary status for a minimum of three years in which you won't be allowed to participate in Council activities and Tierney won't be eligible for a Council seat should one come available."

They wanted power. This offer took the chance away. If they declined, then they'd be forced out anyway.

Tierney huffed. "Right. So you just want us to give up our magic to stay in the Coven. Why would we do that? What's in this deal for you?"

"No. We don't want you to give up your magic." I turned to face Mrs. Clarke. "You said our Coven needed your help. If you decide to stay, we want you to help us. Mom will talk to the Council about an emergency meeting. Gwen's leadership is in question. If she's removed as leader, we would like for you to help heal our Coven."

Mrs. Clarke and her daughter had what appeared to be a silent conversation between them. One would nod then the other. Tierney shook her head a couple of times and Mrs. Clarke responded with one of those mom looks that I could never say no to—tilted chin and narrowed eyes. Whatever she wanted, Tierney didn't agree with.

I waited. Mom silently studied me. We weren't good with non-verbal communication. It didn't help that I avoided her eyes. She still wanted answers and I wasn't prepared to give them. The explanation of wanting to break free needed more than a few minutes of time. If she didn't understand that, I'd add it to my list of reasons to apologize for later.

"There's more that you want," Mrs. Clarke finally said.

"Josh will be here any minute. I want you to release him. Tell him the truth. Then I want you to release everyone else whose thoughts you've controlled."

As they carried on a second conversation, I stood and paced the room. Being the outsider of their silent discussion was more than a little awkward. The book sat unopen on the settee. Questions piled up in my thoughts. Would they want me to show them the names? Would they want to see if they could open the book? It was stupid to bring it. Mrs. Clarke and Tierney both knew I had it. To think I could intimidate them with it was a ridiculous idea.

"I'll talk to Josh. The rest, I won't agree to until after the Council session. I understand why you're here, but you have no authority within the Coven Council."

She wasn't wrong.

"I do have the authority, Addison. Yet, you still refuse." Mom twisted in her chair.

The diversion gave me time to breathe. The whole meeting put me on edge, but Mom's expectant looks amplified my emotions by a thousand.

Just then the doorbell rang. Perfect timing.

"Tierney, please bring Josh in here. I would imagine the three of you have lots to talk about. I'll take care of the rest from my room. Isabelle, you can find your own way out."

Mrs. Clarke left without another word. Weird was the only way I could describe what had happened. It didn't take long before Tierney walked into the room with Josh trailing behind her.

"Josh, I owe you an apology," I said before he made it through the door.

"For what?" he asked.

"The way I've reacted, hitting you, shoving you, all of that. It wasn't your fault and I'm sorry."

He tilted his head to the side. "Umm. I don't remember any of what you're talking about. You haven't been mean to me, Azami. When did you shove me?"

I turned to Tierney.

"Is there something you and your mom didn't tell me?"

She nodded.

"You kind of redirected the conversation before we had a chance. When Mom removes the enchantment, the person forgets everything that happened while they were under the spell."

"What enchantment, or spell, or whatever? I'm going to need one of you to tell me what is going on."

Tierney sighed. Josh pressed his palms into his eyes. He took a seat on the settee and I moved to the chair her mom had used so Tierney could sit next to him. Since I'd shortened the whole conversation, it made more sense for her to talk to him than me.

It didn't take her long to explain the family's ability to read auras and manipulate emotions. She told him her mom hypnotized him to do whatever Gwen wanted. After she finished, Josh stayed perfectly still, his gaze pinned to a spot on the wall over Tierney's shoulder.

"Why?" he asked after a few minutes passed.

"Mom did it to make sure I'd become leader one day."

"No. Why did *you* do it? You could have told your mom no. Instead, you manipulated me into thinking Mila was a horrible person and I needed to do everything I could to hurt Azami." He paused with his gaze trained on Tierney. "You did that. Not your mom. I remember you coming to my house. We went to lunch. That's when you told me Mila stole the book from Azami. She's the wielder of *Mort d'Evanoir*. Was all of that a lie?"

My breath caught in my throat. He was right. Tierney didn't have to help her mom, but she had. Doubt made itself nice and comfortable in my head. If she willingly manipulated people without asking her mom why, what did that make my friend?

"To keep my mom safe. Gwen is not right in the head. We need her out of the Coven. She wanted Mom to poison our whole Coven into thinking Mila was an awful person. Gwen ordered her to manipulate Azami's mom's memories so she believed Azami killed Katie. What kind of person does that?"

She didn't answer the rest of his questions. Tierney came to my side and laid her arm across my back. Her fingers grazed the skin of my arm. The touch was...intimate. Again. Uncomfortable. I did my best to step away from her without making it obvious.

She'd found ways to get closer and closer to me when we were together. Goosebumps rose on my arms along with a tinge of metallic taste in my mouth. Dark magic again. It wasn't strong enough to be Dustin. Every time he'd been around my taste buds wanted to revolt. This was more like when I'd been here with the fire. Present, but not.

There was someone else practicing. It could have been Mrs. Clarke.

"You taste it, don't you?" Tierney's warm breath grazed my neck.

No. For a second I swore she kissed that spot between my shoulder and neck. We were too close. I moved across the room next to Josh. The only way I could have put more space between us was to leave. But I couldn't protect Josh if I wasn't there.

Tierney. A dark magic practitioner.

"What's going on?" Josh considered me then Tierney.

"Mila didn't kill Katie or take the book from me. She's not the wielder." The words came out barely a whisper.

I hung my head. A lump formed in my throat, while my eyes burned with unshed tears. My best friend had turned against me. She manipulated our fellow Coven members. Blamed my ex-girlfriend. A spark of a reason formed, but I didn't want to acknowledge it. I sucked in a breath and shook my hands at my side. We needed to get to the point of the night.

"Oh, good goddess. Mila may as well be the wielder.

Just because it's not her, it's still her family." Tierney chuckled. "Her brother has more power in his pinky than Mila ever will."

"Her brother?" Josh asked.

I nodded. "Mila has an older brother, Dustin. He's the bonded wielder."

"And the guy Katie was secretly dating," Tierney added.

Josh whistled through his teeth when he sucked in a breath. His hands fisted at his side.

"Shut up, Tierney." I put all of my focus on Josh. "Hey, there's something I need both of you to help me with."

He'd want to know more, but the timing was off. Tierney would only pour more salt in his wounds. Later, I'd tell him whatever he wanted to know.

"Of course. Whatever you need."

Tierney took a seat in her mom's chair. She flipped her hair over her shoulder. None of what had just happened bothered her. It was just another day of influence for Tierney.

"We thought the only way to break the bond between *Mort d'Evanoir* and the wielder was death. But I think I can break it with Mrs. Clarke's help. If she erases Dustin's desire to kill, then the bond should break."

"Okay, but what do you need us for?" Josh asked.

"I was hoping you and Tierney could talk to Mila and convince her to come to the Coven house tomorrow. Mom's getting the Council together for an emergency meeting. I would call her, but we're not really on speaking terms."

Including Tierney felt wrong. She hadn't apologized for making Josh think Mila was the killer. I was almost positive she was flirting with me, in a weird almost gross kind of way. Just thinking about how close she'd stood next to me made my skin crawl with a thousand invisible bugs. But I couldn't let Josh know my concerns.

"Of course." Josh took my hand in his.

Friendship warmed the chill Tierney's actions put on my soul: holding hands with Josh felt like every other time we'd comforted each other. We were friends and nothing more.

"Thank you," I said.

Tierney rolled her eyes. "I suppose you think this is your chance to fix things with her."

"Maybe." I shrugged. "Anyway, tomorrow at noon."

Josh nodded then stood.

"She's going to hate you when she finds out I'm the one who messed with her head and convinced her to see you again."

Probably, but it had to be done to save her brother. The sour taste in my mouth added to my discomfort. None of this was right. The three of us walked toward the door together. I was more than ready to get home. Tomorrow would be everything. Josh left first, leaving Tierney and I alone in the front entryway.

"Why?" I asked. My back to Tierney, head bowed to my chest. She'd never answered Josh and I wasn't sure she would answer me, but I had to say the word.

"You chose wrong, Azami."

Tierney reached around me, grazing her hand across my lower back, for the doorknob. That time there was no doubt she kissed the back of my neck then pulled open the door.

If Bennett were still around, I would have asked him if *Mort d'Evanoir* had anything to do with me noticing her closeness now. Or maybe it was my connection with Mila. The determination to break out of my normal routine. There were many reasons why, but it didn't change the fact that she had to stop.

CHAPTER 23

FIVE COUNCIL MEMBERS AND I filled the board room of the Coven house. Addison and Tierney had been invited but told to wait in the library. The Council decided to handle one thing at a time, starting with Gwen. They'd let me sit in because I'd been the one to record the conversation with Gwen talking about using dark magic to get the book.

"I call this emergency Council meeting to order."

Mom stood at the head of the table. Within the Council, each member held a position, which had been decided by other Coven members. The Coven leader couldn't hold the Council president position. A checks and balance system. Three years ago, the Coven elected my mom as President.

"We are here to discuss a matter of abuse of power, the use of dark magic, and the interaction with a banished member. These infractions have been committed by Gwen

Graves on several occasions. Azami Durand is here to share personal grievances against Mrs. Graves."

Amanda, vice president, took to the front of the table when Mom was done. She'd asked that Josh not be part of the meeting. He'd had personal encounters with Gwen, too. Both Mom and Amanda agreed Tierney's influence clouded his judgment on Gwen. They thought his input would make things more confusing instead of helping.

"Before we discuss the counts of misconduct for Gwen, it's important for the Council to know the wielder of *Mort d'Evanoir*. Dustin Hutchings was identified as the wielder this morning. I visited the Hutchings family and spoke with Mr. Hutchings as well as Dustin. He does not deny his involvement in the death of apprentice Katie Guidry or three others within our community. Please remember that Dustin's identity as wielder should not influence our decision on the actions of Gwen. As a Coven, we will review his conduct and Coven actions following the decisions of this review," Amanda relayed the reason for the session.

Once all Council members agreed to the necessity of the meeting, Mom provided the timeline of infractions. She began with the start of Dustin's training and ended with the recording of the meeting she and I had with Gwen.

Gwen didn't dispute the claim that she'd trained with him in both Coven magic and dark magic.

"Why did you choose to break one of the Coven laws to train him, but then condemn Azami for the same infraction?" Pam asked.

"It was to my benefit to work with him. Azami blatantly disregarded the law with no reason."

Pam sighed.

"So you're justifying your actions because of intent. Can you please tell the Council what your intent was?"

Gwen sat up in her chair, prim as always. Not a single piece of perfectly straight, chestnut brown hair out of place. Her three-piece, navy blue skirt suit fit so well I was certain she'd had it made just for her. She dressed like the housewives from the nineteen fifties when they got ready for church.

"My intent was to use him to gain access to *Mort d'Evanoir*. The book's magic would call to a Hutchings, since their family aided in its birth. So I figured I'd use his lack of knowledge to my advantage." She shrugged her shoulders as if using him to gain access to a book of death was no big deal.

I fisted my hands in my lap. The inside of my cheek burned where I'd split the skin in an attempt to keep from bursting out. No matter what I had to keep my mouth shut, otherwise, they'd tell me to leave the room.

Dustin killed those people, but if Gwen had stayed away from him maybe everything could have been prevented. Our beloved Coven leader deserved to be punished for her actions.

"Why did you want *Mort d'Evanoir*? What were you

going to do with it?" Mom asked.

"Honestly, I hadn't decided. If I had the power to wield the magic, I considered trying it once or twice. Then again, that was murder, so I wasn't certain. The main reason was to keep the Coven from finding out my family had lost the book. News flash, if something happens to the book we all lose our lives. It's all part of the magic in the book."

At least she wasn't trying to hold back. I wasn't sure someone in the Council hadn't performed a truth spell, but either way, the facts had been revealed.

"Once you learned Dustin Hutchings had bonded with the book, what were your plans?" Mom asked.

"I was, and still am, willing to do whatever it takes to protect our Coven. I will perform blood magic to break the bond between the wielder and the book."

That wasn't the whole truth. I shifted in my chair, cringing when the metal legs scraped across the floor. Mom and the rest of the Council glared at me.

"Blood magic requires a sacrifice." I slapped my hands over my mouth. "Sorry," I murmured.

Amanda pressed her finger against her lips as a reminder to stay quiet. I nodded then turned my gaze to the floor. To redirect my attention, I drew circles onto the floor with the toe of my shoe.

"Ms. Durand, you're here to share your own experiences. We would appreciate it if you remained quiet otherwise." This from Pam.

"Yes, ma'am. I apologize." I kept my gaze trained on the wood floor.

Heather paused her minutes of the meeting. The heavy silence of the room grew. They had yet to ask about Addison.

"An accusation has been made that you blackmailed Coven member, Addison Clarke, to use her experience with aura magic and manipulate Coven members to do as you asked. Is this true?"

I held my breath. This was the question that would tip the Council's decision one way or the other. Everything else Gwen had done could be argued that it was for the good of the Coven. She'd have a slap on the wrist, but that was it. However, if she admitted to purposely blackmailing a member then manipulating the actions of other members, she'd be removed from the role of Coven leader and possibly banished.

A result I'd wished for. I wanted her out. She'd threatened my girlfriend, would kill my girlfriend's brother, and I wasn't sure she wouldn't hurt me too. After all, I was the one in possession of *Mort d'Evanoir* and accused of killing Katie. As Coven leader, she could force my hand. In fact, I was surprised she hadn't already.

"Yes. That is accurate. I knew Addison would do what I needed with the right motivation."

Each word was spoken without emotion. No remorse. No apology. Gwen had a goal and she'd done what she needed to achieve it. I wasn't sure how to react. Mom surveyed me with a sadness in her eyes I'd never seen before. They weren't wet with tears or empty like my memories of her at Dad's funeral. They were hazy with disappointment maybe. Or loss of respect.

The temperature in the room shifted. Before Gwen's answer, I was pretty sure Pam and Heather were on Gwen's side. They would vote that she stay as leader and get some useless punishment like no vote in Council decisions for six months. After, they both adjusted in their seats. Heather kept looking away from Gwen as if she could no longer meet her eyes. Pam tsked and tapped her pen on the table. Mom and Amanda shared a silent conversation.

Heather turned in her chair to face me.

"Azami, thank you for coming today. While we no longer need your recounting of the events, I would ask that you step outside and bring Mila Hutchings into these proceedings."

I gasped. My pulse picked up at the thought of seeing her. She was less than a hundred feet from me. Right outside the door. It took every bit of control I could find not to run to the door and fling it open. My entire body wanted nothing more than to fall into her caress. Touch the softness of her cheeks.

None of that would happen.

First, I wasn't sure if she even wanted to see me. Second, this wasn't about me. It was for the Coven. For her brother. For her family. I had to put my selfish desires to the side.

It didn't take long to figure out whether Mila was happy to see me, though. I opened the door for her but didn't get a chance to say anything. She walked through without a glance in my direction.

I took the chance to catalog everything about her. The way she carried her head high and shoulders back. Mila had confidence I could only dream of possessing. The light emanated around her. Our Coven believed the entire Hutchings family was bad. Dark magic practitioners, which made them evil. I knew otherwise. Mila was far from dark.

Her hair had been braided and fell down her back in one long weave. The dark purple a stark contrast to the sunlight yellow, Bohemian style dress. She'd completed her outfit with a pair of well-worn, white high tops. Mila made trendy comfortable and her own.

Amanda questioned her about our relationship. They talked about conversations she had with Tierney and Josh. Then they shared the events that took place when Gwen went to her house to deliver the decree from the Council.

"What were you told by Gwen when she came to your home?" Amanda asked.

Mila recounted the threats and insistence that she and I break up. She talked of the promises Gwen made in return for her compliance. Mila also told the Council about the letter she received.

"You know, Tierney is the one who stole the book from you." Gwen pointed at me.

I looked at Amanda before responding and took the tilt of her chin as permission.

"Yeah, we talked last night. Tierney has broken as many rules as you and I both have."

Gwen laughed. "So you admit to breaking Coven rules. When will you find yourself here in my shoes, being interrogated like a common criminal?"

With a sigh, I shook my head.

"It doesn't matter if I am or not. The difference between you and I is that I'm not hiding anything, and I haven't killed anyone either directly or indirectly."

Pam spoke up. "That remains to be seen, Ms. Durand. We're not discussing your transgressions, however, so let's move on." To Gwen, she said, "I would recommend you not interrupt again."

Gwen winked and mimicked zipping her lip closed then tossing the key. I groaned in response. There was a time I would've thought I'd want to be like Gwen, but that was no longer true. The power she had as leader made her forget what it was to be just another witch. The children of our Coven acted more appropriately than she did.

"Thank you, Ms. Hutchings," Amanda said before she sat back down.

Mila left the room without another word. As hard as I

tried to get her attention, she refused to give me a hint of anything. We definitely weren't okay and trying to save her brother wasn't working the way I'd hoped. Somehow I'd get her attention. We would talk before the day was through.

At the end of the session, the Council allowed Gwen to make one last argument. I found it difficult to listen to her talk poorly about Dustin and Mila. She said I was too young to understand how important it was for her family to protect *Mort d'Evanoir*. In a final effort to convince the Council that what she'd done wasn't wrong, Gwen accused Mom and me of trying to overthrow her as leader so Mom could take over.

Rather than analyze every word spoken, I watched the Council. By the end of her speech, I was pretty sure we'd get the result we needed.

Mom stood at the head of the table once more.

"You've asked questions and listened to their answers. You reviewed the evidence and they've shared their anecdotes. We must vote on Gwen's actions. It is recommended she be removed as a member of this Coven for a minimum of one generation. There must be a unanimous decision for this to take place."

To me, Amanda said, "We must ask that you leave now."

I left without argument. It didn't matter what happened next. I'd done all I could do. In the hall, I searched for Mila. For all I knew, she'd left the house right after the Council dismissed her. More than anything, I'd hoped she stuck around at least find out what happened to Gwen—maybe even her brother.

"Did Gwen spill the tea?" Tierney stood in front of me with her hands on her hips. A twinkle in her eye that I didn't trust.

"You mean about you taking *Mort d'Evanoir* from me?" I asked.

She nodded. "But that's not all—"

Mila stepped into the hall from the bathroom across the way.

"Mila," I called out and waved, interrupting whatever Tierney was about to say.

Tierney took my distraction and leaned in closer. Her lips brushed over mine.

"What—" I pushed her away at the shoulders.

"Don't fight. You know you want this as much as I do."

I shook my head. Mila stayed frozen across the hall. I wanted to go to her, make sure she knew Tierney caught me off guard. Tierney took a step in once more. This time I put power behind the shove, not with muscle but with words. Using magic was becoming easier. If I managed to stay with the Coven, I'd work to allow us to begin practicing magic sooner. There was no reason for so many restrictions.

"Walk away, Tierney," I commanded.

Mila stepped toward us. "Tierney, it's time to go," she said.

"You chose wrong. Let me show you." Tierney stepped back toward me, but this time my fist got in the way of her lips.

I stomped my foot down on hers. She jumped back with a yelp. Over her head, I watched as Josh's eyes went wide just before he turned on his toes and ran toward the back exit of the Coven house. I wasn't sure when he'd showed up, but I was thankful.

I swiped the back of my hand over my mouth.

"What was that?" I spit out.

"I was the one you were supposed to pick. Not Mila." Tierney waved her hand in Mila's direction. "She's a Hutchings. We were supposed to stay away from them. You ruined everything. I tried to break you up, but Gwen screwed that all up. Why can't you just let things happen the way they're supposed to happen?"

Mila stood at my side with her arm wrapped around my waist. For all our problems, she was there when I needed her the most. My best friend had tried to ruin my relationship with Mila.

"What are you talking about, Tierney? How did Gwen screw anything up? She was the one manipulating the Coven."

She tsked. "So innocent. Gwen gave me the idea when she talked to my mom, but while Mom worked with all the

Coven members, I was doing my own bit of manipulation. Like telling Dustin who to kill. You don't really think he wanted to kill his girlfriend Katie, do you? I mean, they were in love. Of course, after the first two, he made a few decisions on his own. The librarian who made fun of him when he was a kid. That was all his doing."

No. I couldn't believe what she was saying.

"You're wrong. He told me about the book and his bond. You couldn't have done that. You don't have the magic."

"Oh, I tried, but you're right. My magic is not strong enough, or the right kind. Unlike your ex-girlfriend, and you apparently, I don't have dark magic running through my veins. That doesn't mean I couldn't use my magic to my own benefit."

I didn't want to know anything else. It was too much. My stomach revolted. Tears warred with a sudden need to throw up.

"But why? Why would you do all of this? What did Mila or her family do to you?"

Josh appeared in the hall entrance to my right. I didn't dare look at either him or Mila. Whatever Tierney said from that point on, I'd have witnesses. Mom and the Council stood behind Josh, listening to Tierney's confession.

My heart soared. Magic trickled through my fingers, protecting me. Offering strength to fight Tierney. I didn't have to use dark magic, but the book opened my mind to new abilities when it came to casting. Dustin was right, I had boosted my skills.

"Mila took you from me. Her family...well, they were a bonus."

"Took me from you? We were friends, Tierney. Mila is so much more than that. It's impossible to take something you never had."

Tierney threw her hands in the air. "You are so incredibly thick. You don't get it. I love you, Azami. I've loved you for years. But you've been too wrapped up in being the perfect witch apprentice that you never paid attention. Then all of sudden you find a stupid book, Mila shows up, and you brush me off."

I held up my hands to make her stop. There was too much for me to process. She loved me? I brushed *her* off? Too wrapped up in being the perfect witch.

Tierney manipulated Dustin, Gwen, and Josh. I was awed by her ability to think and act so quickly but disgusted that she'd gone to such lengths. If she'd said something to me before all of this, who knew what could have happened between us. Then again, I tried and she shot me down, so if I guessed, nothing would've grown.

Tierney moved into me, our chests pressing against each other. One step at a time, she pushed me back into the wall. Immediately, my vision began to dull at the edges. Tierney placed her hands against the wall on either side of my head.

"Stop. I need space. Don't..."

I shook her off.

She leaned in. "Feel me, Azami. You can tell Mila no. We can still be together."

With as much non-magical force as I could muster, I shoved Tierney to my left while I took a step to the right. My mind raced with so many thoughts. Mainly, who was the person in front of me. Where had this possessiveness come from?

"Tierney..." I shouted. "You rejected me in high school. Whatever you think you feel for me is wrong. As far as me being the perfect witch, I'm anything but. That's never who I've wanted to be. All I ever tried to do was to stay part of our group. You and Katie pushed me away. So fuck you, Tierney. Quit making excuses and blaming everyone else for your inability to control the need for power."

My ex-best friend ran at me wailing, her arms swung through the air. Her fists hit my shoulder, then my chest. One scraped across the side of my head. For all my new abilities with magic, I'd failed to block her physical attack. Just before the hall went completely black, Tierney was jerked away from me. I blinked a few times, unable to get a clear picture of what had happened.

They were fuzzy, but I recognized Mom and Amanda. They each held one of Tierney's arms. Gwen, Heather and

Pam stood in a half-moon behind them.

"Tierney Clarke, you will be held pending review for the assault of a fellow Coven member," Pam said.

Two sets of arms wrapped around me; one in front and one in the back. A cocoon of safety.

"We've got you. Let us help you," Josh said.

"Come on, babe. I'm here." Mila's voice began to soothe my nerves.

I focused on breathing. One in, two out. Time passed, but my cocoon stayed. Josh and Mila tightened their grip when I started to lose focus. Their strength helped lead me back to the present, away from the images of Tierney pressing me against the wall.

Eventually, Josh pulled away, giving me space. Mila shifted to the side but kept one arm around my shoulders. I was afraid for her to let me go. Worried the loss of her touch would bring the panic back again. The words to tell her wouldn't come. It didn't seem to matter though. Mila sensed what I needed and offered it freely.

Mila and I sat on the floor. I rolled my head to the right.

"Thank you," I whispered.

"Always, Z. I'll always be here for you."

I kissed her. A real kiss. Soft, with more emotion than physical contact. It was right. Perfect. My light.

"This isn't over," Tierney called.

Dustin walked into the hall as Mom and Amanda led

Tierney away. One second, Tierney leaned over and whispered in his ear. The next second, Dustin fell to the floor with a loud thud. Mila and I ran to his side.

While Mila shook her brother's shoulders, I checked the pulse in his wrist. But there wasn't one. Mom called my name, low enough for only me. The question in her eyes gave us the answer we wanted to ask but didn't.

"No," I said.

Sobs broke from Mila's lips. I moved to her side, but she pushed me away and turned to face Tierney.

"You killed my brother."

Tierney smiled. She clapped her hands together then bowed to Mila. I planted my feet shoulder-width apart. Little white bursts blocked my vision as I prepared for round two with Tierney. She'd just killed Dustin.

"He deserved to die. Your girlfriend's stupid fix to wipe away his desire wasn't going to work. The only way to break the bond with *Mort d'Evanoir* is to kill him. I don't need him anymore since it's obvious Azami will always pick you. Now I helped the Coven."

"You call that helping?" I screeched.

Mila raised her hands. She began speaking in a language I didn't recognize.

"Don't, Mila. Please. If you..."

I didn't get to finish my sentence. Tierney went limp in Mom and Amanda's grip. Mila slid her arms under her brother's to lift him from the floor then dragged him out the door.

CHAPTER 24

MOM MET ME AT THE front door of the Coven house with a steaming hot latte. I tried to smile as I took it from her, but happiness brought guilt. I should've been there with Mila, celebrating her acceptance into the Coven. If only my plan hadn't gone so wrong. Since she killed Tierney and left with her brother she'd ghosted me.

Her absence left a gaping hole in my world. Just when I thought I'd gotten her back and we'd get to navigate our way through a relationship, she was gone again. A week had passed and still, I'd heard nothing. She'd missed classes as well.

The Council went to the Hutchings and spoke with Mr. and Mrs. Hutchings about Dustin's death. Mom said they agreed not to take it to the police since they wouldn't understand the implications of using death magic, or how the Coven had already handled the problem so it wouldn't happen again.

Mila's life had to have been in as much turmoil as mine and it was all my fault. If I'd left her alone after finding *Mort*, none of this would've happened. If I'd turned her down when she offered to help me learn more, her brother would still be alive.

Mom and I had the conversation more than once, but each time she reminded me of Dustin's admission that he'd been searching for the book.

The Council called us to the house for the decision of Gwen's punishment. It'd been a week since Tierney's death. They'd planned to review her actions, but that was no longer possible. Addison wanted Mila stripped of magic, punished for her actions, but the Council refused. Because the Hutchings weren't part of the Coven, the Council wouldn't consider stripping her.

But today wasn't about me or Tierney. Today was supposed to be for Mila and her family—I ruined it by trying to have my cake and eat it too.

"You did it. You managed to find a way to save our town," Mom said.

"Yeah, I guess. What's your thought on the decision to reinstate the Hutchings?" I asked.

It was something I'd wanted to talk to her about before we went to the Council with the suggestion, but Mom said it didn't matter. The Council would make a decision on their own. I didn't really have any say.

She shrugged.

"They never deserved the actions handed down. The Coven's finally correcting their mistakes. I just wish it was more of a celebration," I said.

"Me too. Today was supposed to be fun. Not this." Mom wrapped me in a hug and kissed the top of my head.

We walked toward the Council room hand-in-hand. In just a few weeks I'd lost everyone. Katie. Tierney. Mila. Even Josh avoided me. What Mom didn't know was my decision on what happened next.

"I talked to Dustin before..." I trailed off, unable to say death.

"Oh yeah?" Mom turned so we were face-to-face.

"Yeah. I asked him why he killed the others. He didn't answer. Since Tierney had control over his actions, do you think...I mean...I'm the protector...there should've been something I could've done to stop all of this."

She gave a long sigh. "It's not your fault that he's gone. Tierney had problems. I only wish we'd realized it sooner. We could've saved everyone a lot of emotional turmoil."

"Addison believes she was set up," I said.

"Her daughter was killed, Azami. Regardless of the circumstances, that's not something any mother ever wants to experience. To add to the trauma, she wasn't there when it happened. Addison has to take our word that Mila acted out of self-preservation."

"Hey, Azami. How are you?" Josh joined Mom and me outside the door.

I gave him a shrug. The better part of the last week I'd spent in a haze. Classes. Homework. Sleep. Packing. After talking to the counselor, I decided it was time for a change. At the end of the semester, I was going to switch majors to Design. There was a study-abroad program in Denmark that I applied for. Even if I wasn't accepted, I'd already begun making arrangements to move.

Mom wouldn't be happy, but I hoped she understood.

Thankfully, it didn't take long for Amanda to take us into the boardroom.

Once everyone was seated, Mom began.

"The Evanoir Coven Council has voted unanimously to remove Gwen Graves as a member of the Coven. This removal is for the time period of no less than one generation. Should she not have children, the Graves line of witches will no longer be welcome. As for naming a new leader, the Council has decided a vote will take place within sixty days. All full members and third-year and higher apprentices will be included in the decision."

I squeezed Josh's hand. We were fifth-year apprentices. Our vote for a new leader would matter. Even though I'd be in Denmark, hopefully, they'd take my vote.

Amanda stood after Mom finished.

"The Evanoir Coven Council has voted on the proposal to reinstate the members of the Hutchings family. The vote was unanimous."

"Did I hear that right? The whole family?" Josh cocked

his head to the side.

"I don't know." I didn't dare let hope bloom. It would be too much to ask for them to forgive Mila for her actions.

Pam cleared her throat. "Mila Hutchings may join as an apprentice. John and Tracy Hutchings, should they choose, can be full members of the Coven. Their daughters may join as trainees and move into the apprenticeship when they come of age."

"Wow. I don't know what to say," I said.

"Amanda and I will deliver the message to the Hutchings family," Mom added.

Josh clapped and celebrated the—hopefully—new additions to our Coven.

With all the announcements made, I tugged my purse over my shoulder and began to stand. All I wanted was to go home and get back in bed.

"There is one other matter the Council considered." Heather directed her words at me. "Azami, as the protector of *Mort d'Evanoir*, we would like to ask a question."

"Okay," I answered.

"If you were to destroy the book, what would be the consequence for our family?"

I stared at Heather. The answer she wanted was not what I'd give her. This was another reason I intended to move far away. With Dustin gone, the book would need a wielder. If I took it to Denmark with me and hid the book where no one could find it, then the wielder became a nonissue.

"You want to know the consequence of destroying *Mort d'Evanoir*?" I sat back down in my chair. We weren't going to celebrate anytime soon.

Heather nodded.

"We all die. The book is tied to the soul of the Coven. Our souls. It dies. We die. Just like Gwen said."

My answer came out far blunter than I'd originally intended. While I could've apologized, I didn't. If asked again, I'd have given the same, straightforward response.

"As we expected. Due to this, the Council has voted unanimously to name you as the newest member of the Council. As the protector, it is important for you to keep a touch on the goings on of our Coven. The best way to achieve this is to serve as a leader, a member of the decision-making body. This is a position only necessary while the book is in play. Should anything happen to *Mort*, then the seat on the Council is forfeited."

"Seriously?" I asked.

At once, the entire Council answered "Yes."

"Wow. That's—what if I don't want it?"

Mom chuckled. "That's not an option, sweetheart. We need to keep the family safe."

Josh pushed his shoulder against mine. The last person I expected to be happy sat next to me with a smile so wide his lips cracked. This shot my plans to hell. I couldn't leave for Denmark if I was on the Council. All members had to maintain a residence within a one-day drive of the council house.

"All right, then. I would like to consider before I accept."

I would stay the protector of *Mort d'Evanoir* regardless of my status within the Coven. I'd decided to accept the book when it selected me. That was the same day I decided breaking away from what I'd known was a good idea. I wouldn't say I was wrong and made a bad decision, but things became a lot more complicated than I ever expected.

The Evanoir Coven didn't know it was time for a change until *Mort d'Evanoir* came into our lives and turned our world upside down. Gwen had a thirst for power worse than even Dustin. It was my mission to make sure she never had a chance to lay hands on the book again. I doubted she'd be accepted back into the Coven, but stranger things had happened.

I hated that I'd lost two good friends along the way. Katie's death left a mark on all of us. I was grateful for Mila and I would never regret the time we had together.

The Council adjourned and I headed out to my car. If I wanted to seriously consider their offer, I needed space, not to be surrounded by all of them trying to convince me to become a Council member.

Standing in front of my car was Mila. She held her arms out, open for me.

"You're here," I whimpered into her neck.

"Yeah."

"Do you hate me?" The last question I wanted to ask was the one I needed answered the most.

Mila pushed me to arm's length.

"Why would you think I hated you?" She tilted her head to the side.

"If it wasn't for me, your brother would still be here and you wouldn't have had to kill someone."

With one finger under my chin, Mila lifted my head so our gazes locked.

"Azami, you aren't the reason Dustin isn't with us anymore, or why I attacked Tierney. You're the reason my brother is no longer suffering and won't be able to hurt anyone again. You upheld your end of the deal and my famil's name is no longer one of shame. You're the reason I'm here. My whole life, I've wanted nothing more than to have what you have, and now I do. Thank you isn't enough to express my gratitude, but it's the best I have."

I swallowed hard. Twice. When the tears began to fall, I didn't fight them.

"They offered me a spot on the Council."

Mila's eyes grew wide. She bounced on her toes, which was something I'd never experienced before.

"You said yes, right?" she asked.

I shook my head. "I asked for time to consider the offer."

The rest of the conversation wasn't one I wanted to have out in the open, so I walked around the front of the car and got in. Mila climbed into the passenger side without hesitation. At least one good thing had come out of the shit show I created.

"What are you doing, Azami?" She tilted her head to the side, brows furrowed. "I'm with you all the way. I don't care what it is, just let me do it with you."

That was all I needed to make my decision. The Coven would be here when we returned. If the Council didn't accept me back after school then it wasn't my loss, but theirs. If I'd learned anything over the past month it was that taking control of my life meant living for me and accepting the results of my actions. In a year I might decide living in Denmark wasn't for me and return home, but I wanted the chance to figure that out on my own—okay with Mila by my side.

"I'm transferring to a school in Denmark for a year. I changed my major to design and there's a study abroad program that I've applied to. Will you go with me?"

She screamed. "Of course. Oh, my goddess. I've always wanted to travel. I quit school. Toxicology is awesome, but it's not for me. No matter what, I'll pull my own weight. We'll share a place to cut down on costs, and I'll get a job as soon as I can."

I knew I had everything I wanted. With her by my side, I could face anything the next few years threw at me.

I mean, we still had time. Life wasn't done throwing me around yet.

"By the way, after we met the first time, how did you get my number?" I finally remembered to ask.

Mila shrugged. "A witch's secret."

I shook my head before kissing her.

"Pizza?" I asked.

"Definitely." She smiled. "Right after we take this book to your place and put it in the safe I just bought. There are a few too many people running around that still want to get their hands on it. I'd rather not make it easy for them."

Acknowledgments

The idea for *The Coven's Apprentice* came from the darkly creative mind of my kiddo. What started as a fun project for the two of us to work on something together turned into a story I had to put out there for everyone to read.

John, without your support this book never would've happened. Thank you for pushing me to get over my fears. You have no idea how much more I love you every day.

Thank you to #RevPit for putting together a contest that brought together a group of writers who have grown together, leveled up together, and helped me become the author I am today. K.J. Harrowick, Megan Van Dyke, Melody Caraballo, Talynn Lynn, Laura Hazan, Abby Glen, Christy Dirks, Maha Jhalid, and Sanyukta Thakare. Your feedback and motivational pushes helped me finish this story and make it shine.

A special thank you to Megan Van Dyke for

designing this cover. I never understood when others said they cried the first time they saw their cover. Now I do.

I wouldn't have made the leap to publish this book without the team at Portal World Publishing: K.J. from the House of Harrowick, Drinker of Beer, Creator of Worlds, Mother of Dragons, Queen Instagator of Gators, and Wielder of Villians. Taco Fiend be thy name. Megan Storyweaver of House Van Dyke, first of her name, writer of twisted tales, lover of magic and kissing, promiser of happily ever afters. Melody Pie of the House of Caraballo, she drinks and writes things. Lady Talynn of the House of Lynn, Lover of Exquisite Vineyards, Chocolate Connoisseur, Teacher of Pleasantries, and Writer of all things fantasy and science fiction in the world of young adult.

Finally, to my editor Jade Loren. Your edits brought this book from pretty good to great!

About the Author

By day Jen spends her time behind a computer reading regulatory documents (also known as bland writing with no excitement). By night she can be found reading, working on edits for critique partners, writing her next great story, or chilling with her family. Jen's been reading and telling stories since she could talk.

A Texan at heart, it doesn't matter that she transplanted to the Midwest nearly 20 years ago. Rain or shine, humidity or snow, she's happiest with a book in hand.

If you enjoyed *The Coven's Apprentice*, please leave a review. Gain access to exclusive content, cover reveals, and more by signing up for the Portal World Publishing newsletter (https://portalworldpublishing.com/newsletter/)

www.authorjendavenport.com